When I was three years old and in my mother's arms, she looked down at me and said, "Son, the way I'm taking care of you now, when you get old, always have you a woman to take care of you like this." Dig this! All I'm goin' do is rest and dress, buy gasoline and lean. I'm goin' buy diamond rings and have the best of everything. I'm goin' pimp whores!

Holloway House Originals by Donald Goines

DOPEFIEND
WHORESON
BLACK GANGSTER
STREET PLAYERS
WHITE MAN'S JUSTICE,
   BLACK MAN'S GRIEF
BLACK GIRL LOST
CRIME PARTNERS
CRY REVENGE
DADDY COOL
DEATH LIST
ELDORADO RED
INNER CITY HOODLUM
KENYATTA'S ESCAPE
KENYATTA'S LAST HIT
NEVER DIE ALONE
SWAMP MAN

Special Preview of *White Man's Justice, Black Man's Grief*—**page 299**

WHORESON
The Story of a Ghetto Pimp

Donald Goines

An Original Holloway House Edition
HOLLOWAY HOUSE PUBLISHING COMPANY
LOS ANGELES, CALIFORNIA

WHORESON

An Original Holloway House Edition

Printed in the United States of America

WHORESON
ISBN 0-87067-994-5

WWW.HOLLOWAYHOUSEBOOKS.COM
OR
WWW.HHBOOKSTORE.COM

WHORESON

1

FROM WHAT I HAVE BEEN told it is easy to imagine the cold, bleak day when I was born into this world. It was December 10, 1940, and the snow had been falling continuously in Detroit all that day. The cars moved slowly up and down Hastings Street, turning the white flakes into slippery slush. Whenever a car stopped in the middle of the street, a prostitute would get out of it or a whore would dart from one of the darkened doorways and get into the car.

Jessie, a tall black woman with high, narrow cheekbones, stepped from a trick's car holding her stomach. Her dark piercing eyes were flashing with anger. She began cursing the driver, using the vilest language

imaginable about his parents and the nature of his
birth. The driver, blushing with shame, drove away,
leaving her behind in the falling snow. Slush from the
spinning tires spattered her as she held onto a parked
car for support. She unconsciously rubbed her hand
across her face to wipe away the tears that mingled
with the snowflakes.

Two prostitutes standing across the street in the
Silver-line doorway, an old dilapidated bar that
catered to hustling girls, watched her curiously.

Before she could move, another car stopped behind
her. She turned and stared at the white face leering
over the steering wheel. The driver noticed as she
turned that her stomach was exceptionally large.
Guessing her condition, he drove on. She stood holding her stomach and watching the car move down the
street until it stopped near a group of women in front
of a bar. She started to move towards the sidewalk,
but her legs gave out on her, and she fell into the slush
in the street.

From the darkened doorways, prostitutes of various complexions ran to the stricken woman's aid.
Before, where there had been closed windows, there
now appeared heads of different shapes and sizes.

"Bring that crazy whore up here," a stout woman
yelled from a second-story window. While four
women half carried and half dragged Jessie up the
stairs, a young girl, still in her teens, yelled to the
woman in the window, "I think she goin' have that
damn baby, Big Mama."

The large woman in the window looked down at

the girl, amused. "It's about time she had it, gal. Seems she been sticking out for a whole year." Big Mama started to close the window, then added, "You run down the street and get that nigger doctor, gal, and don't stop for no tricks."

The young girl started off for the doctor, muttering under her breath. She ducked her head and pulled up her collar in an attempt to cut off the chilling wind. When a car stopped and the driver blew his horn, she ignored the call for business and continued on her errand.

Big Mama's living room was full of prostitutes sitting and standing around, gossiping. It was rare for a woman to have a baby on the streets; also, it gave them an excuse to come in out of the snow.

"What the hell Jessie working out in this kind of weather for? Ain't she and her man saved no money?" a short, brown-skinned, dimpled woman asked. The room became quiet until another woman spoke up.

"You know goddamn well that black ass bastard she had for a pimp run off last week with some white whore," she said harshly. "He jumped on Jessie and took all the money she been saving to get in the hospital with, too."

This comment started up gossip on the merits of various pimps—then suddenly a slap and the sound of a baby yelling came to them, and everyone became silent.

Big Mama put out the few girls who had remained in the bedroom, then took the baby from the doctor and carried it towards the bed. Her large face was aglow with happiness as she smiled at the woman lying in her bed.

"You can be glad of one thing, Jessie, this baby don't belong to that nigger of yours that's gone," she said while turning the baby around so the mother could see it. "Looks like you done went and got you a trick baby, honey, but for a child as black as you, I sure don't see how you got one this light."

Jessie raised herself and stared at the bundle Big Mama held. "Oh my God," she cried and fell back onto the bed. Big Mama stepped back from the bed, shocked, and held the baby tighter. Her dark face, just a shade lighter than Jessie's, was filled with concern. She had never had a child of her own. Like many women who have been denied offspring, she had an overwhelming love for children. Her voice took on a tone that all of the prostitutes working out of her house respected. When she spoke this way they listened, perhaps because she weighed over three hundred pounds and had been known to knock down men with one swing of her huge hands. She spoke and only her voice could be heard in the house.

"If you don't want this baby, Jessie, I'll take him." Her eyes were full of tears as she looked down at the tiny bundle in her arms. "You can damn well bet he'll have good taking care of, too."

The small, elderly, balding doctor cleared his throat. He held out a birth certificate. "I'll have to get on to my other calls, so please give me a name for the little fat fellow."

Jessie stared at the bundle Big Mama held. All the

black curls covering the baby's head only inflamed her anger. Her eyes were filled with blind rage as she turned and stared at the doctor. He stepped back unconsciously. Here, he thought, was a woman who had been badly misused by some man. He hoped that he would never again see so much hate in a woman's eyes.

Jessie laughed suddenly, a cold, nerve-tingling sound. Big Mama shivered with fear, not for herself, but for the tiny life she held in her arms.

"Well, Mrs. Jones," the doctor inquired, "have you decided on what to call your baby?"

"Of course, doc, I've got just the name for the little sonofabitch—Whoreson, Whoreson Jones."

The doctor looked as if he had been struck by lightning. His mouth gaped, and he stared at her dumbfounded.

Big Mama was the first to recover. "You can't do that, Jessie. Give the child a good Christian name."

"Christian name hell!" Jessie replied sharply. "I'm naming my son just what he is. I'm a whore and he's my son. If he grows up ashamed of me, the hell with him. That's what I'm wantin' to name him, and that's what it's goin to be. Whoreson!"

2

THE SLUM I GREW UP in seemed to me to be the most wonderful place in the world. My early childhood was pleasant and it was a rare occasion when I saw something in a store that my mother couldn't buy for me. Jessie saw to it that I always had money for the candy store. Whenever I lost the marbles she had previously bought, she'd quickly give me money to buy some more. Most of us kids loved the backyards and alleys that we played in with our slingshots made out of discarded tire tubes. We overturned garbage cans in the hope of startling a good-sized rat so we could shoot at it with our homemade slingshots. Between the alley cats, dogs and us, we kept the alleys, yards, and rundown barns clean of rats during summer daylight hours. When night fell it was the other side of the coin. The rats came out in full force, and many children were bitten because they had slept out on the porch to beat the evening heat.

We lived in an upper flat on the second floor. Besides my mother and me, there was a big tomcat that we just called "Cat" who shared the flat with us. Before Jessie would go to work at night, she always managed to run Cat down and toss him in my bed with me. For me to mention sleeping out on the front porch at night was taboo, so I would play with Cat in my large bed until I fell asleep. I didn't know it at the time, but she did it because of her fear of rats. After tucking me into the bed she would ruffle my hair and kiss me on the cheek.

"Well, little pimp, I got to go and catch 'em now. You be good and I'll let you count the trap money in the morning," she'd say before turning out the light and leaving me on my own until she came back sometime in the morning.

On a few occasions she didn't get back in the morning. When this occurred one of my mother's girlfriends would be in the bed with me when I woke up. When this happened, I'd know that Jessie wouldn't be home until later that day, so I would go downstairs and have my breakfast. The woman who lived under us had a bunch of children, so one more mouth didn't make too much difference. When we played in the backyard the boys next door would call them "the welfare's pride and joy." If I'd laugh too much, the little girls who stayed under me would remark, "Ain't no sense you laughing, fool, 'cause your mammy ain't nothing but a whore."

I'd look at them and grin. "You're the fool, girl. You and your sisters and mammy need to get off welfare and become whores." This would cause all of the kids in the yard to laugh and I'd join in with them. At the age of five it's pretty hard for a child to understand the meaning of "whore."

If my mother wasn't home after I ate lunch, I'd wait till the woman upstairs woke up, and then she'd take me over to Big Mama's to stay. This made me think I was the most fortunate boy in the world. Instead of one mother, I had two. Big Mama and Jessie.

With the passing of summer my small world began to change. A big event in my life was my first trip to the neighborhood barbershop. Jessie dressed me with care. She had me put on my new suit and shoes, then marched me out of the house. She had always cut my hair at home, but since I was going to start school in the fall, she decided to have it done at the barbershop. The men sitting around the place stared at us when we entered. I didn't care. The barbershop was a foreign place to me. I stared around in wonder. The tall chairs with men sitting in them getting their hair combed, the glittering mirrors that surrounded the walls, all of this was a new world for me. The loud music from the jukebox made my feet sway with the beat, as I danced along beside Jessie, keeping up.

She seemed unconcerned as she walked me up to

an empty chair. She spoke to a short, fat, balding barber. "I want you to cut it off the back real good, but don't take much off the top."

The barber sighed, "Why is it, girl, every time one of ya bring in a red nigger, you always say just cut a little off, but when you bring in a black boy, you want it all cut off."

Jessie stared at him coldly. "Nigger, all you got to do is look at your head in the mirror, then look at his hair. But that ain't here nor there. I ain't got nothing to do with how you cut some little black boy's hair. What I'm worried about is how you cut my little red nigger's hair. So you pay heed, nigger, this red one is mine, and you cut it like I say." She whirled on her heel and stalked out.

The men lounging in the shop laughed loudly. One heavy-voiced man roared over the noise. "I'll bet you cut that boy's hair right, Lew." Lew seemed to take it as a joke. He smiled, displaying a row of yellow stained teeth. "That's just what I was telling you boys the other day. A nigger couldn't *give* me no black woman. They is the most meanest woman God ever put breath in." He continued, "You damn near got to be crazy to fight with Jessie anyway. She fights like a man."

Another bystander spoke up. "Shit, man, consider yourself lucky if she fights, and don't do no cutting. That black girl there is sure 'nuff mean with a razor."

The barber rubbed my head the way Jessie did sometimes before he started to trim my hair. After he finished with my haircut he bought me a pop and sat

me up on top of the shoeshine stand. "I wonder where
your ma went?" he asked offhandedly.

One of the idle bystanders spoke up. "She probably caught a trick, Lew." Lew shook his head for the
man to remain silent, but the man continued. "Hell,
Lew, don't you never think that boy don't know what
his mother does. Ask him what his name is."

"I know what his name is," Lew answered. I was
too young to understand the pity the man had for me,
but his kindness was understood.

Jessie came through the door, walking as though
the world belonged to her. Her high-heeled shoes rang
louder than the taps on my heels as she took that long
stride of hers. She stopped and swayed, her hands on
her hips. Every eye in the barbershop was on this tall
black woman who carried herself with such pride.
"Well, Lew, I guess I won't have to make you knock
down one of these walls getting out of here this time."

Lew grinned. "I'm sure glad you ain't goin' to do
me no harm, Jess. I sure started to cut a little more
off the top, though. You damn near got this boy looking like a girl with all this hair on his head."

Jessie reached up and removed me from the
shoeshine stand. She picked me up with the same ease
that Lew had shown.

"I'm glad you didn't, Lew," she said. "I know how
I want my pimp's hair to look, and this is the only
pimp I got." With a vigorous shove, Jessie started me
towards the door. I ran out of the shop into the street
I loved so well. There was not much difference
between the daylight business and the night business

on Hastings. The street was full of slow-moving cars, the drivers being more interested in the colored prostitutes in the doorways than on the traffic moving in front of them. I waved at the various girls I knew standing in the gangways. Some of them yelled across the street at me. "Look at Whoreson, ain't he sharp today!"

Jessie caught up with me. "You take your fast ass home and get out of them new clothes." I crossed the street on my way home, and one of the girls came out of a doorway and caught me. She gave me a hug, then pressed a quarter into my hand.

"Let that boy go on home, ya ain't doing nothing but spoiling him," Jessie yelled. I grinned, kissed the girl on the cheek, and went home.

3

MY FIRST DAYS IN SCHOOL were uneventful except for the shock my first name had for my teachers. Of course they quickly solved this problem by simply using my last name. However, this didn't stop my classmates from calling me Whoreson on all occasions, causing my teachers to curse my mother's choice of names. At this stage of life, school was wonderful. On the way to school we used to steal from the delivery trucks making their morning stops.

On a few occasions some prostitute who was still up working, or just coming out, would yell at me, "I'm telling your mammy on you, boy, if you steal that junk."

I don't know if they ever told, but if they did, Jessie never said anything about it. Because the whores always yelled at me, it made me popular with my gang. They commented on the fact that all the prostitutes on Hastings knew me.

My best friend, Tony, would put his arm around my shoulder. His mother sometimes worked with Jessie, so we spent a lot of time together. "Me and you, Whoreson," he would say, "we goin' to be the best pimps in the whole goddamn world."

I would look up at Tony's dark face and grin. He was taller than me, and I was tall for my age. Tony could outrun, plus outfight anybody in our gang except Ape. Everybody knew couldn't nobody whip Ape. He was big, dumb, and strong. There were a lot of grown men who wouldn't tangle with Ape.

We always waited on the corner in the mornings for everybody in our gang before going on to school. If somebody wasn't going, there was always some kid in the gang who knew about it. Tony would stop by for me, then we would stop and get Ape. This way, everybody came to the corner with somebody. After nine or ten of us got together we would start for school, looking for something to steal on the way.

After my ninth birthday I began to really understand the meaning of my name. I began to understand just what my mother was doing for a living. There was nothing I could do about it, but even had I been able to, I wouldn't have changed it.

There was a boy in our gang named Milton, whose mother wouldn't allow Tony or me in her house. She didn't even really want her son to play with us, but he found out it was easier to run with us than to get whipped on the way to school every day. I once heard her yell at him while we were waiting on the sidewalk:

"Milton, if I catch you giving that junkie bitch's son some of your candy, I'll kill you when you get home. That goes for that little half-white nigger they call Whoreson, too. You hear me boy? I mean it now, you take this quarter and save some change for school."

It had been Tony's idea that Milton try and get some money so we could buy some candy. After Milton bought the candy, Tony wouldn't eat any. He told Milton to take it home and stick it down his mother's big mouth. I helped Milton eat up the candy. She wasn't the first person who had said something about me, nor did I think she would be the last. To tell the truth, I enjoyed eating it, because I knew she didn't want me to have it. Tony seemed so pitiful watching me eat the candy that I suggested we stop at Big Mama's. If she didn't give us any money, she'd sure have something to eat. I wasn't hungry but I knew Tony was. It seemed as if his mother never did cook, 'cause he was always hungry.

Milton started to complain. "Ya'll know I can't go up there, Whoreson. You done ate up all my candy, now you don't want me to be with you."

I saw a girl from my class at school going down Hastings Street, and I started to run to catch up with her. "Come on if you ain't scared," I yelled back at

Milton.

Tony ran beside me and laughed at Milton. "Come on, punk, you might get a chance to see somebody doing it, if you don't be so frightened of your mother." We crossed the street at a dead run, causing a driver to slam on his brakes. He stuck his head out the window and cursed loudly, but it just made us to laugh.

Janet turned and saw us coming but before she could get away I had grabbed her and felt where her tits should have been, if she had had any. She called me a nasty thing and tried to hit me, but I danced back out of the way. Tony came up behind her, grabbed her by the ass, then jumped back. She screamed and slapped out at him, but she was too slow. He joined me and we laughed. We had started on down the street when two whores stepped out of a gangway and caught us from behind. Before we could break loose, Janet had run up and slapped both of us. Tony tried to kick her, but the woman holding him got mad and slapped him upside the head harder than Janet ever could have.

"Keep your black ass feet on the ground, little nigger, you hear?" she commanded. Tony complied by keeping his feet still.

Not wanting to appear frightened, I resorted to threats. "When I catch you in school, Janet, I'm going to do more than that."

Janet shook her little skinny hips at me. "You ain't goin' to do nothin', nigger, but try and get along with me," she answered. I tried to get free but the woman held me tighter. "You just wait and see," I yelled. "First time I catch you in school I'm goin' stick it in your little tight puss."

Both of the women who had seized us laughed. The one holding Tony remarked gaily, "Just listen to them. Ain't neither one of 'em got enough to stick in a pop bottle."

I turned bright red, blushing down to my toes. Tony was on the case, though, and he capped sharply, "We got enough to bust your big wide ass open, woman."

Instead of making them angry, his remark only amused them. Then suddenly we heard a voice roar from the window above us.

Big Mama was leaning out of the window. "Bring them fresh little niggers up here. I'm goin' to see how long it's goin' be before they feel on another little girl in the streets."

On hearing the sound of Big Mama's voice, plus seeing that look in her eyes, we really tried to get free. It was useless, though, because after she finished speaking some more girls helped the first two to carry us upstairs.

When we got upstairs Big Mama bore down on us. Both of us were shaking so bad we couldn't get our lies straight. I tried to explain that we were not feeling Janet, just playing with her. For telling this lie, I got a well-placed slap. After that, the women got together and took our pants off. A white man coming out of the back bedroom stopped and gave Big Mama his belt. She took the belt and lit us up with it. After we had begged, cried and pleaded, plus called her

Grandma, she gave us our pants back and sent us into the kitchen to eat.

After eating some ham hocks and greens, we tried to beg some money out of Big Mama. She promised us another beating if we didn't get out of her sight, so we ran down the stairs. The long narrow stairway was dimly lit, so we didn't see the two women who had grabbed us until we got to the bottom. They stood in the dilapidated doorway laughing at us. Tony asked the one who had grabbed him to give up a quarter. She gave him a personal invitation to go to hell, so I tried another approach. I promised the one who had caught me a kiss if she would give up the coin.

She stared at me for a moment. "Give me one good reason why I should want to kiss you," she said, "and I'll give you a quarter."

I stared straight into her eyes and stated, "Since I'm just a little pimp all I'm asking for is a quarter, but you know all you whores love to give pimps money, so just give it up, whore."

Her mouth flew open and she just stared. I stepped back out of the way. I knew Jessie had told all of her girlfriends to pop me upside the head whenever they heard me swear, so I wasn't taking no chances.

The sound of men laughing caused me to turn. I saw two men sitting in a Cadillac who I knew had to be real pimps. They were wearing silk suits and their hair was beautifully processed.

One of the men called over the girl I had been talking to. He gave her two dollars and pointed at us. "You give it to them," he said. "That way they can say they really got some whore money."

She came back from the car and gave Tony his dollar. She held mine in her hand. "You owe me something," she said and leaned down.

I caught Tony's eye. He nodded towards her breast. I winked at him and stood on my toes. I put my hand with the dollar in it around her neck, then kissed her on the mouth. She stuck her tongue into my mouth; my eyes opened in surprise. Reaching up with my empty hand, I squeezed her left breast. I ducked my head to miss the blow, if one was coming, before she could move. Tony moved in behind her fast, sticking his hand as high up under her dress as it would go. She screamed and we ran down the street laughing. Tony yelled to me, "Whoreson, she ain't got no drawers on." People walking down the street stopped and laughed, Big Mama yelled out of the window at us, and the pimps in the car roared with laughter. The other prostitute broke out in a run after us, but when we cut into a gangway that led into an alley she stopped.

After this experience Tony and I stayed on Hastings. When we were on this street of excitement, everything seemed to happen, life was full. Perhaps our introduction to vice was premature for our age, but it prepared us well for our chosen profession. My mother tried hard during this period to stop me from hanging around poolrooms and trick-houses. Her beatings were useless, though. She even tried using coat hangers twisted together. She called them her "pimp sticks" and used them only when I had been exceptionally bad. Even after she had used coat hangers, I wouldn't stay off the corner. For two or three days after a severe beating I would stay close to the house, but when you're young and wild, you soon forget the whippings, or just try not to get caught next time.

Tony had started staying at my house four nights out of a week, so Jessie whipped him as much as she did me. After I turned ten she began to see that beatings were not the answer. She discontinued them, except for when we would sneak back out after she went to work. For some reason she couldn't stand for me to see her working on the streets.

At school our gang had become a terror. We shook down all the kids our age, plus a few of the older ones. We took their lunch money daily, until one day we beat up two brothers who had rebelled against our extortion. Their mother came back to school with the police. The principal informed the officers that Tony and I were the ringleaders. We denied this, but it didn't do any good.

The detectives wouldn't believe our lies, so we ended up by being escorted home by them. Tony said we were half-brothers and lived together. I think he told this lie to stop them from going to his house, where they might have found narcotics lying around.

When the police knocked, Jessie had to get out of the bed to open the door. She just stood there staring at us when the officer pushed us through the door. After listening to the police talk, her eyes began to shoot sparks. We knew there was big trouble ahead. Without answering, Jessie wheeled around and ran to

the bedroom. She reappeared swinging her coat hangers. Her large breasts strained to burst free from the
sheer nightgown she wore. In her anger she hadn't
bothered to put on one of her housecoats, so the officers could see just about all they desired. They stared
with open admiration.

Tony was the one she reached first. I was glad of
this because I hoped that she would be tired by the
time she reached me. As I watched I began to shiver
with fear. She struck with such brutal intensity that I
knew Tony wished he had gone home. I had never
seen her like this before. When she released him, he
squirmed across the floor in torment.

She stood there breathing hard with her hands on
her hips. Her eyes seemed wild, her features were con-
torted by rage. I tasted fear for the first time in my
life. My mouth was dry, my legs trembled. I stared
with fear at this dark, angry woman, who I could hardly recognize as my mother.

When she moved towards me I jerked back, breaking the policeman's hold on my arm. Before I could
maneuver, my progress was halted by Jessie's unyield-
ing grip. It seemed inflexible. No matter how I wiggled I couldn't break her hold. The pain was inex-
pressible. The blows landed first on my back and
shoulders, then moved down to my buttocks and legs,
then back again. I screamed from sheer pain, mingled
with terror. She beat me in such a cold fury, I thought
she would kill me. She didn't stop until an officer
intervened in my behalf. Seething with anger, she
stood over me, her eyes blazing. Her voice was harsh

and deadly when she spoke.

"If I ever hear tell of you taking money from any kids I'll beat you to death. Do you understand, boy?"

Between the whimpers that escaped from me, I managed to nod my head. I believed in my heart that Jessie meant what she said.

Before they left, the officers told Jessie it would be ridiculous to whip us again. They must have thought that after the demonstration they had witnessed, the next beating would kill us.

Tony and I lay on the floor side by side. Without speaking about it, we knew our extortion racket had come to a sorry end.

4

WINTER CAME AND WENT. With the coming of summer Tony and I started dressing neatly every day, for the first times in our lives. Tony got a job delivering papers so he could have enough money to buy clothes. His mother shot up all the money she made, so he had to get his own.

Jessie bought me anything I wanted within reason, so I was just about the best dressed boy in school. One day just after my twelfth birthday, I came home from school and Jessie told me it was time for me to learn my street education. I didn't know what she meant because I thought I'd been learning about the streets without her knowing it. How utterly wrong I was.

While I was eating, she told me she had to make a run, but she would be right back, so stay home. I waited impatiently until she returned. When she got back, she had a tall, dark man with her. I stared at him curiously. Since I had been born, this was the first man she had ever brought back to the house. Whenever Big Mama talked about pimps, she said I was the only pimp Jessie had, or wanted. He was the darkest man I'd ever seem. Actually, he was blue-black, with large red lips. He wore thick, round glasses that made him look like an owl.

Jessie introduced me to Fast Black. For the first time in my life I learned that looks could be deceiving. He began teaching me all the connivance that went into the game. Trickology must be used whenever it was impossible to rip it off. Artifice became my bible, as I learned how to play stuff, the shell game, pigeon drop and three card molly.

Before I turned thirteen, I was on my way to becoming a cardsharp, and with a pair of craps I was becoming a master. I could knock, shoot the turn down, or pad-roll. On sand, dirt, concrete, it didn't make any difference, wherever they played, I just about had a shot for it. Fast Black used to tell me I could never claim to be good until I could take a pair of dice and get down on a blanket, then walk the dice from two to twelve without missing the sequence. My only problem at this time was the hours that Fast Black had me practice. I spent hour after hour in front of a mirror, pulling seconds or dealing cards from the bottom of the deck. When I finished with the cards, I'd have to spend two more hours shooting dice on the bed, with the blanket drawn tight.

To break the repetition of daily practice, Jessie asked Fast Black to teach Tony how to play. We competed against each other for pennies each day. It wasn't long before we were keeping all the boys at school broke. At lunchtime you could always find a game going somewhere on the tiny schoolground.

There was a greasy spoon restaurant across the street from the school. Most of the kids gathered there to play the jukebox. The owner, Fat Sam, liked to watch the young girls dance, so the jukebox kept money in it. After school one day Tony and I saw a crowd gathered in front of the restaurant. Anticipating a fight, we ran over and joined the crowd. Janet, with three of her girlfriends, stood in the middle of the crowd singing. I watched her lead the group. Her small hips swayed with the beat of the tune. I knew then I was through pulling her hair in the classroom.

A police car pulled up and scattered the crowd. I slipped away from Tony and approached Janet. I removed her books from her arms. She turned and stared, astonished. We were too shy to talk much that first day, but after a few days she began to ask serious questions.

"What you goin' to do, Whoreson, when you get grown?"

"Pimp, baby, pimp," I would answer.

She would shake her head sadly. "Don't you know there's better things in life than that? Why don't you finish school and go on to college?"

"I'm ready for the fast track now, baby, I don't need no college," I replied as cool as possible.

She puckered up and tears rolled down her cheeks. I stopped and pulled her into a doorway. Our lips met for the first time. The kiss tasted salty, but it seemed to stop her from crying, so I kissed her again. After awhile, she pushed me back from her. She stared up at me seriously.

"We have to stop seeing each other, Whoreson, 'cause I'm going to be a big singer someday, while you ain't goin' to be nothing but a pimp." I stared at her angrily as she continued. "My mother said singers go with entertainers or businessmen, while prostitutes go with pimps."

I looked at her coldly. "My mother told me something too," I said harshly. "When I was three years old and in my mother's arms, she looked down at me and said, 'Son, the way I'm taking care of you now, when you get old, always have you a woman to take care of you like this.'"

Before she could interrupt, I continued. "Furthermore, before my daddy died, he bought me a graveyard, so that when I got old enough, I could drive my old Cadillacs there and leave 'em." I was talking fast now, 'cause she had hurt me. She started to walk off, but I grabbed her arm. "Before you go, young bitch, I want you to know, you said a pimp ain't nothing, but dig this. All I'm goin' do is rest and dress, buy gasoline, and lean. Now, can you dig where I'm coming from, young whore, 'cause that's all you is.

I'm goin' buy diamond rings and have the best of everything." I turned her arm loose. "When you get home, tell your mammy for me that I want her to know, when I get old, I'm goin' pimp whores." With that said, I turned my back on her and walked off. I felt a large lump in my throat, and my eyes were so watery I couldn't call them raindrops. But I didn't cry. I walked tall proud because I knew I was going to be a pimp.

After I got over the pain of that incident, I started gambling constantly. We were doing so well that Tony quit his job. Our next step was to start skipping school so we could gamble. Soon we both were keeping fifty to a hundred dollars in our pockets at all times. Whenever we did go to school, we had our pick of the girls. They fought constantly over us. While this popularity of mine was growing, Janet drifted completely out of my life.

One afternoon after we had won all the money on the schoolground, we decided to skip the last three periods. After rambling up and down Hastings, we found a crap game going in an alley. We watched for a while. Most of the players were factory workers. Tony caught my eye. I stepped back so we could talk. They were bouncing a pair of red dice off a barn door, plus, there seemed to be a nice amount of money in the game. I knew what was on his mind. We had a set of tee with us, but they were white. Our red set of loaded dice was at the house, and that was a problem. Jessie was at home still sleeping, and we were supposed to be in school. Tony tried to persuade me to slip into the house through a bedroom window. I shook my head stubbornly. I wasn't about to go for that. Jessie would kill me if she caught me skipping school.

Suddenly the lookout yelled cops. All of the guys gambling rushed through the garage door. Tony and I were caught flatfooted. Since we hadn't been gambling I wasn't worried on that account. My main concern was being taken home by the police. I hadn't forgot the beating I got the last time some police took me home.

The two cops piled out of the car as though we had robbed a bank. One of them grabbed Tony and shoved him against the car. "Spread your legs, nigger," he growled as he began to search him roughly. He found Tony's small bankroll and the tee. "Nigger, you must of been doing pretty good in that crap game."

Tony was scared. He answered slowly. "Officer, I didn't even know how to play; we was just watching." The officer slapped him across the face, then kicked him until he scrambled into the backseat of the car.

The other officer, who had been holding me, spoke up. "Boy, what the hell color are you?"

The question took me by surprise. "Colored," I answered. He slapped me in the mouth. "Get up against that car, you black sonofabitch you," he yelled angrily.

Shaking with rage, I leaned against the back of the car. I felt my small roll of money being removed. When I complained the other officer jabbed me in the stomach with his night stick. Bending over, holding my stomach, I began to vomit. Some of the food splashed onto the foot of one of the officers. He cursed angrily. When I finished he grabbed me by my shoulders and pushed me towards the open car door. When I raised my leg to step into the car, pain exploded in my testicles. The floor of the car came up to meet me as I sprawled out on the floor crying. The policeman who had kicked me stuck in his foot and wiped his shoe off on me, then told me to shut up. Tony rubbed the top of my head as if it might take away the pain.

The police rode us around for a while. They told us what would happen if they caught us in the alley shooting craps again. They tried to give us the impression that we were just lucky, since all they were going to do to us was take the money. Not once did they mention school to us. At the time we were only thirteen. They finally stopped and put us out. After threatening us again, they pulled off, leaving us about four miles from home, with no money.

"What we goin' do? Walk, or catch a cab and jump out and run?" Tony asked.

I didn't answer for a few moments. "I don't see no sense in us going home without no kind of money, Tony."

It was Tony's turn for silence now. We walked for about five blocks this way, until Tony stopped in front of a market. I grinned and followed him into the store. In less than ten minutes we were back on the street. We both had six steaks apiece. We continued walking until we found a colored beauty shop. At the first booth inside we pulled out the meat. A heavyset woman doing hair stared at us closely.

"Where ya get that meat at?" she asked loudly. Her fingers were digging into the prime beef. The woman whose hair she was doing picked out four steaks.

"How much?" she asked. Soon the small booth was full of bargaining women.

"Let me get one of 'em," another woman yelled. Fifteen minutes later we were back on the street splitting the money.

"Naw, man, let's try that short con Fast Black showed us. I ain't never used it before, and ain't no better time than now to find out if it works."

We continued walking until we came to a drug store. We entered and tried it but it didn't work. Our next stop was a small grocery store. No luck. The third business we entered was a dime store. I decided to try my luck this time, so Tony handed me the ten dollar bill and one spot.

"Could I have a pack of Camels, please?" I held the ten dollar bill out to the young girl behind the counter. When she returned with my cigarettes and change, she remarked, "Aren't you a little young for smoking?"

For a moment I ignored her question. "Was that a ten, miss?"

"Yes," she replied and raised her eyebrows.

I pushed her a dollar and held on to the change she had given me. "I'm sorry, miss, that's my father's ten. Would you please take the cigarettes out of this? They're for my mother and I can't get the money mixed up."

"Oh," she said, surprised. She took the dollar and went to the cash register. When she came back she put the ten on the counter.

I put the ten spot in my hand with the other money and started counting fast. "Ten, fifteen, sixteen, nineteen, twenty. Just give me a twenty for that change please?"

She looked down at the money and then stared at me. My heart skipped a beat. I almost broke and ran. Panic was setting in. If Tony hadn't come to my rescue I'd have run.

"That other money belongs to my big brother, miss. My, I'm sure going to tell him what a pretty lady they got working in this store." The remark paid off. She picked up the money off the counter and put it in the cash register, returning with a twenty.

"You boys be careful with all this money, now," she said smiling. We showed all of our teeth as we grinned at her on our way towards the door. As soon as we hit the sidewalk, we got in the wind. We didn't stop running until we were four blocks away.

We ducked into an alley and lit up our cigarettes behind a garbage can. We laughed and smoked, then walked on, looking for another opportunity. We found nothing favorable until we came to John-R Street. There we came upon two slick old Negroes playing three card molly with four white men. The whites were being trimmed smoothly.

I was surprised when Tony asked the man handling the cards if he could make a bet. The old guy tossing the boards looked up.

"Your money spends, boy, just like theirs." He laughed loudly at his own wit. Tony bet a dollar and lost. Then two more with the same results. I stared at him and wondered if he could be losing his mind. We both knew how to toss the boards, but he was better than me. He quit suddenly, turned his back and walked away. I followed him down the street till he found a drug store. When he went in he found the women's section and bought some lipstick. Now I was sure he was going mad.

On the way out he stopped. "How much money you got, Whoreson?" When I replied he stuck out his hand. I stared at him foolishly.

Removing the lipstick from his pocket he smeared a little on his finger. "Shell out, man; ain't you got no faith in me?"

I grinned and pushed my small bankroll into his hand. When we returned to the game, Tony watched the cards go back and forth for a while. Then he bet a dollar and lost, picked up the other two cards to see where the queen was, put a tiny mark on it, and dropped it back to the ground with the other card over it.

"Old man, you ain't slick," Tony said. I ain't goin' never let no old man beat me out of nothing. How much money can I bet?"

"All you can get down with," came the reply. The old man switched the cards back and forth, faster than the eye could follow. "Get your bets down, while I'm in town. Money on the wood makes the bets go good," he said while bringing the cards to a halt.

Tony made a thirty-five dollar bet, reached over and turned up the queen. The old hustler swore but, thinking it was pure luck, paid off. Then without hesitating he began to toss the cards again. When he stopped Tony spotted the tiny smear and bet the whole bankroll. He flipped the queen over again. The hustler payed off, while his lookout partner searched the back of the cards. I figured Tony had wiped the back of the queen off on that last catch, but I wasn't taking any chances. I watched the cars coming up the one-way street. As soon as I saw a break in the traffic I hit Tony's arm. We crossed John-R on the run, turning up into the nearest alley.

The hustlers let out a yell behind us, so we knew they must have found part of the mark. The traffic held them up; by the time they got across the street we were cutting through backyards, on our way to another alley.

We bought three cans of reefer for fifty dollars and split the rest of the money. That night we gave a lawn party in my backyard for all the young kids in the neighborhood. There was plenty of wine, weed and beer. We had everything at the party but grass to dance on.

5

WHEN MY FOURTEENTH YEAR on this bitter-sweet earth came, I felt as if I were a man. Jessie and I stood at just about the same height now. My hair was black, with thick curls that hung down upon my brow. Whenever I went up on the corner with Jessie, I could feel the admiring glances the whores would throw my way. A few would even joke with Jessie about when would be my coming-out date. On these occasions I would remark to Jessie that I was ready to pimp, but she would only laugh and cap:

"You think you know how to talk slick, boy, but that ain't the key. Anybody can talk out of the side of his neck. What you got to do is find the key, honey.

I can't give it to you. I can only tell you where to
look for it. You got to learn how to sell conversation,
baby."

At this time I didn't know what she meant by finding the key. I knew I could think and talk fast, plus I
knew all the latest slang. "You just ain't hip, mom,"
I'd cap. "I got some beef that sells better than hamburger." The first time I screamed this on Jessie, I
don't know if she wanted to slap me or not. She had
raised her hand, but I'd stepped back out of reach.

She looked at me sadly. Had I been older, I might
have been able to read doubt in her eyes. "Pimping is
an art, Whoreson," she told me seriously. "There are
very few pimps in this world who can really take the
title of being a pimp. Just because a man gets his
money from a whore, that don't make him no true
pimp. Real pimps are really rare."

To prove her point she reached down in her sweater
and fumbled around. When she removed her hand she
held a small roll of money. She put this into the palm
of my hand, then closed my fingers over the bills.

"Count it," she said. "I'm going to continue working. When you think I've made enough money, tell
me and we'll go home."

I counted the eighteen dollars on my way to the
pigfoot joint on the corner. Tony and Milton were loitering around the jukebox. There was a booth full of
young girls next to the jukebox, and they yelled at me
playfully. I was in the process of convincing the girls
to go up to my house, so that we could use the bedroom, when Jessie entered the restaurant. My back

was turned to the door so I didn't notice her. The kids in the booth got quiet. I turned around to see what the matter was, only to find my mother bearing down on me. She stopped in front of me and held out a five dollar bill. I didn't know what to do so I took the money. Her eyes didn't hold a hint of a smile. Just as suddenly as she entered, she turned and retraced her steps without speaking.

I felt a little self-conscious so I stuffed the five dollar bill down into my pocket without flashing my roll. The last thing I wanted was for the kids to think I got my money from my mother. Tony would know where I got my bankroll at, but they wouldn't, and I had no desire for them to start getting wrong impressions. Had I really understood Jessie's intention I could have avoided the next incident just by going outside. But I was unprepared when she popped back in the door. She hadn't been gone ten minutes.

I stared at her coming across the floor. Bewilderedly, I held out my hand for the ten dollar bill she carried loosely. In a voice that sounded shriller than the one I normally used, I heard myself asking, "You ready to go in, Jessie?"

Jessie had never been ashamed of anything she did, to my knowledge. She knew that she was embarrassing me. This only aroused her sense of humor. "It's up to you, sweetmeat," she said, referring to the statement I'd made earlier. She ran her hand through my hair. "I'm ready whenever you're ready."

I really wanted to stay and shoot the bull with my school friends, but I was embarrassed by the way

Jessie was acting. Given the choice of staying or leaving, I quickly accepted the latter. Had I been as old and wise as I thought I was, I would have realized that many people would get the wrong impression of our relationship. Being as naive as I was, the only thing that disturbed me was that people would think all the money I handled came from Jessie. Many sly looks were cast our way as we walked out of the restaurant, from the older people as well as from the young crowd.

Jessie had a way of walking that made people think a queen was going past. To carry myself with such pride was my desire. On our way home, Jessie started to cough. I held her arm, and she bent over and spit up a mouthful of blood. "You all right, Jessie?"

"I'm as well as any nigger woman can hope to be," she answered lightly. For the first time that night I was glad we were going home early.

When we got home Jessie slipped into a housecoat while I fixed some coffee. She came into the kitchen and sat down across from me. She had removed her makeup and, with it, the professional air she carried when she worked. I smiled with happiness. I realized that I loved this tall, strange, beautiful woman. She gave me one of her rare smiles. There was an understanding between us that was wonderful. Apparently, Jessie understood better than I that we were all each other had.

I went to the cupboard, removed two cups from the shelf, and rinsed them out in the sink. We always took this precaution so we wouldn't have to worry about drinking a roach. I poured us both some coffee before sitting back down. Without taking her eyes from mine Jessie placed a small bundle of reefer down beside my coffee cup.

It wasn't difficult for me to recognize the ten joints I had rolled that morning. They still had my blue rubber band around them. Leaving them under my pillow had been a mistake. I had meant to retrieve them earlier but had forgotten. To try and lie out of it would bring down instant punishment by whatever means lay near her hand. From past experience I knew she wouldn't hesitate to throw the coffee cup at me if I lied. Jessie hated lies with a passion.

I stared at the reefer. Hoping that my hand wouldn't shake too bad, I reached boldly for the reefer. After removing one from the group, I tossed the rest on the table in front of her. Removing a book of matches from my pocket, I lit the joint and took a deep drag.

Jessie silently stared across the table at me. Neither of us had spoken yet, nor was I going to be the one to break the silence. She got up from the table and walked into the other room. Soon the sound of Billie Holiday singing her troubled blues came drifting from the record player in the front room. Jessie returned and picked up a joint and lit it.

We sat at the table smoking reefer and talking till the sky began to get light outside.

Of the many things she warned me about that night, one was never to use any other drug but reefer. She made me promise that for no reason would I allow someone else, or myself, to shoot some heroin in my veins, or snort it up my nose. I wasn't worried about using horse. I had seen what shooting stuff did to Tony's mother, so I had no desire for that form of drug.

We were both lit up pretty well when we staggered up from the table that morning. Jessie had made a short trip down the street and got a bottle of wine to go with the weed, so we had become quite high. Her laughter rang out to welcome the sunrise as I helped her to stand. The flickering rays of the new day played tag across the wall as we staggered towards her bedroom with me holding her up.

After I had put her into her bed, I leaned down to kiss her on her lips, but she turned her head quickly to avoid it. I drew back and stared at her surprised. She drew my head back down and kissed me on the cheek.

"There, you're a big boy now, save your passionate kisses for your young girlfriends." Before I could tiptoe out of the room she had rolled over and gone to sleep.

The following weeks became difficult for me. Jessie continued to hunt me down in whatever restaurant, poolroom or doorway I happened to be loitering in.

It became so obvious that she was giving me her trap money that Tony remarked, "Man, why don't you tell Jessie what people are saying."

I stared at him amused. "If I knew what they were saying I'd tell her." He laughed at my reply. Time after time as we walked home from school, he'd look over at me and laugh. We continued down the street but soon I began to get weary of his humor. The more irked I became, the louder he laughed.

A group of boys came through a yard carrying a case of wine they had stolen. It was Head and his gang. He had received his nickname because of the size of his head. It was longer than a football, with lumps on the back of it. He was short and wide, with a flat nose from too many schoolyard fights. His gang was the only one in the neighborhood anywhere near as tough as ours, and because he was their leader, he was always trying to prove how mean he was.

They spotted us and stopped. All eight of them were roaring drunk. I realized that this could be trouble, so I watched Head closely. In school on many occasions we had started out joking only to end up talking about each other seriously. I knew that for some reason Head had a dislike for me.

He handed Tony his bottle. "I would offer you a drink, Whoreson, but I don't let white niggers drink out of my bottle."

All of us went to the neighborhood movie each weekend, and we had just seen a cowboy picture where an actor had made a similar remark. I grinned at what I thought was his idea of joking and remained silent.

Tony took a long drink and then handed me the bottle. "Man, didn't you hear what I said?" Head yelled angrily at Tony. The children in front of the broken-down houses stopped their playing to watch. Their mothers came out on the crumbling porches, like roaches flocking to garbage, drawn by the imminence of violence. It was in the air, something intangible, felt by all but seen by none.

"Fuck you, Head, in your big black ass," Tony replied quietly. I took a long drink from the bottle and then held it out towards Head. He knocked the bottle from my hand, breaking it on the ground.

"I wouldn't drink after no bastard that pimps off of his own mammy," he snorted loudly.

"Man, why don't you be cool," Tony said softly. "Anytime somebody's mama gives them some money, some ignorant sonofabitch could call it pimping."

"That's different," Head stated and stared at me with his beady red eyes. "This half-white freakish bastard is fucking his mammy."

Before the words had left his mouth, I'd reached across the narrow space and grabbed Head. My right hand seized his shirt, while my left exploded on his chin. I followed this with a knee to his groin, and when he bent over, I straightened him up with my knee. Blood shot all over my clothes and I busted his nose. With left and right hooks to the head, I knocked him out into the street. I ran after him and kicked him in the face. This is how the police caught me when they drove up behind us. I was still kicking him in the head and face. I had learned earlier in my childhood the art of street fighting. Violence was a way of life, and I was dedicated to being good in anything I participated in.

The police took us downtown. Before taking me to Juvenile they dropped Head off at receiving hospital.

He was in need of medical treatment. I sat in a small room and waited for my mother to arrive. After what seemed like a two-hour wait, a tall white-haired man appeared and led me into another room, where my mother waited.

Jessie rushed over and examined me for any injuries. She seemed so concerned that I decided not to tell her what the fight had been about. I didn't want her to have any unnecessary worry, so I remained silent as we left the building. Evening had come over the city; dark clouds covered the sky as we walked down darkened streets in search of a cab. Jessie put her arm around my shoulder and spoke slowly.

"Not that I give a damn about what they say or think, Whoreson, but I just never realized what some low-minded bastards would think after seeing me give you my money every night."

We stopped walking for a moment while Jessie fumbled around in her purse. She removed a small notebook. Each page in the book was dated, with a notation in ink following each day as to how much money she had given me to hold that night. After each week, she had added the total for all seven days. I stared at the book in confusion. I still couldn't comprehend her reasons for keeping notes on the money. I returned the money to her every night after she quit work.

In a sudden fit of humor, she laughed at my perplexity. "Darling, this is just a record to show you what kind of whore money not to accept. If any of your girls should bring you this kind of money, it will mean you're not pimping, you're simping. Oh yes," she added, laughing rambunctiously, "thanks for giving me a vacation."

I have never known if she resorted to scorn intentionally that night, or if my ignorance really was that amusing. Whatever the reason, it got the job done. From that day on, I knew I would never accept schoolgirl money from a woman again.

When we continued walking, with her arm around my shoulder and her laughter ringing in my ear, I clutched the notebook tightly. It served its point. Besides teaching me what kind of trap money not to accept, it taught me that a woman would test her man at all times.

I knew then that I would one day pimp, and pimp good, because I was going to pimp with a passion.

6

AFTER BEING AWAKE all night and most of the weekend, Jessie and I were in a hurry to get home to bed Sunday morning when she finished work. The square working people in the neighborhood had started drifting by on their way to church, dressed up in their Sunday best.

We passed Milton with his parents coming down the sidewalk. He winked at me, but I refused to acknowledge it, since he was damn near grown and still too frightened to speak when he was with his mother.

His mother made some kind of comment, "What a shame," but we were walking too fast to hear all of what she said.

Jessie seemed as tired as I was. We ran up the stairs to our flat. She was halfway undressed before I could close the door. Her blouse was tossed over the back of a chair, and she had wiggled out of her skirt and tossed it on the couch. I was in the process of running her some bath water when somebody started banging on the door.

Before I could get there, Jessie opened the door wearing only her half-slip and bra. Tony rushed into the room with tears streaking his cheeks.

"Jessie," he sobbed, "you gotta come, Jessie. Moms done took an overdose, Jessie, and ain't nothing I do seems to help her."

For the first time in my life I realized that Tony really cared about his mother, though there had never been the harmony between them that there was between Jessie and me. From the many times I had been over to his house, I had yet to notice anything other than indifference between the two.

Idly, I wondered how Jessie would refuse to go. I knew she didn't particularly care for Tony's mother, especially not enough to go back out after working all night. To my surprise she simply turned and began to put back on her skirt and blouse. Unexpected as this was, even more surprising was the fact that she hadn't even cursed.

In less than ten minutes we were climbing the steps to the four-room apartment where Tony lived. The door was already open when we got there. The woman who stayed across the hall was standing in the doorway crying. She looked at Jessie and shook her head. "It's too late, honey, she done passed away."

Tony rushed into the bedroom. Jessie and I followed silently. There wasn't anything anyone could do for her. She lay on the bed, decently covered, with her eyes open. Even for someone as inexperienced as I, the awareness of death in the room was inescapable. The tears that Tony shed seemed inexhaustible; tears rolled down Jessie's cheeks, smearing her makeup. Everyone was crying but me. I turned and left the bedroom,

This was a new experience for me, and I was really shook up. I needed some fresh air to remove the smell of death from my nostrils. Without stopping in the living room I crossed the carpet and opened the door leading to the hallway. Before I could get through the door, two burly policemen came marching into the room. Behind them came the elderly couple who lived downstairs.

"Is this the boy?" the last officer asked the woman following them. I shook my head; this time I knew I wasn't the boy they wanted.

"Naw," she answered, "that ain't him." One of the officers went into the bedroom. In a few moments he reappeared with Tony and Jessie. Before long, the apartment was full of people, most of them police officers.

Jessie went over in the corner and talked to a detective. I saw her write out something on a slip of paper and hand it to him. Then she came over and herded Tony and me out of the room. We walked back home in silence, Jessie in the middle with her arms around both of us.

The sadness of the occasion overwhelmed us, leaving room for sleep only. The week following the funeral our way of living became to some extent more orthodox. Jessie stopped working at night and got a daytime job in a cleaners. She wouldn't allow Tony and me to gamble anymore, plus, we had to be in the house by eight o'clock every night. We were becoming frustrated by this imposed curfew, and this frustration showed in our relations with Jessie and everyone else. Jessie was responsive and sensitive to our feelings, but she would not tolerate any disrespect. She continued diligently with her job while making us walk a straight line. But all her efforts were in vain. After Tony had been with us for a week and a half, a policewoman stopped by the house. Tony and I had just come in from school. Jessie was still at work, so the woman put us in her car and drove over to the cleaners.

The woman went into the cleaners and came out after a short while, followed by Jessie, who seemed to be pleading with her. It was the first time I had ever seen her beg anyone. I hoped it would be the last time. The harder she seemed to beg, the more the woman would shake her head in refusal. Tony realized how useless her pleas were before I did. He opened the car door and got out.

Taking Jessie's hand, he kissed it slowly. She turned and stared at him, surprised. "It's no use, Jessie," he said. "I'll always remember how hard you tried, though."

She drew him close and wrapped her arms around him, tears in her eyes as she kissed him. It was like a hammer hitting me when I realized that Tony was being taken away. I jumped out of the car. We stood on the sidewalk and hugged each other, our tears flowing unashamedly. Had I known it would be years before we would meet again, I still could not have wept harder.

After the woman left with Tony, Jessie went in and quit her job. On the way home she tried to joke about the job, but I believe in my heart that she would have stopped hustling and kept her job if it would have helped to keep Tony. Jessie bought a bottle of gin, and that night she got roaring drunk. At times she would laugh and shout, at other times she would cry. When she attempted to go to work drunk, I went and got Big Mama, and she helped me bring Jessie home and put her to bed.

For a while I was consumed with loneliness. After my initial shock about Tony wore off I resumed gambling and petty stealing. Had I been an introvert I probably would have been more sensitive to my close friend's problem. But after really appraising the situation, I realized that sentiment was useless. Even before Jessie advised me to quit worrying because there was nothing we could do, I had reached the same conclusion. In the slums you have too many problems of your own to cultivate other people's trouble.

Usually I spent most of my leisure time on Hastings, but since I was becoming so well known to

the hustlers who hung out on that street, I had to go
farther to find my action. One day I wandered into a
small restaurant on Brush. A tall, slim, light-skinned
woman was bent over picking up some trash. I leaned
on the counter to admire her legs better. She was bow-
legged, and wide across the rump. Her hair was raven
black and hung down on her back. I knew she hadn't
heard me come through the door, because it had
become a habit of mine always to enter as silently as
possible. She must have sensed my presence behind
her because she turned suddenly and caught me staring in fascination. She seemed startled at first, but her
look was bold and penetrating. Suddenly I became
uncomfortable. She had dark green eyes, which
reminded me of a cat's, and a long keen nose. Her
complexion was the color of burnt copper, and to me
she looked like the Goddess of Love. Usually I could
stare at a woman and make her drop her eyes, but this
time I had to drop mine. She seemed to undress me
with those green eyes, and I got the impression of
something cold and hard about her. I pushed my hair
back off my forehead and gave her my innocent smile
to fake her out. She smiled in return, revealing lovely teeth, and the cattish look disappeared.

After our first meeting I began to stop by the restaurant every day. I knew that Fatima liked me even
though there was a ten-year difference in our ages.

One afternoon I found her sitting at a table by herself, dressed in her street clothes. This was the first
time I had seen her without her white uniform. The
green dress clung to her body. It was cut low in the

front and I could see the roundness of her breasts. My breath caught in my throat and I could feel my blood rushing to my head. Desire for this woman had become an obsession. I wanted to possess her completely.

She stared up at me and I knew she could see the anxiety in my eyes. Without speaking, she slipped out of her chair and stood in front of me. We were the same height, but the heels she wore caused her to tower above me. Taking my hand, she led me from the restaurant. The other waitress stared after us curiously.

Fatima waved down a cab. When we got in, I settled down on the seat beside her. As the cab jumped in and out of traffic on its way across town, her hand found mine on the seat, and she placed it between her legs.

I was in seventh heaven, and until this day I cannot recall the location of the apartment she took me to.

We entered the apartment and stopped inside the door. Somehow she managed to close the door and slip into my arms in the same smooth motion. I could feel her tongue slipping around inside my mouth. It felt like a hot flaming spear. Everywhere it touched, it aroused erotic emotions. I had been kissed by girls many times but nothing like this. Her mouth was hot, her breath felt like a hot wind blowing upon my neck. I could feel her body radiating heat through her dress.

She slipped out of my embrace and, pulling me by the arm, led me into her bedroom. We both began to remove our clothes quickly. Fatima finished undressing first. She helped me remove my pants and lightly shoved me back upon the bed. The room was well furnished. The walls had been lately painted a shocking pink, while the dresser and matching pieces were snow white. It was a showroom, displaying the feminine traits of its occupant. I could feel her kissing me tenderly on the legs and thigh. She removed my silk shorts and I heard her catch her breath in surprise. I smiled because I knew what had given her a shock. I was aware that nature had been exceptionally nice to me in a certain department.

Suddenly I could feel her hot breath on my privates and I began to tingle all over. The boys and I had discussed blowjobs before and while I had spoken on the subject like an expert, this was my first experience. Wow! It was like standing up in bed while still lying down. My head and my heels were the only things touching the bed. I felt like screaming but held back in anticipation. At the final moment, I grabbed her head and pushed against it and held it to me at the same time.

Later, I flopped back on the bed exhausted. Fatima got up and went into the bathroom. After washing up, she returned to the bedroom and asked, "Would you care for a drink?"

I nodded in agreement and watched the sway of her hips as she walked into the living room. In a few moments she returned carrying two water glasses filled to the brim.

I tasted the drink she had given me. It was whiskey

mixed with very little soda. I had drunk wine before but never any strong spirits, because the burning stuff would cause tears to spring into my eyes. I started to set the drink down on the table beside the bed. Fatima caught my hand and pushed the drink towards me.

"Be a big boy, honey! I ain't standing for no shit about you not getting high with me!" she said huskily. I didn't want her to know I hadn't drunk anything stronger than wine, so I turned up the glass and drained it. It was so strong, it almost took my breath.

Somehow, I managed to hold the drink down. Fatima emptied her glass, then lay beside me and we kissed for a while. Suddenly, she got back up and went to refill the glasses. I really didn't want another drink, but my not wanting to reveal my inexperience caused me to try to match drinks with her.

Sitting cross-legged on the bed, Fatima began to shake out some white powder onto a magazine. I watched her in dread. I had never snorted drugs before, but I knew them when I saw them. Removing a book of matches from the table, she tore off a strip from the back cover. Taking the strip and putting a crimp in the middle, she used it like a shovel to scoop up some of the white drug. Holding one nostril, she put the powder into the other one and snorted. The powder disappeared as if by magic.

She refilled the quill and pushed it towards me. I turned my head sideways, and sat up on the side of the bed.

"Don't be afraid, honey, it's only a little cocaine," she whispered, her laughter following, low and husky.

I trembled with an unknown fear. I could hear Jessie's warning roar in my head. Don't ever take any drug other than reefer. The small amount Fatima had taken didn't seem to disturb her much, so I tried a little bit. The more I snorted, the higher I became. Her hands roaming over my body aroused sensual sensations I'd never experienced. Everywhere she touched became sensitive. My nerves became raw, and they tingled with unheard of pleasures. I lay back upon the bed, as my keen sensibilities blazed with passion.

I felt one of her legs rest upon my chest. In moments I became aware of my neck being caught in a lengthwise grip between her thighs. She began to thrust her hips with a steady force until the continuous pressure produced a light discharge that seemed to spray my face. Anger and hate twisted inside my gut, as the notion ran through my mind that she had made a freak out of me.

Pushing her aside, I ran into the bathroom and washed my face thoroughly. I stuck my head under the spigot in the bathtub and rinsed my mouth out. I could hear Fatima standing in the doorway laughing. The more water that ran over my head, the clearer my mind became.

As I stood up, I faked a drunk stagger. She laughed again and came forward to help. I hit her with a straight right to the head, causing her to tumble all the way back into the bedroom. I followed her quickly, but instead of finding an unconscious woman, I ran straight into a wildcat. Her naked body gleamed in the dim light as she met me in the middle of the room, snarling like an animal and clawing like a cat.

I shot hook after hook to her head. She was bleeding from nose and mouth, and for a moment I had doubts about being able to whip this grown woman. She got a grip on my hair and dug her claws into my cheek. I could feel the pain as she raked the side of my face. Remembering that the best way to stop a woman was to hit her in the stomach, I shot a left and right to her gut. She folded up like a bag. I put one on her exposed chin. She exploded against the wall. Most of the fight was out of her as she sank to the floor, but I had no intention of quitting now.

I walked over to the closet and removed a coat hanger. As I twisted the wire together, her eyes followed me the way a hurt animal watches his killer. She began to whimper as I picked up a pillowcase and wrapped it around my hand so the wire couldn't cut me.

Her screams seemed to shake the walls as I laid into her. I continued beating her until I was exhausted. I sat on the edge of the bed resting, as I watched her crawl across the floor towards me. She began to kiss my feet passionately, with whimpers of pleasure escaping from her with each caress. When she kissed her way up to my knee, I kicked her in the head, knocking her back to the floor. I knelt down across her body and slapped her across the face. Then I started to ravish her savagely. She dug her nails into my back while her screams shattered the silence, but I was deaf to her cries and continued to rape her.

7

I STAGGERED FROM THE apartment in a daze, wandering down unfamiliar streets with my face caked with drying blood. The left side of my face had three long scratch marks where Fatima had dug her nails in. I continued on aimlessly until the darkness of the approaching night surrounded me.

When I arrived home I was surprised when Big Mama opened the door for me. I entered the flat and turned my head so she wouldn't notice my scratches. When she spoke her voice was low and urgent.

"Whoreson, you go wash that blood off your face, then change clothes. Hurry boy, Jessie is real sick and she been calling for you."

After washing and changing shirts, I rushed into Jessie's room. Two of the girls who worked out of Big Mama's house were in the bedroom. One of them helped Jessie while she sat up. The other one hand-fed Jessie some soup from a bowl she held. Big Mama towered over the women, watching their movements closely to make sure there were no mistakes.

I walked over to the bed quietly and looked down. Jessie caught my hand and smiled weakly. There seemed to be no strength in her grip and as I looked down on her, I realized that she was very ill. She stared up at me with tense and penetrating eyes. Suddenly she turned her head to cough. My heart shook with fear when her parched lips became covered with blood.

The woman holding her gently leaned her back against her pillows. At times she coughed so hard that her body trembled and shook. She tossed her head from side to side as though the pain was unbearable, then suddenly she would recognize me and the dark shadows behind her eyes would leave for a few moments and she would rest peacefully.

With the arrival of the doctor her breathing became less difficult and she seemed to sleep. I went into the living room and waited until he came out. After he left, Big Mama said something about Jessie having consumption. At that time, this didn't mean anything to me. The following week became a nightmare. Jessie didn't get any better; she just lingered on.

As the days drifted past, I couldn't help but get the impression that the two women from Big Mama's were getting tired of playing nurse. If one of them told me she would be there at ten o'clock in the morning, I'd be lucky to see her before four in the afternoon. Big Mama came every day, but somebody always showed up later in the day to fetch Big Mama to settle some trouble at her house.

Jessie had a little over five hundred dollars saved, and we had been using some of it to pay the doctor and buy medicine. One afternoon the rent man showed up. I left him sitting in the front room while I went to get the rent. Jessie was sleeping when I entered her room, so I tiptoed over to the closet. I put my hand down in the lining of the old coat where the money was kept and came up with my fingernails full of dust.

My mind was rocked by the thought of someone having beat us for our stash. Snatching the coat from the hanger, I turned the lining inside out. The money was gone. In my panic, I ripped the lining completely out of the coat. There was no money. I turned around in a daze, too hurt and dumbfounded to think. I wanted to cry but tears would not come. Suddenly I realized that Jessie was awake and watching me silently. My mind began to function more clearly. I pulled myself together so she wouldn't become aware of our trouble. I knew that Big Mama wouldn't have taken the money, so that left the two whores. My whole being was consumed with a cold, deadly hate.

"Is all of it gone, Whoreson?" she asked in a frightened voice. My silence only confirmed her suspicion. Walking over to the bed, I took Jessie in my arms and tried to console her. I begged her not to worry, but there was murder in my heart.

When she stopped crying I fixed her pillows for her and went back into the living room. The rent man had become agitated over the delay, and when he saw me he started to frown. My anger was just about to reach a boiling point so I walked over to the door and opened it.

"You'll have to pick your money up next week," I said, holding out his hat for him. He must have read something in my face, because he took his hat and left without too much grumbling. I closed the door and leaned against it. I knew what I had to do. With no money in the house and a sick mother to take care of, my childhood came to an abrupt end.

Suddenly the bedroom door opened and Jessie stood there with her street clothes on. There was a stricken look about her, but her face was full of determination. Her body swayed as though she was being driven by a strong wind. I rushed to her side and caught her in my arms before she fell.

"Whoreson, put me down, boy. I'll be all right. I just ain't been on my feet in a long time." There was desperation in her voice, but she was so weak that she knew it would have been impossible for her to even walk up on the corner, let alone catch a trick. Her tears soaked through my shirt as I carried her back to her room.

Much later, after Jessie went to sleep, I went into my bedroom and dressed with the utmost care. After combing my hair the way the girls liked to see it, I closed the door silently behind me and left the house.

The kids running up and down the street waved in my direction. Milton and two other guys from my gang met up with me and walked along until I came to the restaurant. We stood outside and looked through the window. Fatima was bending over the counter taking a customer's order. Cautioning the guys not to follow me unless they saw me get into trouble, I entered the restaurant.

Fatima didn't notice me until I reached the counter. After placing a hamburger on the cooking grill she turned and saw me. Her hand flew to her mouth and her eyes grew large with fear. Making my stare cold and harsh, I beckoned towards her with my head.

My voice snapped at her like a whip. "Take that apron off. I got something else for you to do other than fry hamburgers."

She stood there too shocked to move until I stepped behind the counter. I don't know what I would have done if she had continued standing there, but she saved me the trouble of finding out. She took a quick look at my set face, then removed her apron and started to climb over the counter.

"Not that way, bitch," I growled. "Come on around this way." She recoiled slightly when our eyes met. "Why are you looking at me like that?" she asked as she started past me.

When I slipped my arm around her waist I could feel her stiffen. I remained silent until I had led her out of the restaurant, ignoring the inquiring stares that followed us. When I ran my hand down over her body she relaxed under my arm. Her mouth turned up in a smile and I knew she was scheming fast and furious. I decided to keep her unbalanced. Seeing an empty doorway, I pushed her into it and slapped her. Stark fear sprang up in her eyes and she backed up in panic.

My words drummed at her, giving her no time to think. "Bitch, I'm taking you up on the track to work. The tricks spend from three dollars on up. It's up to you on how much they spend. I just don't want to hear that you turned down anything over three dollars. That's rock bottom, do you understand?"

She was slow in answering so I slapped her again. Her head bobbed up and down in reply. "I want you to turn at least three tricks an hour. At three dollars a lay, that's nine dollars an hour. Ninety dollars in ten hours." I stepped back from her. "Now bitch, do you think you can get my trap money together without causing me to kill you?"

She mumbled something in agreement. Taking her by the arm, I led her to Hastings Street. I stuck so close to her on the track that she didn't have the time to try to run away. While she stood in a doorway hustling I'd stand across the street and watch her. When she caught a trick, I'd follow them into the trick house and wait until she finished. After the trick left, she would come out of the bedroom and give me the money, before going into the bathroom and washing up. That night, after she had finished catching dates, I knew she was hooked. Fatima had taken to whoring like a fish takes to water.

Because of my concern for Jessie I pulled Fatima up from the track before midnight. Earlier in the

evening I had given a girl I knew from school five
dollars to go to Jessie and stay with her until I got
home. Just like a good whore, Fatima complained that
the tricks had just started to ride good, so she wasn't
ready to go in. The money she had made was in the
eighties with out counting the five I had given away.

We stopped in a greasy spoon restaurant and
ordered two dinners to go. While waiting on our order,
Fatima walked over to the jukebox. Loud laughter
caused me to glance around and see a tall, brown-
skinned stud with a thick mustache getting up from a
booth occupied by the two whores who had been coming to see Jessie. I felt like exploding on top of both
of them, but I curbed my anger. Walking over to the
table I stared down on them. They stared up at me in
mock surprise.

"Hi, Whoreson, I see you done got chose," one of
them said before they both broke out in laughter.

It was easy to see that they were high off weed or
coke. They were not aware of the deadliness welling
up inside me. I had to turn away or I would have
killed one of them. My glance went to Fatima. She
was trying to pry their pimp's hand loose from her
arm. A blinding rage consumed me. My control
slipped completely away. Grabbing a pop bottle off a
couple's table, I rushed at the tall man's back. He must
have heard me coming because he dropped her arm
and turned quickly. With the full swing of my arm, I
caught him square in the face. If I hadn't caught him
by surprise he probably would have killed me. He was
full grown, while I was only sixteen. The surprise

attack plus the bottle equalized the fight.

I didn't give him any air. He fell back against the jukebox with his arms outstretched. I kicked him viciously between the legs. He almost turned green. As he fell forward I grabbed a handful of processed hair with my left hand and burst the bottle with my next swing in his face. Blood and teeth spattered the floor. A warning scream from Fatima caused me to whirl around. Both of his whores were charging and they meant business. The first one had a knife, while the second one had a bottle. Fatima tripped the first one when she rushed past to get to me. I stepped back as she sprawled out on the floor in front of me and kicked her in the face. The second one was on top of me with the bottle. I took the first blow on my upraised arm. Before she could hit at me again, Fatima caught her behind the head with a chair.

After that I could take my time. While Fatima kept one girl busy, I stomped the other in the face till her nose broke and most of her teeth were stomped out. When I finished with her, I turned and pried the bottle loose from the one Fatima was tussling with. Breaking the bottle, I bent down and pinned the second whore to the floor with my knees. With the knowledge of what they had done to me and Jessie burning in my breast, I took the jagged edge of the bottle and cut up her face.

Fatima turned as pale as death when the blood flowed. She twisted her head away and started to puke. I didn't give her time. Grabbing her arm, I hustled her out the door. Before we had crossed the street

a police car squealed to a halt. When they rushed into
the restaurant I led Fatima through a gangway that ran
directly to an alley. We cut across alleys and between
houses until we wound up in my backyard.

Dropping her hand, I led the way up the stairs. She
followed me into the house like a well-trained French
poodle. Just about out of breath, I sat down in a chair
in the front room. I caught her staring at me with a
look of horror on her face, mixed with something like
admiration.

Betty, the young girl I had paid to watch Jessie,
stood in the bedroom door smiling. She was a tall thin
girl with big eyes and so knock-kneed you could pick
her out in a crowd.

"How is Jessie doing?" I asked quietly.

"She fell asleep just before you came in, Whoreson,
but your mother is sure sick," she answered.

Fatima spoke suddenly. "You ain't afraid somebody
might bring the police, Whoreson?"

I hadn't given the problem any thought. Now that
she had brought it to my attention, I realized that it
wouldn't take long for some informer to lead the
police to my house. I had enough game about myself
not to allow my woman to see me undecided. Since
I really didn't know what to do, I decided to play
strong. Pimping was a twenty-four-hour job, but I
meant to pimp twenty-five.

"Bitch, turn that wall loose and get in the bedroom
and find you a housecoat. I want to hear your bath
water running in three minutes, plus have a sweet
smelling whore in five."

She moved like she had been shot out of a cannon. When she came out of Jessie's room with the house-coat, she was running so fast that before I could point out the bathroom, she had run into another bedroom. Before I could call her a bunch of dumb bitches, she had found the bathroom and the sound of running water could be heard.

Betty stared at me in wonder. "You always said you was going to pimp, didn't you, Whoreson?"

Our eyes met. She was looking at me in a peculiar manner. "Ain't your mother goin' worry about you, Betty, if you ain't home?"

She laughed harshly. "Shit, Whoreson, my mama done got drunk off that five dollars and went to bed with some man somewhere. Besides, it don't make her no difference if I don't never get home. That's one less mouth for her to feed."

"You mean your mom won't say nothing if I pay you to stay here and take care of Jessie?" I asked quickly.

She replied bitterly, "My mother wouldn't say anything if I moved in here with you, Whoreson, except to warn me not to bring no babies back expecting her to take care of them."

There was a strange light in Betty's eye that I couldn't make out. "You wouldn't mind sleeping on the couch, would you?" I asked.

She wet her lips with her tongue. Betty was staring at me the way a hungry dog watches a bone. It made me uncomfortable. There was something inflexible about her look, causing me more discomfort than

I'd ever felt from a woman's stare.

It seemed like an eternity before Fatima finished her bath. When she came out I had her stretched out on the couch. Just to have something to do, I massaged her back, legs and shoulders. She purred like a large cat under my hands and my gentle kisses on certain parts of her body.

We were interrupted by heavy footsteps on the stairway. I snatched Fatima up from the couch and we ran in the bedroom. Someone began pounding loudly on the door. With a warning to Betty that she hadn't seen us, I closed the bedroom door. Leaning against it, I took Fatima in my arms and held her close. I could feel her trembling from head to foot.

Big Mama's familiar voice relieved some of the tension. "Whoreson, damn you boy, get out here."

Opening the door slightly, I peeped out. Big Mama was standing in the middle of the floor with her hands on her mammoth hips. "Move boy, damn it," she roared, "you ain't got too much time."

Fatima and I entered the room like two frightened chickens. Big Mama glared at me with eyes blazing. "I ain't got the time now to find out why you and that yeller whore of yours messed up them two girls, boy, but you better have a good reason when I have time for you to explain it."

I started to sputter out an explanation but she cut me short.

"Boy, the police is coming. They know your name, they know you did the cuttin', now all they got to do is to get someone to show them where you stay."

My mind was racing a mile a minute. I knew I had to get away, but I didn't have the slightest idea where to go. Fatima was staring at me with complete confidence. If she had been able to realize how completely at a loss I was, I believe she would have run off.

Big Mama came to my rescue. "I left a car downstairs, Whoreson. The driver knows where to take you." Her voice was full of fury as she continued. "I want you to make damn sure you stay there, and keep that whore with you, too, until I get there."

I could tell her temper was just about at the exploding point, and when that happened, Big Mama went into her violent bag, so I got out of her sight real quick. The last thing I wanted was for Fatima to see somebody whip me. With a few clothes tossed together, I stopped in the bedroom and spoke with Jessie for a moment, then departed. Not aware that it would be the last time I'd see my mother alive.

8

WE HAD BEEN HIDING in a flat right off of Hastings Street. After two weeks the rooms had started to become smaller and smaller. Big Mama had stopped by on three different occasions. The first time she showed up there had been nothing but smiles for us. Jessie had explained to her about the five hundred dollars getting stolen, and since the girls had been wife-in-laws, all of us figured that the money had been taken by both of them.

Betty came over twice a week to do our shopping. The only thing Fatima had to do was cook and pester me about making love. When we went to bed she seemed to have more arms than an octopus. After I

72

pried one hand loose, she always managed to secure a firm hold with the other.

One afternoon while we were going through our wild wrestling match on the living room floor, we were interrupted by someone pounding on the door. Fatima went to the door. I was surprised to see Betty, because she had done our shopping the day before. There were tears in her eyes when she stopped in front of me. A sudden apprehension overcame me. Before she spoke I knew that what she had to say would be bad.

"You better come quick, Whoreson, 'cause I think Jessie is goin' to die."

Fatima and Betty ran after me as I rushed from the flat. Die, Jessie couldn't die, I thought while making that frantic dash. In my shock, I didn't even notice the cab sitting in front of the house. The girls jumped in the cab and caught me before I reached the corner. When we reached our destination I leaped out of the vehicle before it came to a halt. I ran up the stairs. Entering the living room I was vaguely aware of the people milling around. I rushed into the bedroom. Big Mama, tears streaming down her cheeks, stood aside to let me reach the bed. Jessie lay as though she was sleeping, except that the chill fingers of death had given her a tranquility that would never again be disturbed.

Falling upon her, with my arms clutching the slim body to me, I remained motionless with my head pressed to my dead mother's bosom. Realizing that I would never see her smile again, hear her laughter, have the joy of just being with her, was unbearable.

The sobs started deep within me, where they hurt.
There were no tears. Just long body-racking sobs that
shook my whole being.

I can't recall how they pried me loose from the
body. I remember that Fatima and Betty kept calling
for Big Mama to give them some help, but I can't
recall whether she helped them or not.

For the next two days I wandered around our flat
in a daze. Big Mama took care of the funeral arrangements. Betty, not wanting to return home, moved in
with me and Fatima. All three of the women who really cared about my welfare had a difficult time convincing me not to attend the funeral. Big Mama swore
up and down that the police were looking for me more
than ever now, and if I wanted to join up with Tony,
then go on to the funeral.

I was still so set on going that Big Mama, as a last
resort, hired a man to take me and my two ladies out
of town. The same day that they buried Jessie, we were
on the highway. I sat in the front seat next to the driver.

It was a short trip. An hour and a half after leaving
Detroit we stopped in front of a hotel in Flint,
Michigan. The driver began setting our bags on the
sidewalk. Fatima went in and got us a room with twin
beds. I followed them into the hotel and up to our room
as if in a trance.

Day turned into night and I still remained in a state
of total bewilderment. Fatima undressed me and lay
down beside me. I remained motionless even after the
sounds of the night people ceased to be heard from the

street. Fatima called my name softly twice. Then the springs of the bed sounded as she got up. I could imagine her staring down at me, but I kept my eyes closed.

In a moment I heard the bed that Betty was in squeak. They whispered to each other quietly. I turned my head slightly. My eyes were already accustomed to the dark, so I could see them embracing very clearly. I watched in silence. The bed they were in began to squeal from their contortions. Without being observed, I reached the lamp and pulled the lamp cord. Light flooded the room. Both women were nude, with Fatima on top. They reached hastily for the sheet, but it had slipped or been pushed to the end of the bed.

Fatima's eyes grew large with fear as I stood up. I smiled down at the prone women. "Don't let me disturb you, ladies," I said, then walked into the toilet. I removed my silk shorts and stepped under the shower. It was hard for me to accept the fact, but I realized that it wasn't the girls' fault they didn't feel the same grief that I had to endure. Jessie had been my mother, and mine alone. Then the tears began. I hadn't cried before, but now the tears flowed fiercely. With the door locked and the noise of the shower covering my sounds, I let loose all my pent-up torment.

After quite a while, I stepped from the shower and stared in the mirror. I knew that Jessie would have been ashamed of me. Here I was, acting like a baby the first time pressure was put on me. Jessie had always thought she was raising a man. Now I was flipping over to a punk's role. This wouldn't do at all. Her words rang in my mind: "First be a man, Whoreson, then be a pimp."

Shoving the door open, I stepped into the bedroom. I felt that I was already a man, and pimping was my destiny. Leaving my shorts on the floor in the bathroom had been an oversight. Standing between the two beds naked made me regret this absent-mindedness. No man is at his best when he confronts two women in the nude. Fatima had climbed back in her own bed, so this eliminated most of my problem.

I stared down at Betty coldly. "So you want to fuck, huh, bitch?" I sneered. Reaching down, I ripped the sheet from her hands. She had been clutching the sheet up around her neck, and now she put her hands unconsciously over her breasts for cover and lay there staring up at me in terror. I lay down on top of her and grabbed a handful of hair and kissed her ruthlessly. The more she tossed and turned and tried to get away, the more my passion was aroused. When I penetrated her, she screamed. I took her the way a stallion would take a mare. With ruthless strokes I pushed myself deeper and deeper. She began to moan feverishly. Raising up on my elbows, I started to pile-drive my way to the promised land.

Hearing a wild laugh behind me, I looked over my shoulder and saw Fatima trying to spread Betty's legs wider. Betty started to scream again at the top of her lungs. Fatima let go of her legs and clapped a hand over Betty's mouth. With her other hand she grabbed a handful of hair. Releasing Betty's mouth, she bent down and hushed her cries of pain with savage kisses.

When the pre-dawn light began to show through the window, I rolled over on top of Betty again.

Her voice quivered. "No, no, not yet, please."

"Shut up, bitch," Fatima snarled as she rolled over to enjoy herself. "You know goddamn well you like it."

For an answer, Betty put one arm around Fatima's neck and pulled her down to kiss. With her other arm, she pulled me down towards her bare breasts.

Later in the afternoon, I awoke to find both of the girls gone. A chill ran through me. This was a strange new terror, one that stays with any man who lives off the earnings of a woman. His very existence depends on the loyalty of that woman. When his woman goes to a store and stays too long, he begins to worry. If she should stay exceptionally long on a date, fear builds up inside him until he hears her steps upon the stairway.

A prostitute will run off from a man she has been staying with for the past ten years without any warning. She will leave him at any minute, hour, day or night, taking with her only the clothes on her back. The only thing a pimp can be sure of is that the rent is due, or his car note needs to be paid.

Jumping from the bed, I rushed to the closet with fear pounding in my heart. Their clothes were still there. I slammed the door and leaned against it weakly. Where could they be? I didn't think they would have run off without taking some of their clothes. I reopened the closet and counted the suitcases.

There was nothing missing that I could see. I sat

down on the bed with my head in my hands. Suddenly
I heard steps in the hallway. My heart skipped a beat.
Holding my breath I waited and prayed. The sound of
the key being put in the lock put an end to my anxiety. Lying back on the bed I cursed my stupidity. The
first thing I should have checked for was the key.

They came into the room laughing and carrying dinners. The aroma from the soul food caused my stomach to ache from too many missed meals.

I ate slowly and listened to their constant chatter.
They had never seen so many white tricks as they saw
up on Industrial Street. This was due to the fact that
a car factory was right across the street from all of the
bars there.

"Whoreson," Fatima said happily, "I met a girl who
was working the streets and she took us to a trick house
where we could turn our tricks for a dollar." She went
on excitedly, "A dollar each time you use the bedroom
ain't too much, daddy, cause the tricks up here don't
spend under ten dollars."

Betty was just as happy. She pulled out a twenty
dollar bill and held it out to me timidly. "While we
was at the house, Whoreson, this man come in and he
didn't want to see nobody but me," she said cheerfully.

"The John thought Betty was a schoolgirl," Fatima
added, without malice. "You know I couldn't get that
bitch to spend no part of that twenty. She borrowed a
dollar from me for the use of the room, then the hussy
wouldn't break that damn bill to pay me back."

At that moment I really believed I held the world

in my hand. I smiled at both of them. Then I lay back on the bed and relaxed. How sweet it is sometimes to get your money off the top of the dresser.

The following week my bankroll grew swiftly. I met a pimp who went by the nickname of New York, and moved my small stable over to his house, taking the upstairs flat. There had been a family of squares renting the three-bedroom flat from him, but when they found out he was running a whorehouse downstairs they got indignant and moved.

New York had five prostitutes living with him. Three white girls and two colored ones, plus four French poodles running around the downstairs apartment. It was a madhouse, also one of my favorite homes. New York pimped, and pimped hard. The only time I can remember one of his demands being ignored was when he spoke to the dogs. New York was not only a small-built man, he was short. With his shoes on, he couldn't have stood over five-five. He wore his hair processed, and he always kept it neatly done. His eyes had a coldness that was hard to overlook, but when he smiled he revealed beautiful, evenly spaced teeth. He dressed the way only a small neat man can; his personal grooming was perfection in motion.

Our flat became the trick house. All the girls from downstairs brought their dates up to my flat to take care of their business. Our three bedrooms in my flat stayed in constant use. When the girls from downstairs came up with a carload of white tricks, I'd make myself scarce by taking the back stairway down to New York's house. We did this so that, if the police raided, everyone wouldn't go to jail.

After I moved upstairs, New York made it a house policy that no white men were allowed downstairs. In fact, he wouldn't even allow his white insurance collector inside his house. His reasons for doing this were logical. If the police had his flat under observation, any white man entering would give them reason to kick the door down. We had an agreement that, if my door got kicked in, he would pay half the fine. I was young and both of my ladies were just as inexperienced as I, so we didn't realize that New York had everything in his favor with this arrangement, while we had everything to lose. Lady Luck was smiling down on me at this stage of life, and I didn't have to pay any dues for my ignorance.

With the money rolling in daily, I started taking my two ladies shopping regularly. We would go downtown and spend the whole afternoon going in and out of various stores. Fatima picked out a diamond-studded watch for me that cost seven hundred dollars, then she talked me into buying her a mink stole that cost fourteen hundred. Betty, on the other hand, got to bring her present home the same day. With Fatima pushing her, she picked out a leather coat for two hundred fat ones, and I paid for it out of my pocket. It took a little while to pay off the bill for my watch and Fatima's mink, but she arranged the payments in such a way that we paid off both articles on the same day. When we got home after picking them up, she ran upstairs to change clothes while I went to find New York to show off my watch.

9

NEW YORK LISTENED silently as I raved over the delicate quality of my watch and the exquisite beauty of Fatima's mink. He removed his watch from his arm and put it beside mine. There was no comparison. To match my watch against his was as disastrous as pitting a baby kitten against a full-grown dog. His watch had two rolls of diamonds going completely around it, while mine had one. Where the bands connected, there was a cluster of diamonds, whereas on mine there was none. I had always known that his jewelry was superior to anything I could purchase off the whore money I was getting, but my excitement over buying my first diamond-studded watch had led me to act rashly, and now complete embarrassment was my reward.

All five of his girls were lolling around in the front room watching us. When he compared our jewelry they giggled. New York caught them with his glance, and the sound froze in the air. But the damage had been done. I felt like jumping in a hole and covering the top up for the duration.

There was a knock on the door. Before anyone could open it, Fatima came parading into the room, hands on her hips, impudently flaunting her mink. She moved with the grace of a lithe, sinewy leopardess.

"How do I look?" she inquired and turned with that leopard-like motion.

Instead of looking at me for an answer, she stared directly at New York for her compliment. Her face was lighted up with a rare beauty. It was almost shocking; it demanded that you acknowledge its superiority.

New York returned her stare as though in a daze. I think he realized at that moment that Fatima was the most beautiful woman in the house.

I sensed something passing between them, but I couldn't understand what it could possibly be.

"Whoreson done gave me the night off, New York," she whispered, "but he can't get in no bars 'cause he's too young, so I'm stuck for a date."

If I hadn't felt foolish before, I did now. I wanted to choke her till she turned blue. I wished I had never purchased that damn mink. I was beginning to learn, but my dues hadn't come up yet.

"If Whoreson don't mind," New York replied easily, "I'll take you out so you can show off your new outfit."

I wanted to say no, but the angry looks on the faces of New York's ladies caused me to give my agreement. They were staring at Fatima with pure hate. I couldn't understand why they resented Fatima going out with New York. She was my woman, and if I didn't show any resentment over the date, I felt they shouldn't either. Had I known then what I know now, I would have realized that they just considered me a young fool.

Fatima rushed out to take her bath and put on her evening clothes. New York asked me to take a ride with him while he waited on Fatima to dress. I followed him out of the house and waited in the driveway till he backed his Caddie out of the garage. I sat back in the car seat and tried to look clever. The motor ran so smooth and silent that I wished for the thousandth time I was old enough to buy my own car.

"Whoreson," New York began, "I'm going to run something down to you, man, 'cause I kind of like you. You know about as much about pimping as a monkey knows about flying an airplane."

I was stung and hurt by his words, but before I could stutter a reply, he continued, waving me to silence.

"Just listen, baby, just listen. First of all your main lady is a bull-dyker."

He didn't ask me, he just made a frank statement, and he went on ruthlessly.

"Fatima likes pussy as much as you do!" His voice was harsh. "That bitch of yours will spend money to freak off, I know this for a fact because she done already turned tricks with three of my girls."

I muttered something about killing the whore, but he didn't give me time to finish the sentence.

"Whoreson, I ain't telling you this so that you'll go home and jump on Fatima. Baby, I'm pulling your coat so that you'll never let another bitch tell you how to spend your money."

"You're wrong, New York, I don't let my women tell…."

He interrupted me with laughter. His laugh was so hurting that I stopped trying to explain.

"What you mean I'm wrong, baby? Just what the fuck you think you been doing?" He cursed sharply, then lowered his voice. "Listen baby, I'm going to explain it to you just one time, so listen close. Your main lady played on you! Ain't no ifs and buts about it, the bitch played boss game on you! First, the bitch had you spend fifteen hundred for the mink. Plus, two hundred for an alligator purse, then a cool hundred for some matching shoes, and we don't even have to count all the dresses you bought her that cost over fifty dollars." He paused to catch his breath before continuing. "Add up all the money you spent for your watch, suits, shoes, then maybe you'll dig just how far ahead that bitch done got on you."

There was no need to count. Once New York had mentioned it, I realized how the bitch had played on me. He didn't even know about all the cash money

I'd given her to send home for the care of her two children.

Stopping for a red light, New York lit a cigarette. "Dig baby, it ain't no sense in violence. If you're as cool as I think you is, just give Fatima her propers, baby, she put boss game on you. Can you dig it?"

I'd give the bitch her propers all right, I thought angrily.

"To pimp, Whoreson," he said arrogantly, "you got to have style. I don't mean copy it off of somebody. Like for instance the way you imitate my walk. I've even heard you try and mimic the way I talk. In fact, baby, I've seen you duplicate my hand motions."

I blushed like a schoolgirl. His words hurt, mostly because what he was telling me was the truth. I had tried to walk, talk, even act the way I thought he would on certain occasions. But for him to put it out in the open like this really showed me how foolish I'd been acting.

Ignoring my embarrassment, he continued. "Now I'm not the only one who has noticed this, Whoreson. My girls remind your ladies of this fact with expressions that have made serious problems flare up."

He reached over and turned the radio off. His next words exploded in the silence.

"In fact, Whoreson, my whores have made fun of your limitations so much, that your bitches are so tired of being mocked about it, that they're both going to choose another man."

His words jerked me upright. "You better take me home, New York," I replied with more firmness than

I felt. "I'll try and straighten this matter out." I hated to make an apology, but I managed to stammer out a few words. "The only reason man, uh, try and dig this, I've uh, ya, idolized you, I'll admit, and copied your walk...."

He interrupted. "Don't make no excuses, baby, and not to me. I realize you're still a kid, Whoreson, and for a kid your age, you're doing all right. But you still got a lot to learn. That's the reason I'm going to the trouble of pulling your coat, baby, 'cause I don't want to see you blow no more whores like this."

I knew what he was saying, and then again, I didn't. I hadn't blown any whores yet, and I didn't plan on losing any. "I dig what you're saying, New York, so I'll be able to tighten my game from here. I ain't planning on blowing no whores now, since you done pulled my coat."

He smiled at me real friendly, then pulled my world down on top of me. "Whoreson," he said quietly. "You ain't got no whores, baby. When we left the house, my girls went upstairs to help yours pack. They done chose me, Whoreson."

The words had been spoken quietly, but the message came to me loud and clear. I had taken him for a friend, but the friendship had only been respected by me. At that stage of my life, I wouldn't have accepted one of his girls if she had come to me. That was something Tony and I never did, mess with each other's girls. But New York wasn't Tony. I trembled with rage. Not because I had lost my whores but because I'd let my admiration for New York make me completely forget Tony. I realized with anger that I'd forgotten to send Tony any money since my involvement with this so-called "friend." New York said something. I had to bring my thoughts back from the spreading fog to understand what he was saying.

"Dig, baby, I ain't going to let you down uptight, Whoreson. I'm going to give you the money both girls make for the next two days, baby, that way you can get yourself together, baby, 'cause I really dig you."

I laughed sharply. "If them whores done chose you, mister, the only thing you can do for me is have some bitch call me a cab, so that I can get the fuck out of your house."

New York got mad. "You ain't got to take that attitude, baby. After all, the game is cop and blow."

I was quivering. I had to fight down the urge to kill him. "One day, New York, I'll see you, and instead of looking up to you, I'll be looking down."

"You was blowing the bitches," he yelled angrily. "If somebody was going to cop them it might as well have been me. You might as well learn now than later, Whoreson, when it comes to whores, you don't trust your brother. Anyway, you ain't ready for no bitch like Fatima. Me, now, I know how to handle her. What you should have did, Whoreson, was send her to a whorehouse, so that when she freaked off with another bitch she'd have a chance of pulling a new whore for you." He shrugged his shoulders to emphasize how simple it was.

"What you did wrong," he added, "was to let Fatima tighten Betty. Now, instead of losing one whore, you blow two."

He pulled the Cadillac into his driveway and stopped. All the lights were out in my flat.

"Whoreson," he said quietly, "you ain't got to take no cab. I'll drive you wherever you want to go."

This was too much. I had stepped out of the car, but at the sound of his voice I stuck my head in. Motherfucker," I screamed at him, "I don't want you to do nothing but stay the fuck away from me. My understanding is completely zero, so you and them bitches ain't got nothing to say that I want to hear. Do you understand, bitch ass motherfucker?"

New York didn't answer. He just stared at me and shook his head in agreement, and I realized that he was frightened. The fear in his eyes smoothed my anger. Some of his girls had heard us pull up in the driveway, and now they were standing on the porch. I knew they had heard everything I'd said to him, so before I closed the car door I tried to humiliate him.

"If I ever see you anywhere, punk, downtown, on the track, in the streets, and you look at me too long, sucker, I'm getting knee deep in your ass." Then I added for emphasis, "If you keep frowning, sucker, like you don't like what I'm saying, I'll get in your ass now."

He stared straight ahead, not looking in my direction, his hands frozen to the steering wheel. I could sense the struggle he was having with himself. Even a fool can comprehend certain facts at certain times, and I began to grasp the reason for New York to ignore my insults. It wasn't that he was so afraid of me, he just didn't want any trouble. He had copped my girls, so why fight? Later in life I would meet up with Betty in Detroit, and she would remind me of this night and tell me that New York had a pistol, but he really liked me too much, so he didn't shoot me.

He slowly regained his composure and smiled coldly. "We'll meet again, Whoreson. Maybe by then you'll have learned something about pimping."

I slammed his car door shut. His girls watched me climb the stairs. There were contemptuous glances shot in my direction, but I stared at them so scornfully that they dropped their eyes. There was a burning passion in me to kick New York's door in and drag both my whores out and kick them in the ass till their noses bled. The only thing that kept me from going on the wild was my earlier teaching. Jessie had always taught me that I was better than five whores. If a bitch ever left me, it wasn't my loss, it was hers.

Her words rang in my mind! "You don't need no bitch. The whores need you. Don't fight a woman just because she wants to leave you. Help her pack. Give her cab fare. Then go out yourself and have big fun. Don't let a bitch living get the idea that she is hurting you by leaving. If anything, make her believe she is doing you a favor. Tell the bitch that since she is leaving, that's one less worry you'll have."

With these thoughts in my head, I straightened my back and went on up the stairs. My bags were sitting in the front room, packed. I smiled. They had really crossed me out of the picture. I sat down on top of a suitcase and pondered my problem. I still couldn't shake the feeling of shame. The sound of a horn blowing in front of the house woke me from my stupor. I walked to the window and looked out. A taxi was parking in front of the house. Raising the window, I yelled down for him to wait. I picked up my bags and went down the stairs. I knew that I had blown my first whores, and I also knew that they wouldn't be my last.

10

THE MATTRESS IN THE small, dingy hotel room was lumpy, and I shifted positions to keep a button from pinching my back. It didn't do too much good, though, so I just tried to forget my surroundings. My eyes followed the progress of a roach as he crawled across the ceiling. He finally darted into one of the hundreds of cracks in the wall. The small light that hung from the ceiling cast shadows against the walls. To amuse myself I began to make silhouettes. Holding my fingers up, I'd make a donkey head. Quickly growing tired of this, I began to pace up and down. The three days I'd been cooped up in the room were beginning to tear on my nerves.

The radio in the next room went on. That would be the pregnant woman next door getting up. Without even trying to listen, I could hear the water running in her facebowl. Soon the sound of her brushing her teeth came through the thin wall. I knew her next movement before she performed it. She would open the door and go down the hallway to the toilet, then spend the rest of the morning there, doing God knows what. I stood by my door and waited. Soon as I heard her come out, I opened mine. I stared at her as she paddled down the corridor towards me wide-legged. She smiled as she passed. Again I was shaken by the sight of her. She wasn't beautiful, not the way most men would judge beauty. To me she seemed like an untamed queen. She was tall, taller than me. I had always been drawn to dark women, and she was by far the most attractive black woman I had ever seen. She was jet black, and her skin seemed to be as soft as velvet. I watched her wide ass as she waddled down the hallway. It was extra-large, but in her condition that was expected. Oh well, I cautioned myself. You can look but don't get involved. I had enough problems without getting the responsibility for some pregnant bitch didn't nobody else want.

I stopped at the desk and paid my rent. It was ten dollars a week, or two dollars a day. I had no desire to stay there permanently so I paid mine daily. I caught a cab outside the hotel and went downtown. I found a drugstore and went in to the money order counter. I counted my bankroll. Fifty-two dollars was the family jewels. For a moment I hesitated, then went on and had a twenty-five-dollar money order made out to Tony. Next I found the food counter and ordered breakfast. While waiting for it I wrote a short note to Tony, then mailed it. After that I got down to serious business.

I spent the whole morning and most of the afternoon running in and out of stores, short-changing the salesgirls. After that I hit a men's store and played for two suits that came off a clothing rack where the prices started at a hundred or better.

With both suits tucked under my armpits in a booster fold, I scanned the moving traffic until I saw an empty cab. After waving it down I had to outrun two women shoppers to the cab door. I slammed the door in their faces and grinned at the driver. He smiled in return as I gave him the directions, then pulled out into the moving traffic. Stopping a block away from my destination, I paid my fare and started walking. My purpose for walking paid off quicker than I hoped. Towards the middle of the block I entered a barber shop and sold both suits. When I came back out on the street, I felt pretty good with myself. I had made over two hundred dollars hustling that day.

The Ding-Dong Restaurant was partially empty when I entered. It was a large, greasy spoon slop house. In the middle of the floor was a horseshoe counter with two waitresses on the inside of it, each working a different side. I sat down in the curve of the counter so that I could watch the pinball machines lined up against the wall. The sound of laughter caused me to whirl around on my stool. Four sporting girls still in their teens entered with two young pimps I had seen around. One of the men nodded towards me, while the other ignored me and went to the jukebox.

As soon as the music began two of the girls started dancing. George, the fat white proprietor of the restaurant, came out from the back and stood at the counter watching the buttocks of the dancers. From the gleam in his eyes, I knew that the sign on the wall, NO DANCING, meant nothing.

When my food came, I just picked over it. The short, thin, light Negro who had gone to the jukebox took a seat near me and began speaking to the girls.

"I got to pimp or die," he yelled in a shrill voice. "If a whore don't give me no money, I'd starve to death. I don't know how to do nothing but pimp. Pimp, or die." He continued to babble. "Some people think the game is cop or blow, but it ain't. It's cop, lock, and block. Cop and hold."

The girls shot me a startled glance. His remarks were directed at me. Everybody in this town seemed to know that I had lost my ladies.

"That's why," he continued, "it's pure delight for a bitch to choose me. I'm the sweetest thing this side of heaven. Why, a bitch would have to be crazy to leave me. Ain't that right, baby?"

He turned to the girl sitting next to him for agreement. Her head bobbed up and down stupidly. If he had stated he could fly, she would have given the same answer.

The jukebox went silent. George came from behind

the counter and put in some more money. He motioned to one of the girls dancing, and she ran over to punch some buttons. George slipped his arm around her waist and got a few free feels. She squealed with laughter, punched the last record quickly, and expertly slipped out of his grasp.

Loudmouth jumped up with a yell. "Everything I do I do good," he shouted and pulled the nearest girl from her stool and started dancing.

After watching him a few moments, I knew I could make him wish he had never learned to dance. From close observation I knew the smaller of the two girls dancing was the better dancer. Without hesitating I grabbed her arm and pulled her towards the middle of the floor. I gave her a spin before she was ready and caught her hand when she came around. I dipped and started doing the new bop. She smiled up at me. All women love to dance with a man who knows what he is doing, and she quickly realized that I was exceptional. We danced as though we had been doing this together all our lives.

Out of the corner of my eye I could see the other couple. Loudmouth was doing the split and whatever else came into his mind. He tried to outdo me, but it was useless. The harder he tried, the sillier he looked. The record ended and I went back to my seat, with Tiny following me.

"You sure are mellow, baby," she said, sitting down on the stool next to me.

Her compliment was sweet to my ears. I turned around on my seat and stared at her. She was smaller than I'd thought. With shoes on, she still wouldn't stand over five feet. That was the only way you could call her small, in height. Her legs and hips were extremely large for a woman her size, while her breasts would stand up to measurement in any company.

"You like what you see?" she asked softly.

I smiled and continued my meticulous examination. Her hair had been processed and she wore it flat combed to the front. It gave her the look of being fast and slick. She was golden brown, and her skin didn't have a blemish. There was a look about her eyes that seemed older than her body. She had the eyes of a woman who had been hardened by life, yet she couldn't have been older than eighteen.

"Everybody calls me Little-Bit," she informed me. "So now, Whoreson, we know each other, don't we?" Her laughter was harsh but pleasant at the same time.

I remained silent and smiled at her knowingly. I knew she had used my name for the sole purpose of getting me to ask her how she found it out. I listened to her simple chatter. After a while I came to the conclusion that Little-Bit wasn't too bright. She talked constantly, in an unceasing flow, about various people in show business. It would have been impossible for her to have known all the entertainers she spoke of.

After we had danced a few more times, Little-Bit chose. I had copped a whore by the simple fact of being a good dancer, not because I'd run some heavy game down to her or impressed her with how clever

I was. She talked so fast that I hadn't been able to get my few words in.

We left the restaurant and headed for my place. I was still trying to pimp from between my legs. Little-Bit laid up with me till close to midnight, before she got up and started to dress. She dressed slowly and ran her mouth constantly. Having my own racehorse on the track meant a lot to me, but her persistent gibbering had destroyed the satisfaction I had felt about copping another mud-kicker.

Normally I would have gone up on the track with her. The main reason for doing this would have been to protect her from the man she had left, but Little-Bit claimed she hadn't had any pimp. Common sense should have warned me. Most of the time when you find a prostitute who doesn't have a man someplace, something is wrong somewhere.

Being at that stage of life where impressing people meant so much, I lay back on the bed and imagined what the whores would be saying about my quick cop. When she returned at about six in the morning, she shook my shoulder and started chattering. I rolled over and mumbled for her to put the trap money on the dresser. Then I quickly covered my head up with the pillow and pretended to sleep. I lay there silently and listened to all the sounds of morning life, cars starting up to take men and women to the factories and shops.

Finally Little-Bit settled down and soon the sound of her gentle snoring came regular to my ears. I drifted off again and slept until the door next door, opening and closing, reawakened me.

After lighting a cigarette I got up and walked over to the dresser to find my trap money. If I hadn't been fully awake at first, I was now. I recounted the six crumpled one dollar bills. In two giant steps I was at the bed jerking the covers back. I shook Little-Bit until her eyes opened wide with fear. Holding the money under her nose, I slammed her back against the bed.

"Wait, daddy," she managed to say. "I didn't break luck till early this morning. You know you kept me in the bed till late, and when I got up on the corner, there wasn't many tricks riding."

Releasing my grip on her nightgown, I stepped back from the bed. She was awake now and talking a mile a minute. The floodgate was open, and I really didn't know how to stop it unless I put my fist in it. Since this was Friday, it would be a good night in the streets for a whore, so I didn't want to jump on her. It was the only thing that prevented Little-Bit from getting a good ass-kicking that morning.

She was talking so fast I couldn't get a word in. Stepping up to the bed, I grabbed a pillow and covered her face with it, not to scare her, but just so I could get a word in.

"Bitch," I yelled angrily, "I'd rather toss bricks at the penitentiary then allow a whore of mine to bring me short money." She was kicking so hard I took the pillow from around her head. I didn't want to smother her. Had she realized that I lived by this code, she could have avoided a lot of future grief. All she had to do was gather her few belongings and leave. Even though I was still immature and too unseasoned to be a good pimp, I'd set certain standards and any whore that chose me would have to live up to them.

Soon as she caught her breath and figured I wouldn't kill her, she opened the floodgates again. I turned my back on her and slammed the door on my way out. I stormed down the hallway in a rage.

My pregnant neighbor was coming into the hotel when I crossed the lobby. She smiled brightly at me, but I frowned down so tough that her friendly greeting froze on her face.

I went downtown and started playing con with a deadly intent. I short-conned my way down one side of the street and back up the other side. After playing one supermarket cashier out of a ten-spot, I doubled back and got into another line and played another cashier out of another bill. We were having an Indian summer and the day was too hot for good boosting without a shot box, so I just kept on playing stuff.

Traffic was backed up on the streets with workers changing shifts when I started back towards the track. The bars were full of workers cashing their checks. I cursed my youth with a passion. Had I been of age, I could have mingled in the barrooms with those veteran prostitutes, and in my daydreams I imagined myself the master of fifty hard-working whores.

I strolled on down towards the poolroom. That was one place I could get into without too much trouble. I could easily stand to lose twenty dollars or more to improve my game. After all, I had close to three hun-

dred dollars in my pocket. It was just dark when I
emerged from the poolroom. My bankroll was fifteen
dollars shorter than it had been, but I counted that as
cheap fees for learning how to play nine ball good.

On the back table in the poolroom a crap game was
in the process of starting. I knew that it would start
off with small bets, but as the night advanced, it would
gradually accelerate until most of the players were
wagering the don't-go money.

I stopped and peeped through the Ding-Dong window on my way home and spotted my paltry whore.
She was in the middle of the restaurant floor doing a
bump and grind. Two prostitutes leaning on the front
of the building watched me closely. I spoke to them
and continued on down the street.

Back at the hotel I pulled my suitcase out and rumbled around until I found my bag of tee. Removing
three pairs of white, green, and red dice from the bag,
I tossed them on the bed while I put the suitcase back
up. Returning to the crooked dice, I made a few practice knocks with the bust-outs. I practiced switching
the dice until my movement was so graceful I felt I
could swindle the game without fear of being detect-
ed. I carried all three sets of dice with me, in case the
house man should change the color of the dice in the
game.

My nerves were tingling at the prospects of winning. I walked down the hallway with a light gait.

"Whoreson, Whoreson, wait a minute. You going
up on the corner?"

I turned to see my neighbor waddling down the hall

towards me. Her belly was protruding in front of her so far that she seemed deformed. She was grinning at me as if I were the expectant father. There was something about her that I liked, so I returned her smile. Actually I wasn't in any rush. I wanted the game to be going full blast whenever I got back to it.

"Ya baby, I'm going up on the set." I took her arm and helped her down the stairs. "Big as your stomach is, honey, I'm kind of curious about what you goin' have. Bull or elephant?"

She laughed and leaned on me. It was a gay sound and I liked the huskiness in her voice.

"I'm a big girl, Whoreson, look at me. Can't you tell? Everything about me is big."

I tossed my hands in the air in mock alarm. "You mean to tell me everything is large, honey?"

That deep beautiful sound of gaiety escaped from her again. "Yes, baby," she replied smiling. "Even that's getting large, but that's one problem I'll correct as soon as I drop this load."

Without seeming to do it, I examined her closely. With the heels she wore, I was a couple inches under her.

She inquired casually, "Now that you have smoked me over at close range with those bewitching eyes of yours, would you care to know my name? That is, if I've passed your inspection."

Actually I was ashamed of living next door to her and not having taken the time to ask her name. She sensed my embarrassment. Putting her arm around my shoulder, she drew me closer. "Marie Wilson, that's my whore name, and my real name too. Even though don't nobody call me that. They all call me Boots. Don't feel bad, now," she admonished me. "I didn't know your name until your girl came to my room this afternoon and talked me to death."

The night had grown chilly, so I slipped my arm around her waist as we walked. Boots waved to a couple of girls working out of a doorway, then snuggled closer in my arms as we walked up to the poolroom.

She looked at me sadly. "I'd heard about you, Whoreson, before I ever knew who you was, and I think I know just what you need. My only regret is that I didn't meet you before I got pregnant." She walked off and left me staring after her in surprise.

Before going into the poolroom I walked to the restaurant and peeked through the window. It wasn't too much of a shock for me to see my whore in her favorite spot. With a boy about my age, she was dancing in the middle of the floor. It wasn't hard for me to figure out why my trap money was shitty. I slowly walked back to the poolroom. If the crap game went off the way I anticipated, I had one hell of a surprise in store for her.

THE SMOKE WAS THICK inside and you could hear the sound of balls being broken open from the rack. Voices were raised in loud bantering, while shooters leaned across the tables shooting with deadly eyes. The house man stood behind a glass counter selling pop and cigarettes, plus stale candy, to the few junkies sitting around nodding. Three street whores stood around the counter sipping pop while they stared towards the back table, where their men were gambling.

As I walked past them I capped, "You want me to check and see if they done blowed the trap money?"

A small thin girl with a coke in her hand shot back,

"At least my man got some trap money to blow. That's more than that honkytonk bitch you got is doing for you, yellow ass nigger."

My ears burned from her scream, and the loafers sitting beside the wall watching the pool players broke out in laughter. A short, fat, brown-skinned hustler I played pool with sometimes remarked, "Whores can be awfully cold at times, Whoreson."

I grinned at him. "You're right about that, Fatdaddy, but I brought that on myself," I replied and kept on walking towards the crap table. I tried not to let it show, but I was warm. If I had anything to do with it, I was going to make sure her old man didn't have any money when I pulled up. I knew him by sight, plus that his name was Ray, but that was all I knew about him.

The crap game was roaring when I got there. I stood on the sidelines and watched the dice go around. It was mostly factory workers playing, with a sprinkling of hustlers. As I watched I realized that very few of the so-called "hustlers" really knew how to get down. The game was ripe. Each shooter could pick up the dice and shoot them like he wanted to. If the fader didn't catch the dice, point seen, money lost.

The dice finally came to Ray. He got covered for twenty dollars. I groaned when he shot the dice out. He was using the turn-down. The same shot I was going to shoot. And he knew what he was doing. My plans for busting him began to dim as I watched the diamond on his little finger glitter.

My diamond-studded watch needed some compa-

ny, so I promised to buy myself a ring in the morning if I won. The house had a limit on passes. After
you hit five licks, you had to pass the dice. Ray
jumped a four for his fourth shot. He tried to get faded
for a hundred and twenty dollars, but wouldn't anybody fade him. Since this was his last shot, I decided to try and set him up. I knew he was crap-wise,
and also wouldn't catch a point if I covered such a
bet, so I wouldn't have time to slip in the bust-outs.
I stepped over beside him.

"I got you faded for the twenty, baby. I want some
of that whore money you be getting," I said, talking
hip out of the side of my neck.

He grinned at me. "Going for your twenty, baby
boy," he said and just as quickly tossed a seven in the
door.

"Man," I exclaimed, "I'm glad I didn't fade the
whole thing."

The stickman, keeping the game moving, yelled,
"Next shooter!"

I tossed a hundred dollars to him. "Shoot it," I
yelled. "I almost blowed it fading, so I might as well
bet it." I shot the dice out of my hand all the way
down the table the way a square would shoot. The
dice stopped on seven, too.

The stickman yelled. "Wait a minute, Red, you ain't
even faded."

Putting on my good square grin, I smiled. "That's
all right, houseman, I got plenty more of them sev-
ens. Get me on."

That kid jive stung, but I waited till his money was

in the houseman's hand with mine. I picked the dice
up and shot them away from Ray, so he couldn't catch
them. The dice spun like tops, neither one turning off
the five-deuce I'd set them on. Ray almost broke my
ribs trying to push me aside so he could catch the
spinning dice. I had braced myself though, and he
couldn't have moved me out of the way with a Mack
truck.

"Seven," yelled the gamekeeper. "Shooter shootin'
two hundred."

Ray stared at me angrily. His eyes were slits.
Suddenly he grinned. "Boy, when you got me, you
got a good one," he said quietly, then yelled, "Bet the
shooter hits."

I couldn't get covered for but fifty dollars the next
shot, then twenty; the last two fades were for ten dollars. I caught four on my last shot, and between the
bets I could beat Ray to, I picked up forty dollars
more on side bets. I jumped four and passed the dice.

I waited until the dice had gone halfway around the
table before I made another killing. A large, pot-gut-
ted, light-skinned factory worker wearing bib coveralls was shooting. He had started with a twenty-dol-
lar bet, hit, then shot the forty, hit, and now was trying
to get on for the eighty. I covered the whole bet, then
prayed that he didn't come out the door with seven
or eleven. When he caught six, I bet fifty more around
the board that he would miss.

Ray was betting the odds, percentage and hunch,
so he spread about fifty around the board that the
shooter would miss. When the shooter turned the dice

loose, I caught them and asked him to give me a shake. The dice I tossed back in his hand were bust-outs. When he sevened out, I grabbed the dice and switched the proper ones back in the game.

"You sure know when to get down, kid, and I mean, and I mean get down," Ray said and slapped me on the back.

I didn't know if he had seen me switch, but for the rest of the game, we both bet the same way. I was holding over two hundred dollars in my hand when Little-Bit came barging up to the table.

She grinned. "Daddy, give me some money so I can eat."

Looking up from the table I growled, "Eat when you break luck, bitch."

She whirled around and ran out of the poolroom angrily. Two colored factory workers showed up with three white guys from the afternoon shift with fresh money. They must have played with Ray before because they were all trying to bet that Ray would hit. He couldn't get faded, so I tossed up ten dollars and winked at him. The dice came out with a seven. His thin woman squealed with joy. She was holding on tight to one of the white players. I tossed up another ten, again a seven. I kicked his leg and held my right hand below the table and flashed the tee. Putting ten more on the table I said, "Ain't nobody goin' pass all night. If your money is long, the dice goin' show wrong." Everybody around the table wanted to make a bet with me.

"Wait till he comes out and catches a point," I

yelled. "Then get your money down; I'm covering all bets."

Ray tossed a six. I laid him a fifty-dollar bet that he would miss, then laid two hundred around the table. I didn't take any chances. When he came out, I caught the dice and tossed my tee in his hand. His next roll was seven.

"Shoot that money," I yelled while picking the dice up and switching. I picked my side bets up.

After two more shots I left the crap game and moved to the front of the poolroom. The wineheads started begging for quarters. I gave them ten dollars to go and get ten bottles of wine, then sent three more wineheads with the first one to make sure he came back.

When Ray came out and got in his car, I was standing outside drinking wine. Between the poolroom and restaurant twenty whores paraded back and forth. I walked over to the car and asked Ray to wait a minute.

Looking up and down the sidewalk, I couldn't spot Little-Bit anywhere. I stepped inside the restaurant and spotted her sitting with two other girls.

"Did you break luck yet?" I asked slowly.

"How you expect me to do something, huh? I'm too weak from hunger," she cracked loudly and her girlfriends laughed.

I wheeled around and retraced my steps out of the door. On the sidewalk I found three wineheads and paid two of them five dollars apiece to go in the alley and get me two half-full garbage cans. They stared at me as though I were going crazy, but finally realized

I was serious. I paid the other man ten dollars, five now and the rest when he returned, to run to the hotel and gather up Little-Bit's clothes and bring them back in a paper bag.

Ray was sitting on the passenger side with the window down. "Hey, baby," he called, beckoning to me. "What's the deal here? Sit down mellow and run it to me."

He moved over under the steering wheel and I sat down on the passenger side. His woman stopped and peeped through the window.

"Get on, bitch, you ain't goin' make no money staring at me," he said brutally.

I pulled my roll out and split the money I'd made when he shot at the six.

"You didn't have to take the chance and put that tee in my hand, Whoreson. I was going to miss anyway." He added, "You sure got a beautiful motion, Whoreson. I know you be knocking, but I'll be damn if I can see you doing it."

Our conversation was interrupted by the return of two of the wineheads. Each of them was rolling a half full garbage can. They left the cans standing in front of a darkened doorway and came over to the car. From the doorway infuriated whores screamed curses at the wineheads for leaving garbage cans in front of their working spots.

I leaned my head out of the car window. "I'm going to give you ten more dollars to do two more simple things for me."

"What's that?" they asked in a chorus.

"First," I said, "I want you to make sure don't nobody move those cans for a few minutes. Can you handle that?"

They shook their heads in agreement, so I continued. "Second, I'm going to put some garbage in those cans, and I want you to make sure it don't get out till you got it back in the alley where all garbage belongs."

"Man, I don't know what's going down," the taller of the two stated, "but if that's all you want, we can sure handle it."

The guy I had sent for the clothes walked up with a brown paper bag in his arm. He handed me my key through the car window. I opened the car door and got out. After I took the bag from him, I became aware that we were getting a lot of attention. Ray got out of the car and came around and sat on the fender.

I sent the man who had brought the clothes in the restaurant to get Little-Bit. Walking over to the nearest garbage can, I began dropping the feminine apparel down on top of the garbage. Looking up, I saw Boots staring, apparently shocked. The girls with her watched me with open curiosity.

Suddenly the air was ringing with curses. I whirled in time to catch Little-Bit's arms.

"What the hell you call yourself doing with my clothes?" she screamed. "Goddamnit, Whoreson, you bastard. Turn me loose, you red motherfucker."

Realizing that it would hurt her more if I humiliated her, I held back from cracking her head. Picking her up, I pushed her down inside of the other garbage can. Each time she tried to climb out, I pushed her down deeper in the can. She eventually stopped trying and just sat there and cried. Some of the pimps and wineheads and other night dwellers laughed loudly. The prostitutes stared angrily at me for my treatment of their sister.

Removing my large bankroll, I beckoned to the wineheads I was paying. "Take this garbage to the alley where it belongs with the rest of the trash," I commanded, peeling off some bills.

The anger in the prostitutes' eyes only added fuel to the fury inside of me. My voice was full of contempt as I tongue-lashed them. "I'd rather sleep in shit or suck a dog's dick than let one of you funky bitches think for a minute that you got enough sense to put game on me. If you feel sorry for that trampish ass bitch, don't. The bitch is where she belongs, with the garbage."

Ray slapped me on the back. "Pimp hard," he yelled. "Let these whores know that a hard pimping young man is on the set."

The prostitutes began to slip away. Ray, with his arm around my shoulders, led me towards his car. We got in and he started across town to get some cocaine and reefer. The night was young, I had a pocketful of money, and I believed in my heart I could make as much money as any whore that peed between two heels.

We came back to the track around four in the morning. My nose felt like it was frozen from so much coke. We sat in the car, high, smoking reefer with the windows rolled up tight, watching the girls work.

Boots walked up and down the street. Even with her belly stuck out a mile, she tried. Every time she stopped a car and waddled out to haggle with the men, some other girl would always come off the sidewalk and stand conspicuously behind her. The men constantly passed over her for the other prostitutes. As the time passed, I began to feel sorry for her. Finally, Ray's woman got in the car. Her trap was fat, and she was ready to go in. I said good night and got out. He reassured me that he would pick me up later in the day and take me to a pawnshop so I could buy me a ring.

Moving back in the shadows, I stood and watched Boots try and work. A carload of young white boys stopped in front of her doorway. When she didn't come out, they just sat there and heckled her. All the other traffic on the street had to go around the jeering teenagers. Since this ruined her chances of stopping a date, she came out of the doorway and started walking down the street. The car moved slowly along beside her. She turned and came back. The driver put the car in reverse and backed up slow, so that he could keep up with her pace. When the light from the restaurant outlined her pregnancy, they really began to harass her.

Two prostitutes walking past began to take up for her. They berated the kids in the car viciously, their words dripping venom. Where the kids had found Boots vulnerable, they now found themselves defenseless. The prostitutes heaped abuse upon their mothers, fathers, sisters, no one was left out. An empty beer bottle came sailing out of the car in the direction of the girls. They ducked, and the driver roared off with his tires squealing.

I stepped out from my dark concealment. "Hi baby," I said, putting my arm around her waist. "You ready to go in?"

She tried a halfhearted smile. "I ain't got my rent money together yet, baby."

"Don't worry about it," I replied, and took her arm. Boots shook her head. "I couldn't, Whoreson. If I took the money from you, I'd still have to try and make it to give it back." She added, "Besides, I'm too big to be stuffed in a garbage can."

Since I still held her arm, I didn't leave her any alternative. "Listen, nut," I said, "I'm going to spend twenty dollars with somebody tonight. If you don't want to make that money, that's okay with me, but I'm going to find me a working girl somewhere who ain't so choosy."

My proposition was the answer to her problem. Shrewd as she was, she saw through my little plot. Boots was well aware that I wasn't planning on spending twenty dollars on a whore. But handling men was her profession and she was professional enough to know the error of calling a man a liar to his face. For her to yield to my request now was a simple matter. Her ego wouldn't be hurt, and she would still be independent.

Mischievously, she put her head down on my shoulder. "You really make me feel wanted," she said and laughed lightly before adding, "sweetie."

My muscles tightened involuntarily. The term "sweetie" was mostly reserved for tricks, black or white, as long as they spent cash money. Genuine laughter erupted from deep in her throat. She had immediately realized my extreme dislike for this term of endearment when it was used in connection with me.

Loneliness was a part of life that I was not used to. As we walked towards the hotel I was overjoyed at the prospect of finding temporary release in the warm embrace of Boots' arms.

Later, much later, Boots lay in the crook of my arm with her back pressed against me. The sound of her light snoring was pleasing. My thoughts were troubled as I pondered the future. I kept trying to push the idea from my mind, but it was no use. I recognized the truth of my problem. No matter how much inconvenience it would cause me, Boots would have to be mine.

Instead of going to sleep, I rolled her over on her back. Then I kissed her eyes, nose, neck, till she moaned and came awake.

Blinking her eyes, she stared at me in surprise. "What, baby," she asked sleepily, "ain't you goin' get no rest?"

I kissed her until I could feel her really responding. "Tomorrow, honey," I whispered, "you goin' move your clothes in here. I'm not giving you time to choose, I've already chose."

I had her complete attention now. She twisted

around affectionately so that I was gazing down into her beautiful dark eyes.

"Whoreson, don't do nothing for me out of pity, baby. I can make it."

I replied crudely, "Don't you understand, bitch, that I really want you. Pity ain't in it. I know you're a good whore, big belly or not. So I'm going to hook up with you now."

She raised up on her elbows. Not truly convinced of my sincerity, she apparently was trying to reach an honest decision. Her acceptance of my proposal was a must, especially since I had committed myself. If she refused me now, my pride would be hurt. Determined that she wouldn't deny me, I enclosed her in my arms and compelled her to surrender. Her nipples grew firm under my caresses, and I made love to her till her voice trembled with erotic weakness.

Sometime in the early morning I relaxed against the sweat-soaked sheets. Her murmur came to me low and husky. "I can't describe how you make me feel, but I'm yours, Whoreson, as long as you want me."

It was late in the afternoon when Ray showed up. I had just come back from the bathroom after taking a hot bath. He nodded and smiled warmly at Boots propped up in the bed with both pillows.

"Hey girl," he yelled, "what you done gone and did? Copped you a mack? I know you ain't laying up in no pimp's bed-yarding, girl, so tell me the real deal."

While straightening my tie, I watched her in the mirror. I couldn't help but appreciate her. Her low

laugh was deep and sexual. When she smiled her face
took on a rare beauty.

She asked lightly, "Are you congratulating me on
my choice or warning me, Ray?"

I slipped on my overcoat before interrupting. "I'm
ready whenever you're ready, Ray."

"Wow!" Ray exclaimed. "Man, what's the deal?
You done got sharp, and even choked up tight on me."

I laughed and opened the door, ignoring his remarks
about the suit and tie I wore. He was just as immaculate in his attire as I was, except that I wore a tie
and he didn't.

Two hours later, after visiting five different pawn-
shops, I sat down in the car and relaxed. Glittering on
my little finger was an exquisite diamond ring. I stared
at it proudly. It had cost seven hundred dollars but I
didn't care. My bankroll was down to nine dollars,
yet I didn't have a concern in the world. Whether I
was stupid or just didn't realize the value of money,
I can't say. After all, I was only sixteen. Still, I wasn't
doing too bad. Jessie had made a better hustler out of
me than I realized. It was many grown men who
couldn't compare with me when it came to getting
down and gettin' cash money. Here I was, in a strange
town, with a pregnant whore to support, and yet I
didn't have any doubts about living. Because if the
sun came up, by the time it went down, I'd have figured out a way to get fresh money.

12

I STARED OUT OF the car window glumly. The feel of the steering wheel didn't excite me as it had the past week, when I'd received the keys to the Cadillac from Ray. For a few moments I let my mind dwell on Ray and his predicament. Last week the police had picked him up for draft evasion. I had gone down to visit him and he'd given me the car keys. After being introduced to his mother and promising to give her five hundred dollars, she'd given me the papers to the car. Everything was still in Ray's name, but I had the payment book.

Sleet beat a tattoo against the windshield. I stared at the mess falling. It wasn't snowing or raining; this slush was a mixture of both. Visibility was slight, so I strained my eyes trying to pick up Boots, who was standing in front of the restaurant in an attempt to pull a trick. I let out a sigh of relief. Boots came out of the restaurant door with a white john in tow. At least we would be able to pay the rent in the morning.

I watched them make their way to the trick's car. I wondered idly how she would handle him. He was just about the biggest, fattest man I'd ever seen. If we hadn't needed the money so bad, I would have told her to pass him up. She was about seven months gone now. I pictured her and the honkie together and grinned. The trick had a potgut on him as big as the one she was sporting. I left the curb in pursuit of the trick's car. I had no fear of being seen, because the john's back window was completely covered, like mine, with frost.

I found a parking spot a few doors down from the hotel and I left my motor running, absorbing the heat. I watched the couple dash for the entrance of the building.

Boots had turned out to be an asset instead of a hindrance during the past three weeks we had been together. Time passed slowly as I sat there with the radio swinging. I glanced at my watch for the tenth time. They had been gone over fifteen minutes. I lit a cigarette to help pass the time. Angrily, I realized that, if something didn't jump off soon, I'd have to pawn my jewelry to raise the five hundred dollars for the car.

After smoking the cigarette down to a butt, I put it

out in the ashtray. Cutting the motor off, I jumped out of the car. Tomorrow was my birthday and I'd be damned if I'd spend it cooped up in a car. I pulled my coat collar up and glanced at my watch. Damn tomorrow; today was the beginning of my birthday, and I was poor as hell.

The hotel lobby was empty as I crossed it and started up the steps. The night clerk had a small room behind the desk and you had to ring the bell if you wanted a room after midnight. Stopping in the hallway leading to my room, I glanced at my watch. They had been up there for over thirty minutes now.

Hesitantly, I stood in front of the door holding the key. I was undecided on whether I should knock or just barge in, when the sound of a muffled scream came from behind the closed door.

I inserted the key and lunged into the room. The sight in front of me enraged me. Boots was completely naked, while the trick was wearing only his shorts. He was so obsessed with beating her that he hadn't heard me enter the room. He was using an ironing cord to whip her. Blood was running from her nose and mouth, from the punches the trick would give her each time she tried to grab hold of the cord. Boots was so engrossed in trying to avoid the cord and punches that she didn't hear me either. She tried to cover her head with the pillow, while pulling the sheet up around her body to protect as much of it as possible.

Picking up a chair sitting beside the dresser, I slipped up behind the trick and tried to cave his skull in. The chair splintered on the back of his head. He whirled around and reached for me. His face was covered with blood from the long nails Boots had raked him with. With the remains of the splintered chair, I struck him in the face.

The chair didn't stop him. He grunted and wrapped his arms around me. He was as hairy as a gorilla. His chest, legs, arms and back were covered with a thick, filthy mass of hair. For the first time since I'd entered the room, fear filled my mind. His foul breath was smothering me from our nearness. In desperation I swung my knee up between his legs as hard as I could. A cry of pain exploded from his lips and I kneed him again. His big frame began to fold up. Catching him by the hair, I pulled his head down and lifted my knee with all the force I could put into it. I caught him full in the face, crushing his nose and causing teeth to scatter about the room. He had false teeth, because when he fell to the floor he spit out the rest of them.

He stared up at me with fear in his eyes. When I saw that fear, I knew I had him. Grabbing up the ironing cord, I began to beat him viciously. His screams had the effect of waking up everybody in the hotel. The trick crawled towards a corner and I beat his hulking body unmercifully. Every time he tried to get off his knees and come out of the corner, I'd kick him in the face.

Suddenly he screamed, "That's it! That's it! Don't stop!" He gasped in shuddering ecstasy.

I stared at him in astonishment. He held his penis tight and moaned sickeningly.

The doorway was filling up with couples trying to peer in. The clerk stood in the doorway and stared in horror. His eyes kept going from the sickening sight of the perverted trick in the corner to Boots, naked and bloody, stretched out on the bed.

Not realizing that I still held the ironing cord, I started towards the door to close it. Everybody in the doorway backed up in a hurry.

"Listen here, boy," the clerk said hotly. "If you start beating them again, I'm calling the police. I don't give a damn if that freakish honkie in there wants you to beat him or not, I ain't having that kind of shit in this hotel." I slammed the door in his face. When I turned around, the trick was putting his clothes back on.

My voice was cold and deadly. "Leave your money on the dresser, all of it, honkie. Just consider yourself lucky that that's all it's goin' cost you, too. I should kill you, peckerwood."

He took all the money out of his wallet and placed it on the dresser. Then, clinging to the wall till he reached the door, he snatched it open and fled down the hallway.

My heart began to beat normally again after he left. I realized that he could have beaten me to death if he hadn't been an arch coward. Assuming an air of compassion I moved over to the bed and began to examine Boots. I found a pan, filled it with warm water and washed her wounds gently. All the while I'd ignored the money on the dresser, but my mind was in an uproar from wondering how much was there.

After I finished washing Boots and got her to go

to sleep, I rushed over to the dresser. There was only eighteen dollars there, all the bills were one dollar ones. I had been hoping for a couple of hundred, at least, but the singles had faked me out.

It didn't take acute perception for me to realize that I would have to play some stores in the near future. Like early in the morning. I needed cash money, quick.

Under the facebowl, I had hidden the last of a twenty dollar spoon of cocaine. I sat up with the coke and some weed till daylight invaded the room. The sound of the morning traffic had dwindled slightly when I got up and slipped on my booster overcoat. It was a coat with shot pockets sewed onto the inside lining. Two exceptionally large pockets, I might add. After smoking the last joint, I was ready for work.

I glanced at the clock on the dresser. Just a little after seven. Boots moaned in her sleep as I gave her a quick check on my way out the door. Out on the street I pulled my collar up. The hail had stopped, but a freezing wind was blowing. I started the car and climbed back out to clean the windows. The car was warm by the time I got back inside.

Traffic moved along at a brisk pace as I drove downtown. I stopped off and had breakfast, killing a little more time. Most of the main stores were still unopen. I parked on a side street and started walking. The first store I entered turned out to be a blank. There was nothing above the counter I could swing with, and not enough money in the till for me to note.

Hitting the street again, I fell in step behind two

well-dressed ladies. They walked fast in an attempt to escape the chilling wind. When they turned down a side street I stopped and watched them run across the street and enter a modern looking building.

That made my mind up for me. I crossed the street and examined the name on the building. Ruben-Donley Publishing Co. I started to examine it more closely as two secretaries rushed past. I followed them into the building. The corridor was empty. The lobby had been scantily furnished. Just a few chairs. Next to two pay phones, I found a directory. I scanned it quickly. The building had six floors. The printing department was located on the second floor. I quickly decided to bypass that floor. I passed the elevators and found a door marked "stairway." I took the stairs two at a time until I reached the top floor. I crept down the deserted hallway and discovered I'd reached the floor the cafeteria was on. Peeping through the window, I saw the sister I'd noticed enter the building. She seemed to be fixing up the counter. Except for the two women in uniform, the place seemed empty.

Retracing my steps, I took the stairs down to the fifth floor. I hesitated before opening the door until the sound of high-heels faded away. Straightening my coat, I removed a newspaper from my coat pocket. It was already turned to the want ads. Gripping the paper firmly, the way I imagined a good job hunter would do, I stepped into the hallway. I smiled at the fleeting thought that it would really be amusing if I got hired. I walked down the hallway briskly but silently. The first office I stopped at, I could see someone silhouetted through the shaded glass so I crossed the corridor to another office. With my head beside the door, I listened patiently. Not hearing any sounds I took the plunge. I stepped inside the office.

The office was deserted but the door leading to an adjoining room was open. I could hear a woman's voice coming from the other office. As I listened I heard a man speak, but I couldn't make out the words. Quickly I examined the room I was in. There were two desks in the office, both on the other side of the room from me.

To reach either desk I'd be in view of whoever was in the other room. The only thing in my favor was the thick carpet on the floor. I held my breath and began creeping. The woman had her back to the open door, while the man was sitting at his desk with his head down, examining a cluster of papers. I passed the open door without being observed and reached the first desk. I bypassed it for the second desk, where a chair had been pushed back, as though someone had just risen. As quietly as possible, I opened the second drawer. The bottom one on the right had held only paperwork. It was empty, too. I moved over to the other side of the desk, and pulled out a drawer. The first thing that met my eye was a large black pocketbook. I removed it and closed the drawer. The damn thing was too large to fit the pockets inside my coat, so I stuck it under my armpit.

My heart skipped a beat as I heard the woman start for the door. I froze as the door opened wider. Should I break and run? Maybe I could brazen the bust out.

I stepped from behind the desk. The sound of the man's voice halted the woman in the doorway. When she turned to answer, I made my move. Moving quickly but silently, I recrossed the short distance and reached the door, praying all the while that the woman framed in the doorway concealed me from the man's view. I opened the door and stepped into the hallway, leaving the door ajar. Without looking back, I rushed towards the stairway. Before I reached the stairs the elevator stopped and a woman got out. I gave her my dazzling smile and stepped into the elevator. I pushed the button for the first floor, then tried to arrange the awkward pocketbook under my arm so it wouldn't be conspicuous.

At the second floor the elevator stopped, causing my heart to flutter. An elderly woman peeped into the empty elevator.

"Up?" she asked stupidly.

"Down," I replied as I pushed the button for the door to close.

When I got downstairs and out on the street, I looked back over my shoulder at the building. This was one hell of a way to be spending my seventeenth birthday, I thought bitterly. I reached my car and rode away from the downtown district. After I found a small deserted side street, I parked and started searching the pocketbook.

The purse had ten dollars in cash in it. I cursed for about ten minutes, then investigated the rest of the contents. The bank book I inspected with care. The fourteen hundred and fifty dollars she had deposited in the bank really interested me. I examined all of her identification. Only her driver's license had the revealing "W" on it. I tossed the license out the window and started the car up.

There was no way in the world for Boots to pass for white, but the rest of the I.D. could be used by her. The woman was twenty-eight years old. Boots could pass for twenty-eight with her belly sticking out in front of her a mile. Providing we found a white bank teller. They always said we looked alike to them.

Taking my time on the slippery streets, I reached the hotel with time to spare. The bank didn't open till nine. Whereas I was completely unfazed about stealing the purse, I did have a few qualms over Boots withdrawing the money. Despite my concern, I was going to make her try and withdraw all that cash. After all, I reasoned, if she fucked up and got caught, being pregnant would be in her favor when she went before the judge.

Boots was lying on the bed moaning when I entered the room. I put my hand on her head. It was hot.

"I'm bleeding, Whoreson," she whispered.

I stared down at her for a moment. "Listen, baby, ain't there something you can do, like pack yourself, or something? Just slow the bleeding down. I got something I want you to do, now."

"I might not be able to stop the bleeding, Whoreson. I done already soaked through two pads and the sheet. I think I'm hemorrhaging."

My mind was running super-fast. I needed her now. "I'll tell you what, baby, take and pack yourself with cotton, then get dressed and I'll take you to a doctor."

There was no compassion in my heart, nor was I conscious of any concern about her having a miscarriage. In fact, I hoped that she would lose the baby. If my mother could see me now, she couldn't help but be proud. At seventeen I was developing into a cold, vicious pimp. This is the way I reasoned with myself, but in my heart I knew that, if Jessie could see what I was doing, she would have thrown up in my face. I needed that money, though, and time was something I didn't have. If I didn't get it this morning, it would be too late later on in the day.

Boots was too slow getting dressed for me, so I helped her. After getting a maternity dress on her, I grabbed a spring coat and tossed it across her shoulders. She was in too much pain to notice that I had left her heavy winter coat on the rack by mistake.

The mistake had been made on purpose. I wanted the bank teller to be sure and see she was pregnant.

Finally we got ready to go. I had to just about carry her down the stairs. I began to have doubts about her holding up long enough for us to make it to a bank. At no time did I even think about taking her to a hospital or doctor. I wanted the money before the bank could be notified.

There was another stop I had to make before going to the bank. I parked in a no-standing zone and rushed into a drugstore. I bought a pair of round rimmed glasses and some pain pills. The eyeglasses she put on, the pills she couldn't swallow without water, and I didn't have the time to stop and get any.

Driving towards the outskirts of town, I searched frantically for a branch office bank. I finally found one near the city limits. By this time Boots seemed nearly delirious. Her legs were stretched out towards me, while her head was against the door. When I shook her, she didn't wake up completely. I got out of the car and picked up a handful of slush. Opening the car door on her side, I held her head and washed her face with dirty snow.

She sputtered and spit, but the ice shocked her awake. "Listen, baby," I whispered, "you goin' have to be kind of sharp now. I done told you a dozen times how to do this, and how simple it is."

I had to help her out of the car. "All you got to do is fill out a withdrawal slip, give it to the teller, and get big bills."

"You going with me, daddy?" she asked, clutching my shoulder for support.

"You know I am, baby; you don't think I'd send you by yourself, do you?" I said. I hadn't planned on going in with her, but a blind man could see she would never make it herself.

I steered her through the bank entrance. While she filled out the slip I arranged her coat so that her protruding stomach couldn't help but be seen.

It's a belief of mine, I don't know if it's true or not, that people will never suspect pregnant women of a hoax. The mother image is so strong that most people wouldn't imagine a woman in this condition swindling anyone, let alone them.

The only doubt I had after entering the bank was

when the teller picked up the phone. The only reason I didn't run was that my hands were full trying to keep Boots on her feet. She had put most of her weight on me, and I was really holding her up. When I turned back towards the bank teller she was already talking on the phone. If I ran I would have to drag Boots, 'cause she was holding on to me for dear life. The teller hung up and smiled. She started counting out the money. To be fair to the lady whose money I was taking, I left fifty dollars in the bank.

Back in the car I just about got Boots settled before she passed out. I pulled out into traffic and drove back towards town as fast as I dared. I still hadn't learned to drive too well, and not having a license, the last thing I wanted was to be stopped.

I spotted a doctor's office on the other side of the street. Making a U-turn, I pulled up in front of the building. Some kind of way I got her half awake so she could stand on her feet if I held her, and I managed to get her into the doctor's office. The receptionist took one look at me holding Boots up and rushed into another room. The white patients sitting around the room stared at us curiously.

It wasn't long before she was back, followed by a baldheaded fat man. He was blowing as though he had just run a mile.

He tossed his hands in the air. "No, no, no! You must take her to her own gynecologist. Better yet, take her to an obstetrician, but this is the wrong place, young man."

I was dumbfounded. I hadn't understood much of

what he said, but I did comprehend wrong place.
"You're a doctor, ain't you?" I asked belligerently.

The doctor stared at me as though I were losing
my mind. "I'm a dermatologist," he yelled. "Didn't
you read the sign outside?"

Boots slipped out of my arms and fell on the floor
at my feet. The doctor looked as if he were going to
have the baby. The nurse rushed to a telephone while
the doctor and I raved. I pulled my large roll of money
out. Behind all I'd heard and knew of white people,
I knew this would get results.

"Look, doc," I started to say, "I'll pay…."

The doctor raised his hands toward heaven, spoke
for a few moments in another language, then said, "I
don't want your money. I'm a dermatologist. Don't
you understand? There is nothing…."

I interrupted him harshly. "Why you colorstruck
bastard, you. You'd allow this young girl to suffer…."

At the sound of my words the doctor turned bright
red. The nurse spoke up. "Don't worry, I've called an
ambulance. It will be here shortly."

The doctor and I exchanged a few more choice
words before the ambulance crew arrived. When they
did arrive, we were standing over Boots glaring at
each other, while the nurse knelt beside her, giving
her a shot.

As I followed the stretcher from the office, I turned
in the doorway. "You're about as useful as a doctor,"
I said loudly, "as a penis is on a sissy."

As I started my car up to follow the ambulance I
glanced at the sign. Dermatologist. I couldn't pro-

nounce the damn word, let alone spell it, and I sure didn't have the slightest idea what it meant.

Later, at the hospital, an intern thinking that I was the grief-stricken husband, stopped and explained. "Your wife has had a miscarriage. The membrane was punctured, causing the fetus to die, and when that happened, the uterus started to expel it."

"You mean she goin' lose the baby?" I asked ingenuously.

The young intern stared at me for a moment to see if I was serious. Then realizing that I was just young and dumb, he said, "She has lost the baby. Now we are trying to stop the hemorrhaging, so that we don't lose the mother, too."

That rang a bell. The last thing I wanted to do was lose a good whore. After waiting all this time for her to get streamlined, I didn't want to lose her now that she was ready for the track.

When he saw the shock in my face, the intern walked away. I felt the bankroll in my pocket. It was four hundred dollars short because of the hospital bill. I shouldn't have paid the damn bill so fast. If she died and I hadn't paid the bill, all I'd had to do was deny being her husband and the hell with the bill. The thought of her dying rang in my mind, followed by the frightening knowledge of what a funeral would cost. I sat down suddenly and began to pray. Please Lord, don't let that young girl die.

For the next two hours I sat there with my head in my hands. Whenever a nurse came by, she would try and console me. They must have imagined me as a grieving husband, for they were all very kind. They didn't realize that I was just as concerned about my four hundred dollars as I was about Boots.

I don't want this misunderstood, so I'll try and explain it better. If Boots lived, the hell with the four hundred, but if she died, it was then a two-way blow. A good whore is always worth more than four hundred dollars to a good pimp. One of the nurses stopped and persuaded me to go home and get some rest. It didn't take much urging. I'd been trying to figure out a good excuse for departing. That way, if something happened, I'd make damn sure they couldn't find me to stick with the burial expense.

The next few days were days of worry. I called the hospital constantly. Most of the nurses knew my voice by now, and they kept me up on the latest. She was out of the worst of it, so I could start relaxing. This was really beautiful news.

I knew that in the near future I would be pimping again, and doing it sure'nuff big.

13

MY THOUGHTS WERE SHARPLY interrupted by the ringing of the telephone. I picked up the receiver and listened to Boots' excited chatter.

"Okay, Boots, just grab a cab, I'll have everything ready when you get here."

Things had begun to get damn hot in this small town for us. I had moved from the hotel one jump ahead of the vice squad. Everybody on the track knew the police were looking for a light-skinned Negro with a pregnant woman. Now the search had moved to the hospitals. Some black-ass nigger had done some tall talking to the police, 'cause Boots had just been interviewed by two detectives.

Removing my bankroll from under the pillow, I sat up and counted the money. There was still three hundred dollars in my roll. After paying Ray's mother five hundred, the cost of living in a motel the past few days was beginning to eat up my stash.

A car pulled up outside. I pulled back the curtain and looked out. It wasn't Boots, but she wouldn't be long. As soon as she could steal some clothes, she would slip out of the hospital.

It didn't take long for me to come to a solution to our problem. Put some highway between us and the police. Our bags were already packed, so I carried them out to the car and put them in the trunk. After that I removed the silk scarf from around my head and combed my hair, then put our toilet articles in an overnight bag and laid it on the arm of a chair. I examined the room carefully, making sure I hadn't overlooked anything.

The sound of a car stopping in front of my unit gave me a start. I peeped out the window cautiously. Boots was getting out of a cab. I rushed to the door and opened it, and handed her the cab fare.

We stood in the doorway and watched the cab until it turned out of the driveway. "Let's go, baby."

She asked, "Ain't you goin' give me enough time to change clothes?"

I removed the overnight bag from the chair. "You can change at some gas station on the highway, baby. Right now we goin' get the hell out of here before we end up locked up tight."

The mention of jail put wings on her heels. I didn't begin to relax till we got out of the city limits. The farther I got away from the city the better I felt.

After I got out in the country, I stopped at a gas station and filled the tank up, while Boots went to the rest room and changed clothes. When she came back to the car I helped her put her suitcase in the backseat.

I pulled the car out onto the highway again. I was undecided on where to go, Detroit, Chicago or New York. With Boots sitting beside me pouring the drinks and lighting the reefer, I was at peace with the world.

"Where we going, daddy?" she asked, crossing her legs and leaning towards me. She rubbed the back of my neck, titillating me slightly.

Driving with one hand on the wheel, I put my other one between her legs and rubbed her smooth thighs affectionately. Her long, shapely black legs seemed to vibrate with heat. She moaned softly and nibbled at my ear.

"I can't do nothing for at least four weeks, Whoreson."

"You can do something," I replied with a grin. "I ain't heard nothing about your head being dead."

We both laughed raucously. Boots lit up another stick of weed and choked on the smoke. She coughed for about five minutes while I laughed all the while.

When we reached Detroit, we were still in a jocular mood. Driving down Hastings Street was a thrill for me. The appalling deterioration of the tenements, gloomy and frightening to some people, filled me with joy. This was home to me. I didn't know any other way of life. The women huddled in the doorways, trying to find some measure of warmth and shelter while plying their trade, didn't arouse commiseration in my heart, only regret that they weren't in my stable.

Boots' impression was altogether different from mine. "I sure feel sorry for them bitches. I bet they done damn near froze in them doorways." Then she added, "If it was me, I'd walk up and down instead of standing still, that way at least you might stay a little bit warm."

Some of the more notable pimps could be seen sitting in their cars with the motors running. Sometimes a girl would run out of a doorway and get in a car. After sitting in the car for a few moments to get warm, she would run back to her doorway and continue working.

I parked in front of Big Mama's. Most of the women standing in her doorway knew me. They began to yell before I got out of the car.

"Look at Whoreson, honey. Driving a Cadillac, and diamonded down," Marge yelled, a healthy coffee-colored woman.

Boots got out of the car and waited for me at the curb. She put her arm around me and tossed her head up. Her attitude revealed beyond a doubt that I was her man and that she was plenty proud of it.

We walked up the stairs, arrogant and self-sufficient, without a care in the world.

Big Mama, her face all aglow, smothered me in her huge arms. "Whoreson, boy, why didn't you write or something? Here I been worried to death over you, and you don't even bother to write."

I finally extricated myself from her embrace. I hadn't realized how much I had missed this big woman who cared so much about me. There was a lump in my throat and I hoped that my eyes wouldn't betray me by glittering with tears.

"Come here, baby," I said to Boots, "and meet my grandma." Boots was a big woman herself, but when Big Mama embraced her, she was completely lost in those enormous arms and bosom.

Big Mama removed a bottle of wine from her refrigerator and we sat around in her kitchen drinking and reminiscing.

"Whoreson," Big Mama said, "I still got your flat, boy. If you want to move back in, it's okay with me. I been paying the rent and sleeping there sometimes. It does my poor heart good to get away from all these silly girls at times. I'm sick of hearing them talk about their damn pimps."

My acceptance of the flat seemed to bring joy to the old woman's soul. I guess she just felt as if I were her wayward child. On my part, I not only felt but knew that, except for Boots, she was the only person in the world who really cared about what happened to me.

Quite a bit of time had elapsed since we entered the apartment. I stood up. "Well, Big Mama," I said, "I guess we had better be going. We been traveling all morning and need some rest."

Boots stood up and clutched my arm for support. The drinks and weed had finally caught up with her.

"That child sure can't drink much, can she?" Big Mama asked.

"We been drinking all morning," I replied, "plus, she just got out of the hospital today."

"If that's the truth, Whoreson," Big Mama said plainly, "don't you go putting that girl to work too soon. You wait till she ready, you hear?"

She followed us to the door. "I mean that, Whoreson. If you need any money, boy, let me know. But you better make damn sure I don't hear about that girl out there working sick."

Her friendly warning followed us down the stairs. It was obvious that I wouldn't work Boots until she was in good shape. Amusing as Big Mama's threat was, it would benefit me to pay heed to it. If I put Boots out on the streets working and Big Mama got the wire, she wouldn't hesitate to lock Boots up in her flat, and there was nothing I'd be able to do about it. It was a sure bet that I wouldn't try kicking her door down. Any time a man has been raised by a woman, his mother or not, there are certain liberties she can take with him that no other person in the world would dare do.

By the time I got Boots in the car and was starting the motor up, someone knocked on the window. I glanced over my shoulder and saw Ape grinning at me. Reaching over Boots' sprawled-out form, I opened the car door and let him in. He waved back at the men he had been with as I pulled away from the curb.

Ape had filled out quite a bit since I'd seen him

last. He had been big before, but now he was huge. When he smiled, he still resembled a titanic gorilla. He didn't have but two teeth in the front of his mouth, and his lips were large and blubberish.

When Boots got sober enough to look up at him, she tried to climb on top of my lap. "Watch out, woman," I yelled. "What you goin' do, sit on the steering wheel?"

"How far we got to go to find some good reefer, Ape?"

He hesitated for a moment. "Billy got some light green, Whoreson, while Eddie's smoke is good, it's got a lot of sticks and stuff in it." He added, "Eddie's dealing out of the poolroom."

"I don't care nothing about the sticks, Ape, if the smoke is boss."

"The smoke is mellow, baby," he answered. "The sweet thing about it is that it don't take no time to cop. When Eddie ain't at the poolroom, he leaves his bag with the rack man."

The poolroom was on John-R, so I turned down a side street. "Give him fifteen dollars, Boots, out of my inside pocket. Cop me a half a can of weed, Ape, and pick up a couple of bottles of wine. We'll be around at the flat where I used to stay; is that cool with you?"

He took the fifteen dollars out of her hand. "That's swinging, brother. What should I do if some of the mellow fellows want to come around to your pad with me, cut 'em loose?"

I laughed. The expression on his face revealed all

he didn't say. I knew that he was wondering if I would cut all of my old partners loose now that I had a Caddie and a whore.

"Bring whoever you want, man, this is Whoreson, not John Flippinggates."

He stuck his hand back in the car. I leaned over and smacked his hand hard with mine. He yelled, "Mellow, mellow, mellow, I can dig it. I can really dig where you coming from, baby boy." He turned and catted towards the poolroom.

Boots looked at me amused. "Baby, I can really tell that you're at home."

14

EMPTY WINE BOTTLES and overflowing ashtrays littered my apartment. For the past two weeks our flat had become an open house, with wild parties continuing for three or four days without stopping. Since Friday I'd promised myself that come Monday morning the party would end. At long last, I had got the last drunk started down the stairs. It had taken over an hour to get rid of all of them, but now I could sigh with relief.

Now with dawn breaking through the early darkness, I watched from my window the working men of the neighborhood preparing to depart for work. Milton's father, dirty as usual, stood in the street

beside his car talking to one of his neighbors. I
watched him with disdain. His coveralls were grimy
with filth. The old model car he drove matched its
owner in shabbiness.

My gaze flickered to my Cadillac. There was a feeling of triumph inside of me. I wasn't even half his
age and I'd already accomplished more than he ever
would. Milton's mother could look down her fat nose
at me if she wanted to pretend, but we both knew who
had the sweetest end of the stick. Exultation overcame
me as I turned and watched Dianne dumping ashtrays.
With my chest pushed out with pride, I walked over
to the bedroom and opened the door. Boots and Vera
were both laid out, side by side. They had danced so
much over the past few days that they were just worn
out.

"Dianne, why ain't you in bed gettin' some rest,
girl?" I asked quietly. "You know I'm sending you to
work later on today."

She looked up from her cleaning and smiled shyly.
"I just want to clean this mess up a little, daddy," she
answered innocently.

A good pimp should try and know what his whores
are thinking. Sometimes you would be put in an awkward spot, but most of the times you can guess just
about what they have on their mind.

"Quit lying, bitch," I replied coldly. "I know the
only reason your lazy ass is up, faking like you're
working, is on the slim chance that I'll give you some
meat this morning when I go to bed."

Her eyes dropped and she tried to look rejected,

but just as quickly she rushed over and hugged me. "You goin' do a little something for me this morning, ain't you, Whoreson?"

This was an ideal time to act chilly, but my defense was weakening. She was light chocolate, and her skin was as smooth as a baby's ass. When she smiled and looked up at me with her big bedroom eyes, I couldn't refrain from taking her in my arms and kissing those tender lips. As she pressed her young body against me, I knew that fate had dealt me a terrible blow. I had been gifted with a tender dick.

Bending over, I caught her legs and carried her towards the other bedroom. Her body had the smell of fresh roses and her arms around me had the same effect as alcohol to the senses. When our bodies met, a shock of electricity went through my mind. We were caught up in the passion of youth, and my excitement exceeded all bounds.

Later, with Dianne snuggled against me gently snoring, I shuddered with horror at the thought of having to leave every morning for a job. I had never had a job and because of my environment and training, plus my dexterity at getting money, employment was unnecessary.

My stable was growing. My mind wandered to the other two girls in the house, Boots and Vera. Now that I had three girls, it wouldn't be long before I was the best young pimp in the city. Here I was, at seventeen, with three of the youngest, wildest and fastest whores in the country. How sweet it was. Pimping really had its good points.

With the passing of Christmas and the following holidays, I was in good shape for the new year. Boots was able to go back to work, so I stopped her from doing any more boosting. Her boosting bloomers were packed away for later use.

Many pimps would disagree with me, because quite a few pimps would rather have a booster than a whore. But to me, at this stage of my life, I didn't want anything but a flat-backing whore.

The neighborhood theater, which went by the name of Duke, used to put on talent shows every Saturday afternoon. Since I was too young for the bars, I'd dress my three ladies up, get the car washed, and make my grand appearance, amidst much head-turning and adulation from the young would-be pimps in the audience.

Ape, with a few more of my old gang, would have two rows of seats saved down in front for the selected ones in our crowd. My girls enjoyed the adulation as we walked slowly towards our seats. My popularity was rising. The fastest young girls in the neighborhood would crowd down near our row trying to catch my eye. This theater was to become the best establishment in the city for meeting potential prostitutes.

One Saturday, while sitting down front, crowded in between many admirers, a group came out on the stage and swept the spotlight from me with their swinging arrangements. I stared in wonder at young Janet. She was still singing and getting better than ever. I watched her capture the crowd with song after song.

The audience wouldn't let them leave the stage. Every time they tried to leave, the crowd would become so unruly that the owner would call them back on stage.

After doing one more number, Janet must have decided to put a stop to the commotion herself. She came down off the stage, followed closely by the two girls who sang with her.

She stopped in front of me and leaned over. "Whoreson, how about trying and getting us out of here," she yelled in my ear.

"Don't worry, baby," I said, standing up. "I can handle it," I replied with more confidence than I felt.

The crowd was really yelling and kids were crowding into the aisle. I had grave doubts about whether I could get them out. One thing kept ringing in my mind, though; this young girl had STAR written all over her, and I meant to shine bright in her eyes.

Embracing Janet, I pulled one of her trembling girlfriends into my other arm. Catching Boots' eye, I yelled, "See if you can get Ape and some of the fellows to clear a path, baby."

She nodded and ran over to him. With Ape and five more of the bunch in front of her, Boots started breaking through the crowd, with us right behind. With kicks and punches, they soon had kids climbing seats to get out of the way.

Finally we reached the protection of my car. All the girls piled in. I gave Ape enough cash for cab fare and some weed before driving off.

"You can drop us off anywhere, Whoreson," Janet said quietly.

I smiled and kept on driving. "I know you ain't goin' be rude enough to refuse an invitation to my place, Janet."

She sighed and settled back against the seat, compelled to accept my offer by my apparent refusal to stop long enough to let them out.

Within thirty minutes after our arrival, the capacity of my house was being tested. Teenagers were everywhere except the back porch, and that was only because of the cold weather.

Janet sat down on the couch beside me. She was breathing heavily from continuous dancing. "This is the first time I've sat down since we got here," she laughed. "I've heard about some of the swinging sets you gave, Whoreson, but I didn't realize just how renowned you are."

"I'm glad you're really enjoying yourself, Janet. You seemed so set against coming here that I figured you'd leave before everybody arrived."

"Actually I'm having a better time than I thought was possible, Whoreson." She touched my arm and gestured towards the dancers. "Seriously though, Whoreson, just how long do you think this can go on?"

"What do you mean, baby, the party?" I asked, looking down into her large serene eyes.

Yielding to her female wiles, she laughed lightly and gave my arm a pinch. "You know what I mean. These parties, prostitutes, you not working. How long, Whoreson, do you really think you can last? Noticeable as your Cadillac is, successful as pimping might be, you still don't have any solid foundation under you."

It finally occurred to me that she was serious. Probably this was her way of letting me know that she would be available if I would give up the game. Naturally I had no intention of ever giving up the game, but I didn't want to hurt her feelings.

"Listen, sugar," I said softly, "name me one good job that I could get. Don't think about the Caddie that I drive, or the diamonds that I wear, nor the silk suits that I look so good in. Just forget about those things, and name me a decent job that I could get."

She bit down on her lip for a moment. "Well," she began, "you'd probably have to go back to school for a while." She hesitated to see if I was taking this seriously before continuing. "Then after you graduated you could...," she finished in a rush, "get all kinds of jobs."

"Be a little more precise, baby," I inquired of her jokingly.

She frowned and became very nervous. "Well, let me see," she said quietly. "You could uh...become a policeman."

I laughed harshly. "At what police department, honey, one in China?"

"No, no, Whoreson. It's the truth. I ain't joking. My mother read it in the papers this morning. She said they're hiring colored men for all kinds of jobs on the force now."

Instead of being amused by her behavior, I was ashamed of myself. I realized that she was so inno-

cent she believed I might give up my precious pos-
sessions for love.

"Whoreson," she said, her face shining with sincerity, "there are many girls who would marry you
and not care if you didn't make a whole lot of money
at work. They wouldn't care if you had to sweep
floors, wash cars, anything. Just as long as you were
theirs, it wouldn't make any difference what you did."

She was looking at me with so much tender love
in her eyes that I tried to joke her out of the mood.
"You can easily say that, Janet," I said, "but I ain't
seen none of these girls you keep talking about."

Her eyes had tears in them as she stared up at me.
"Just look at me, Whoreson," she said, "I'd gladly be
your wife, but never your whore."

After quite a circular route, there it was, out in the
open. I had tried to keep the naked truth of her feelings from coming to light, but now the cards had been
spread on the table, face up. She seemed so lovely sitting beside me that the thought of losing her was like
taking a liquid bath with loneliness. I knew that my
answer would hurt her. Even while I wanted to spare
her pain, my customary glibness vanished.

To me, the sound of my voice was harsh and sharp.
"Janet, I wouldn't be a flunky to the white man for
you or the Virgin Mary. Car washing, truck driving or
working in some honkie's factory is out of the question for me. Wait," I said, and grabbed her arm to pre-
vent her from leaving. "If my mother had left me
enough money to set up a business or something,
things would have been different, but since this didn't

happen, the only way I can get big money, without selling drugs, is to manage sporting ladies."

She listened to my raving until I was finished, then removed my hand from her arm. "Good-bye, Whoreson," she said bitterly. "Again I wish you all the happiness in the world."

Instead of following her I watched her walk quickly to the door and leave. If there was one thing I disliked, it was to watch a woman cry, and I knew she was crying. Trying to maintain my air of composure, I turned and examined the crowded room.

Boots dropped down in the vacant seat. She patted me on the cheek. "Don't worry, daddy. You miss one shot, you get another." She added, "While you was talking to Janet, that light-skinned girl over there asked me if I'd mind having her for a wife-in-law."

Copping was just that simple. My fourth girl came to me just like that. I stared at her without too much interest. Boots' sharp remark brought me back out of the clouds.

"What you looking so mournful about, Whoreson? I know it ain't over that skinny ass Janet. 'Bout all she could do is sing to the tricks, 'cause she ain't got enough ass to stand no heavy pounding."

I whirled around to give her a chilling rebuke, but her eyes were deadly cold, unflinching.

Her voice dripped with venom when she spoke. "Whores go with pimps, Whoreson, barbers go with manicurists, and square bitches go with square niggers." She pivoted on her heels and walked across the crowded floor. Her back was straight, her head held high.

With the coming of summer, my stable of whores stayed anywhere between six and a dozen good prostitutes. Pimping was good and my bankroll continued to swell. At times I would hear reports about Janet singing at different places, but I made it a point not to go anywhere that I might run into her. For some reason she stayed in my mind, no matter how many different women I slept with. As the summer wore on and my stable grew, I tossed myself into one party after another, and started trying to teach myself to take the bitter with the sweet.

15

I AWOKE MONDAY afternoon with a splitting headache. My mouth was dry and my eyes were bloodshot from too much entertaining without sleep.

I reached over one of the ladies in my bed and removed the last stick of weed from the night table. Before I could finish smoking the joint Boots opened the bedroom door and walked in.

Her sharp glance briefly lingered on the two sleeping forms I was lying between. "Whoreson," she said, "why don't you get them lazy bitches up and on the track? Shit, they ain't done nothing but pop their fingers and shake their ass since Friday night."

Before replying I sat up in the bed and inhaled

deeply on the tiny cocktail between my fingers. "Bitch," I replied coldly, "until you grow a pole you leave the pimping to me."

Boots put her hands on her hips and leaned provocatively towards the bed. "Yes suh, master suh," she said sardonically. Amused at her answer, I climbed out of the bed and stretched. Since the miscarriage Boots had developed into one fine bitch.

You couldn't have paid one of my other whores to speak to me in such a flip manner, but Boots knew that she was my main lady, so at times she acted just like a black queen. And to me that's just what she was.

"Since I'm up now I guess I'll take a hot bath," I said.

Boots hurried over to the dresser and took out a large towel. "Whoreson, I went over to the hotel like you said, daddy, but I couldn't get the top floor like you wanted. It was already rented out, so I rented a suite on the second floor."

"How much did that one rent for?" I asked sharply.

She hesitated for a moment. "Thirty dollars a day, daddy, but I didn't pay but a week's rent on it." She rushed her words out, afraid of my reaction.

More from habit than anger, I yelled, "Bitch, dumb bitch, ignorant bitch, did it ever occur to you that I might not want the suite on the second floor?"

I walked out, leaving her to stare after me dumbfounded. Pushing the bathroom door open, I stopped at the sight of another one of my whores. "Damn," I exclaimed irritably. "When you get finished, Jean, run me some bath water." Before slamming the door, I added, "Get some spray, or either burn some goddamn incense in there, and please mix some water with it."

The girls in the kitchen burst out laughing. I stared at the women preparing breakfast until silence greeted my smothering glance.

Boots came quietly into the room and put on a stack of records. "Any of you bitches got some reefer hid, set it out for daddy," she ordered.

Dianne, small, thin, with features that seemed to have been carved from a bronze statue, danced out of the kitchen. She held up two joints proudly.

"Here, daddy." Her voice belied her small frame with its deep sensuality. Her large hazel eyes twinkled as she held out the weed.

Without commenting I removed the reefer from her outstretched hand and watched her dance back into the kitchen. If all my girls had the vim that Dianne displayed at all times, my pimping would be a relief. Next to Boots, she was the best moneymaker in my stable.

Jean came out of the bathroom. She was almost as tall as Boots, but that was where the comparison ended. Where Boots was dark, Jean was light, with yellow teeth full of gaps. Ordinarily, I wouldn't have accepted her in my stable, because she was lazy and virulent. At the time she chose me, I was just beginning my stable. She came to me after ripping off three hundred from a trick.

I finished off the joint I had started before traipsing off to my waiting bath. The mellow weed plus the hot bath eliminated my slight irritation. Living in a house full of women had its drawbacks but I found it much more rewarding than living in a house without any women.

Slipping deeper into the tub, I splashed water up on my chest and shoulders. With the rental of the suite, I would eliminate the problem of some of the worrisome women in my stable. When I moved out, I reasoned, I wouldn't take but Boots and Dianne with me.

My meditation came to an abrupt end with the entry of Dianne. She closed the bathroom door behind her, and by the time I turned to see who it was, she had slipped out of her duster and leaped into the tub naked.

Now I have heard many people speak of how wonderful it is to make love in the bathtub. But to me ain't nothing happening with it. First of all I don't enjoy a woman bathing with me, and as far as I'm concerned, when it comes to having sex with a person in a tub, I think it's foolish.

As small as Dianne was, she still hurt my legs when she sat on my lap. I pushed her up so she turned around and sat down in the bathtub facing me.

She was so full of mischief that she made me grin in spite of my attempt to look stern.

I put my knee between her legs and began to probe for the right spot. Her lithe and graceful body began to move in a most assertive manner.

She looked up at me and groaned enthusiastically, "Oh, Daddy, daddy, you sure know how to make it good to me."

Before the sound of her vibrant voice descended to

its normal tones, Boots had shoved open the door and stepped in. She stood in the doorway, glaring, with the reefer I had given her hanging from the side of her mouth.

Dianne broke the silence. "Whore, you don't own this dick, bitch," she yelled. "So, try putting an egg in your shoe and beat it."

Boots ignored her and came over and sat on the side of the bathtub. "Little hot cunt heifer," she said. "Why don't you get your ass out of there so that Whoreson can enjoy his bath."

The weed had put me in such a mellow mood that I just sat back and enjoyed the byplay.

Dianne snorted. "Huh, whore, I like your nerve. There you sit on your wide ass smoking my reefer and talking shit."

Before Boots could retort, Dianne followed up her verbal attack with action. Using the palms of her hands she began scooting water in Boots' direction. Boots took to her heels while I tried to save my towel from getting soaked.

Cursing, I climbed out of the tub. "It would be my luck to get hooked up with a bunch of crazy bitches."

Dianne jumped out of the tub and snatched the towel from me. Resigned to my fate, I stood docile while she rubbed me down. True to her impetuous nature, as soon as she got below my waist she began to act up. Using the towel with an imp's delight, she took to her task vigorously.

I laughed at her unruly behavior, but before I became too aroused I decided to put a stop to it. I slapped her wrists, but it didn't do any good, she just got a tighter grip. Trying to pry her hands loose was more difficult than trying to get free from an octopus.

"Bitch," I yelled. "Enough is enough, turn my jones loose." Instead of obeying she dropped to her knees and opened her mouth as though she were going to eat some rare delicacy.

I grabbed a handful of her hair and pulled her head back. Only the sudden opening of the door stopped me from slapping her.

Boots charged in carrying a bucket of water. Dianne uttered a scream and scrambled behind me. I leaped sideways but I was too slow. Most of the cold water landed on me.

I shook like a dog shaking water from his fur. Boots turned and fled and I leaped towards the doorway in hot pursuit, cursing every step of the way.

Shrill, piercing shrieks greeted me as I ran bare-ass into the living room. All of my women were sitting there eating, and three other prostitutes that didn't belong to me had stopped in to roll up some reefer.

My predicament was embarrassing even for me. There I stood in the middle of the floor, naked as a newborn baby, with no less than ten women evaluating my prodigious instrument. I looked down unconsciously. Because of the vicious tugging by Dianne a few moments ago, I had nothing to be ashamed of.

Gathering up as much dignity as the occasion would allow, I ambled towards the bedroom amidst catcalls, much laughter and sly insinuations.

"Muh-huh," one girl exclaimed. "I see why

Whoreson got all ya whores in his stable now."

Another one cracked, "I don't know what ya got between your legs, but if I dreamed I took that much meat, I'd wake up with female trouble."

Amidst much loud laughter I slowly dressed, listening from behind the door to their frank appraisal of my merits.

Once again I became aware of the fact that whenever a group of women got together they discussed private sex matters much more openly than a group of men would.

To a stranger their conversation would have sounded vulgar, because they discussed oral sex as though it were a hat they had just purchased. But to me, their conversation was as normal as eating and sleeping. They were discussing their work, and the easy way of doing it.

I hadn't turned eighteen yet, and prostitutes were the only kind of women I had ever known. If someone had inferred that the life I led was quite different from the rest of society, I wouldn't have given it a second thought. From the factory workers I knew, and the ones I saw coming home from work, I didn't have a doubt in my mind as to my role in life. As far as I was concerned, there were two categories of people: one group consisted of tricks and the other of players, and I knew I had been born to play.

I finished dressing and glanced in the mirror. My apparel consisted of black pants, a gold hi-lo shirt, and black alpaca sweater. The black alligator shoes set off my casual dress to perfection. I put on my diamond ring and took one last peek in the mirror, fixing my features in a cold unruffled mask. I opened the bedroom door and stepped out onto my stage.

All pimps must be actors to some degree; not to act spells failure in their field. When a woman comes to your bed in the early morning hours with a fistful of money for you, you are forced to act. No matter how much you may detest this certain lady, you cannot allow your true feelings to show. Being aware of the possibility that she may have consumed a bucket of sperm in the course of a night, you don't display any aversion if she wants to kiss you. You just send her to the bathroom with the Listerine and toothpaste.

So instead of her ever becoming aware of your true nature, she only sees the part you act. Instead of scorn she finds acceptance, instead of hate she finds her conception of love. Thus, many people believe that prostitutes are the biggest tricks of all.

Closing the bedroom door behind me, I yelled, "Dianne." My voice was cold and harsh. "You and some of them other bitches clean up that water on the floor. Then you get Boots' clothes and your own packed. I'll be back for you in a little while."

Fear leaped into her eyes. She searched my face for a clue, then turned and stared at Boots. Their eyes met and whatever transpired seemed to relieve her. She was laughing as much as ever when Boots and I went out the door.

16

THE FOLLOWING WEEKEND Boots and I drove up to visit Tony. He had grown quite tall, with a swell of muscle in his forearms and chest; wiry, but with more than an intimation of great physical strength in the young, cleanly built body. His face, with its deepset black eyes and aquiline nose, showed the fierceness of his African heritage, tempered by the compelling beauty of a black starless night.

His broad features burst into a genuine grin of happiness. "Damn, Whoreson, I done damn near gave up on seeing you until I got out."

Without any embarrassment he embraced me and crushed me against his broad chest. I had to blink to hold back the tears of joy that were filling up my eyes.

The other inmates ignored their visits to watch us curiously. Just as suddenly as he grabbed me, he released his bear hug and swooped down on Boots. She uttered a startled yell before being swept off her feet. While swinging her back and forth as though she were a toy, he planted wet kisses all over her cheeks.

"Damn it, girl," his voice boomed out across the visiting area, "you better stay out the sun; you get any blacker I'm going to disown you as being my sister."

He winked in my direction and I grinned. Knowing him as I did, I knew he had said it to embarrass the white people who had stopped visiting to watch us.

Boots hadn't realized why he did it so she kicked him sharply on the leg. He set her back down.

"God damn you, Boots," he swore, and then added quietly, "I was just showing the white folks we was true to form."

The frosty glare disappeared from her eyes and she smiled suddenly. "Well, just don't use me for any more of your demonstrations."

Tony put his arm around my shoulder. "I don't see how you do it, Whoreson," he said, shaking his head at Boots. "Me now, I ain't goin' have nothing but white girls; they know their place. You show me a black girl, and I'll show you the most evilest, meanest, muleheaded woman God put on this earth."

Glancing out of the corner of my eye, I could see that Boots was steaming. She managed to control her temper until the visiting period was up. We were just about the last ones to leave and all of Tony's friends who had had visitors joined us.

The lush green lawn was almost free of people; before it had been full of running and screaming children, but now most of the lawn chairs were empty. A guard started towards us. Boots stood up.

"Oh ya, Tony, I almost forgot to give you Jean's message," she said quietly. "She said…."

Tony interrupted her. "What Jean you talking about?"

"Don't try and act clever, nigger," Boots replied sharply. "She asked me to tell you that she wanted you to know that she sure liked that hot head you laid on her before you left the streets."

The cold, harsh words fell on a silence like a void. For a moment there was total stillness, then Tony's friends broke out in laughter. Some of them laughed so hard they fell down and rolled over on the grass holding their stomachs.

Amidst the uproar Boots stalked off towards the car. Tony stared after her in wonder. "That's what I call a dirty black bitch, Whoreson," he muttered angrily.

I watched her feline grace until she entered the Cadillac. "Well Tony," I said amused. "Looks like you got a lot of explaining to do to your friends, baby."

He grinned. "That's a topnotch whore you got there, Whoreson. In fact," he continued soberly, "there's something about her that reminds me of Jessie."

Later on as I drove back to Detroit his words stayed in my mind. I'd take my eyes off the highway and glance in Boots' direction. After catching me looking at her a few times, she asked, "You ain't mad with me about what I said about Tony, are you, daddy?"

Since Tony mentioned it I could see some similarity between Boots and my mother, though Jessie had been slightly smaller. Both were tall, dark, beautiful black women with forceful personalities. Whereas Jessie had been quiet, content to live within herself, Boots was the opposite. She enjoyed the company of others, and when she was by herself she became miserable.

I roused myself from my thoughts as her voice penetrated my daydreams. "Ya baby," I said lightly. "Just you be careful who you say such things to, baby, 'cause some niggers get awful mad when people infer that they go in the bushes."

She slipped her arm over the back of the seat and laughed lightly. Her skirt inched up above her knees and I put my arm in her lap. As we neared the city I pulled her skirt up higher and caressed her smooth thighs.

I let Boots out of the car in front of the restaurant connected to the hotel so she could pick up some cigarettes. I parked the car and walked slowly back. The lavish hotel lobby was crowded with people sitting around and talking. Upon entering, I stopped and looked around casually.

Boots came out of the side door of the restaurant without seeing me and started towards the elevator. There were four men sitting at a table playing cards, and one of them reached out and grabbed her arm as she went by. His voice came across the room to me clear and sharp.

"Hey honey, what's your hurry?" he asked. "That young boy you got upstairs got too many girls to be worried about you."

"That's my arm you happen to have hold of," she replied coldly.

"Dig how cold she is," he said sarcastically. "Honey, you ain't cold, and that young punk you got for a man ain't got enough sense to tell you how to respect a man."

A few of the whores and pimps sitting around began to laugh. I watched Boots with amusement. I knew she had a sharp wit and I hoped that she could handle him. If she couldn't, I was pretty sure that I could.

Boots' voice began to rise in anger. "I don't care what you say about my man, at least he don't have to sit out here in the lobby and molest other people's women."

"You got it wrong, baby," the tall thin card player said. "First of all, you ain't got a man, you got a boy, and second, you have to be a man to hang out down here."

Boots laughed sarcastically. "You say my man is a punk, huh. Why don't you come upstairs and tell that to them ten black whores he has sleeping up there. Better yet, why not try and tell the six white whores, three bull-dykers and two punks, and one gold-toothed mule that looks like you, that he ain't a man."

The card player's friends laughed at her retort, but I noticed that he was getting mad, so I moved in. I grabbed the arm that he was holding Boots with. "If you don't mind, buddy," I said softly, "I'd like to see my woman go on about her business."

"Sure, man, sure," he said and with insolence slowly released her hand. He turned his back on me and started laughing and talking to his friends as though I didn't exist.

As Boots took my arm I could feel my temper mounting. "Next time one of these tricks stops you," I said loud enough for the whole lobby to hear, "you find out how much money the sissy is spending, baby, and if he ain't spending any money, don't waste any time with him." And then I added as an afterthought, "You know how some freaks are, baby, they come just by holding a whore's hand."

When the elevator stopped I turned around before entering it and saw that two of the card players' friends were holding him in his seat.

We entered our apartment and hugged up, laughing our heads off. The smell of burning hair was strong in the air. I could hear the chatter of many feminine voices coming from the kitchen. I sighed with resignation. Moving from my flat hadn't done any good. The girls just found an excuse to leave a dress or coat whenever they visited my penthouse, and before I knew it they had just about moved in.

Boots uttered my very thoughts. "Oh Whoreson.... Every time I enter this suite I'm overwhelmed by its beauty."

"You should be," I answered. "For thirty dollars a day it should have a swimming pool in the front room."

I walked into the lavishly furnished living room. The deep blood-red wall-to-wall carpet felt plush beneath the eighty-five-dollar lizardskin shoes I was wearing. The carpet alone seemed to trumpet my arrival as an up-and-coming young pimp.

"Whoreson?"

I turned as Boots glided to a stop before entering the bedroom. "What, baby?"

"I'm going to change into something more comfortable." she said. "How about twisting me up a joint?"

"Okay pothead," I said grinning. "We done already smoked a matchbox since this morning, woman, but just for you, I'm going to smoke some more."

"Oh baby, you sure treat me good, don't you?" she said gaily. She dipped down in her bra and came up with a small brown envelope.

I took the weed from her and as she turned towards the bedroom door I playfully slapped her on her wide ass."Ouch! Whoreson!"

I sat down on the white sofa and placed the envelope of marijuana on the coffee table in front of me.

My eyes roamed around the room. The architectural design was typical of middle-class hotel suites around the country. However, whoever did the decor knew his business. Everything was ultra-modern. My fingers savored the smooth texture of the fine material covering the sofa, as my mind received vivid impressions from an abstract oil painting on the wall in front of me.

I rolled a stick of weed for myself. Relaxing against the soft cushions, I enjoyed the mellow feeling of contentment that flowed through my body. I realized that, with the house full of women, I should value this stolen time. To be alone for just a few moments gave me a tranquility that was indeed rare.

I had never before seen a wall painted black, that is, not in a hotel. It complemented the blood-red carpet. Turning my head, I took in the enamel white wall with its louvered door through which Boots had walked. At the far end of the room, set between the flat-black wall and a mild orange-colored one, was a Nero reclining couch. Placed between this and another like it, both upholstered in leopard skin, sat a large palm plant that appeared to be growing out of the carpet.

By a large window, behind the sofa I sat on, stood a floor-to-ceiling cylindrical lamp. It seemed to be made of frosted glass, with small curlicue designs etched into its surface. Looking up I felt a strange sensation as the zebra patterns on the ceiling gave an illusion of melting together. To me, this was a hip joint.

I stood up and walked over to the Grundig stereo sitting below the abstract painting. As I turned on the switch the sounds of violins filled the room. Although I'm strictly a blues and jazz fiend, the mellow sound of strings in that room seemed appropriate, so I left it on.

"Whoreson! What the hell is that on the box?" Boots asked me from the opened bedroom door.

"It's music, woman. You think the whole world listens to nothing but Jimmy Smith and Little Richard?"

"Oh, daddy, I was just asking."

I walked back to the sofa and, taking some Zig-Zag papers from my coat pocket, sat down and opened the envelope, pouring its contents of dark green reefer onto the long glasstop coffee table. Boots walked over and said in a sexual voice, "Lace me up, daddy."

"Turn around." I stood up and made a bow in the two silk strings hanging from the back of a transparent, hemmed in mink, pink silk negligee.

"Boots, call down to room service and have them send up a fifth of Johnny Walker Red and six bottles of beer."

As she walked towards the telephone she reminded me of what a topnotch whore should look like. The mink that ran around the hem of her negligee bounced softly from her half-exposed buttocks. They were large for her size but without flaws. Her dark thighs and legs were second to none I had seen, and she drew tricks like bees to honey. After reseating myself, I began to roll a few joints.

"And a bucket of ice," I called after her. She stuck her tongue out at me but relayed my message to the desk. After hanging up she came over and lowered herself to the carpet in front of me. I lit up a joint and handed it to her.

"Now be good, honey," I said and pried her inquiring hands loose.

"Daddy, I'm always good," she said and then started doing what I knew she would do. I took the joint from her hand and leaned back on the sofa. Smiling up at me, she unzipped my pants and began fumbling around for the separation in my shorts.

"Why don't you just ask me to take 'em off?" I asked.

"It's more fun this way," she said, and after finally getting a grip on what she was after, she began squeezing and pulling gently, then lowered her head. I felt the warmth of her mouth move up from my thighs and settle deep into my stomach. Each movement of her tongue sent frantic sensations up and down my spine until I didn't think I could stand it any more.

Through the pounding of my heart and the roaring in my mind I heard a metallic sound. The door opened and Dianne walked in.

"Goddamn!" she yelled. "Every time I look around that bitch got a yard of dick down her throat." Dianne pulled her wig off and walked across the room. "Damn, I'm tired," she said as she sat down.

She stared at Boots for a few moments. "Damn, bitch, ain't you got no shame, cum-loving whore."

Boots stopped and looked around. "Why, tramp? You jealous?"

"You damn right I'm jealous, dick-loving whore! I've been out catching tricks all day and you sit up here with your black ass sucking all the life outta Whoreson."

"Well.... Don't worry, little white girl, you'll get your chance."

Dianne capped. "I know damn well I'll get my chance if you ever turn the meat loose, black ass cow."

I stood up and straightened up my clothes. Dianne looked down at Boots and removed a large roll of bills from her bra and laid them on the coffee table.

With her last remark aimed at Boots, she said "With tricks outside riding bumper to bumper, all this sorry bitch could catch would be a cold." She turned on her heel and walked into the bedroom.

Boots got up off the floor and sat down on the couch. "Daddy, I was thinking you might have some trouble out of that fellow that was down in the lobby."

I stared at her silently for a few moments before answering. "The only thing that nigger better do, baby, is try to get along with me, 'cause I ain't letting nobody put no static in my game."

The telephone rang and Boots answered it. I had made it a point never to answer a phone whenever there was a woman in the house, because sometimes tricks called and, if a man answered, they would hang up.

Boots waved the receiver towards me. "It's for you, daddy." I took the phone out of her hand. "Who is it, baby?"

"It sounds like Dot."

I frowned at the receiver. Dot was one of my most recent cops. Ever since I'd had her, she seemed always to get into difficulties.

"What is it, honey?" I asked into the phone.

Her voice came over the line shaking and scared. "Whoreson, I'm…, I'm sorry about not being on the track, but my brother seen me standing on the corner and made me go home with him."

I shouted into the phone. "Bitch, you mean to tell me that your brother is the reason that my trap money is going to be shitty?"

"But Whoreson, he seen me on the corner and made me go home with him."

I snarled, "Tell the real, whore. I don't hear no babies screaming in the background, so I know you ain't over to his house now, so just what is the reason, the real deal, bitch? Just why are you presenting this weak shit to me? Is your money funny, whore? Or have you been out yarding somewhere?"

She started to cry into the receiver. "Daddy, I'm not lying, I had to climb out the bedroom window to get away."

"Bitch!" I exploded. "I should make you go back to his house and walk out the front door. Dumb ass bitch, don't you realize that when you're out there on the corner you're representing me, and what you do reflects on me? Now how do you think I'm going to feel if people get to talking about my woman had to climb out of a window because her brother didn't like what she was doing."

"But Whoreson, didn't nobody see me come out the window."

"Shut up, bitch, and listen. It ain't the idea that anyone saw you come out the window, it's the fact that I know that you came out of the window. My whore had to climb out of some goddamn window because her winehead brother took her home!"

I interrupted her reply. "Just shut up and listen. I ought to kill you, bitch, but I ain't. I'm going to give you another chance. Now I want you to get your ass back up on that track and get my money right. If your brother should come back up there looking for you, don't hide, just tell him that you're up there taking care of my business, and I don't want him blocking my game." I continued, "If he should take you home anyway, don't climb out no windows, bitch, just walk out the front door. Now if you don't think you can handle this, I'll take you back over to your brother's house and talk to him myself."

Before she could hang up mad, I smoothed her feelings so she wouldn't go to work mad. "Listen, honey, all young girls make mistakes when they first go to work, so don't feel bad about it. This all goes along with the making of a good whore. If whoring was easy, every woman you see would be out in the streets with her legs in the air, but it takes a certain kind of woman to be a good whore, so most of them back up from it 'cause they be lazy and it just ain't in them."

She was quiet for a moment. "Daddy, I'm going to be a good whore, ain't I?"

"Sure you are, baby, but it just takes hard work. Now, don't forget, I don't want to see you getting in your father's car, if he ain't spending no money, you understand?"

She laughed. "Whoreson, you wouldn't want me to trick with my daddy, would you?"

"Not really, honey," I grinned, then added, "unless he was going to spend a sure'nuff big buck, then I think you could handle it."

She was still laughing when I hung the phone up.

Boots picked up a joint from the coffee table. "Pimp hard, daddy, pimp hard."

I laughed coldly. "Ya baby," I said and looked at my watch. "You can start getting ready for the track, too, Miss Fine."

Dianne came into the room with the bellboy who was bringing up the whiskey and beer I had ordered earlier. She was wearing a pair of very tiny panties with a see-through bra. The bellboy, who was about forty, couldn't keep his eyes off her.

The hallway door opened and a troop of my women came in. They were all scantily dressed, and the bellboy didn't know which one to look at. His eyes were going back and forth like pinballs. The girls, noticing his excitement, began to harass him. Dianne stepped up and took control. "Honey, you saw me first, didn't you? So why you making all them eyes at them sluts? Don't you think I can handle your problem, honey?"

He shook his head up and down dumbly, and she took his hand and steered him into the bedroom. In less than five minutes he was back out of the bedroom looking around sheepishly.

Dianne escorted him to the door. "Be sure to ask for me the next time you come up, big fellow, hear?" she said sweetly.

As soon as he left Dianne pulled a ten dollar bill out of her bra and twisted her hips provocatively as she crossed the living room. "You see, girls, what a good whore gets? He paid for the drink that you all are trying to consume, and plus, he tipped me this for being so sweet."

The girls laughed and talked and gossiped until I interrupted. "Well, ladies, the party is over and I know you have all had your kicks, but the time has come for you all to catch some tricks."

I settled back on the couch with Dianne in my arms and watched them prepare to go to work. It still took better than an hour before they had all dressed and departed, leaving just Dianne and me in the suite.

17

DIANNE HELPED ME out of my car, and the early morning chill wind helped to sober me up. She had come down to Carl's after-hours club and waited patiently until I had finished gambling and drinking. The sun was just coming out as we staggered down the street. By the time we reached the hotel I had got control of myself enough so that I could walk without any help. The lobby was deserted at this time of the morning except for the night clerk and a couple of fags.

When the elevator went up I had to fight to hold down the hamburgers I had eaten earlier. The sound of loud music reached us before we could even get the apartment door open.

"Sounds like somebody else is up besides us, daddy," she said.

I pushed open the door and the sound of loud jazz blasted me in the face. For a few moments the women's faces in the room were a blur, but I finally managed to focus in on them and what I saw came as a surprise.

Boots and a tall white blonde were dancing together. They were both about the same height and they were swaying to the beat of the music with an intimacy that suggested a strange relationship between two women.

Boots broke away when I entered. Dianne poured coal oil on the fire. "Don't ya stop belly-rubbing just because we showed on the set."

"It ain't what you think it is, bitch," Boots said. "Whoreson, this is Jerry," she explained. "I met her downstairs and she wanted to know who you were, so I told her to come on up and meet you. Oh ya, I also told her that you didn't have girlfriends, only whores, so she brung her clothes. Oh, ya," she added, "she belonged to that damn nigger that's always downstairs bothering us whenever we come in. You know, the one you had some words with yesterday."

So, out of spite, I let her stay. Jerry was twenty-four years old, and the first white girl I'd ever had. Not really having any connections for a white girl, I allowed her to lie around the pad for about a week before deciding to let Boots take her down to my whorehouse on Hastings. The colored tricks went mad over her. It lasted exactly one week before the police caved the door in, taking all the whores in the house to jail.

I knew that my whorehouse was busted before the police came out the door with the girls. I joined the crowd, like a fool, and watched the police load the cursing women into police cars. Before I could leave the crowd, two tall white vice officers walked up from the rear of the crowd and arrested me.

Another group of my girls were in the crowd and they caused one hell of a commotion before some more police busted them. They put me in a car with three of my girls from the crowd. I yelled out the car window to some friends, "One of ya get in touch with Big Mama and have her get the bondsmen on the case."

This was the beginning of the end. From here on out, my luck changed. I had been enjoying the sweet without the bitter. Now my turn had come to start paying dues.

Everybody made bond except the white girl. They held her as a witness for the state. The rest of my girls were fined fifty dollars for loitering in a house of ill repute, while they charged me with pandering and Boots with aiding and abetting.

My bond was set at five thousand dollars, while Boots' was set at three thousand. We both came out on bond at the same time. The lawyer socked it to me for a big fee, and my bankroll began to dwindle at a shocking pace.

It turned out that this was Jerry's first arrest. Because of this, the police contacted her parents out in Bloomfield Township. When they found out that their precious daughter had been staying with a black man, they went through the roof of the police station. With the police browbeating her and her parents screaming at her, she became a cooperating witness for the police.

We stayed out on bond for two months before going back to court and being found guilty. One week later we went back to court for sentencing.

My lawyer promised me probation because of my age. "Don't worry about a thing, Mr. Jones," he said. "How could a seventeen-year-old kid possibly corrupt a twenty-four-year-old woman? If anything," he told me jokingly, "the judge should give her ninety days for teaching a young boy bad habits."

So the day of my sentence, I went to court snug as a bug. Between me and my lawyer, we had a tacit agreement. Boots was in a cross. I figured she would get about six months, but she could stand it better than me.

The first one the judge passed sentence on was Boots. He looked down from his bench at us as though we had crawled out from under a rock. He gave her three to five years in the Detroit Women's House of Correction. Before he could announce mine, I knew the cross had gone down, with me caught in the middle. He said something about my behavior and also mentioned the cutting I had done on the girl's face last year. Then he finally lowered the bomb. He sentenced me to from six to seven years. Instead of probation, I had got prison, and I hadn't known that white girl two weeks. I was in a state of shock when they led me from the courtroom.

I stayed in the county jail for two weeks, waiting to be shipped out to Jackson Prison. This was to make me be glad to get to prison, because couldn't nothing be worse than a county jail. We had to sleep on mattresses on the floor, because there wasn't enough bunks to go around. The food was just enough to get by on, and the weak didn't get theirs. Bowls were fought over just because some men wanted another piece of meat. The weak, the scared, the timid, made it a point to give their meat to one of the stronger inmates. This way, they had someone to protect them on the ward, not only because of the food, but because rape was a way of life when the lights went out at night. On my first day in the county jail I had three fights before the night was over. After that, the wild young boys on the ward gathered around me and we started a wolf pack. If one fought, we all fought. In less than one week, we ruled the ward.

My day finally arrived. With two other prisoners, we were handcuffed together and loaded into the rear seat of an auto. Our hands were cuffed tightly behind us and leg irons were firmly secured to our ankles. One long chain went through each man's leg iron securing all three of us together. In the two-hour drive to the prison, I watched the passing scenery with unseeing eyes.

When the car pulled up in front of the gate, I stared at the huge walls surrounding the penitentiary. I watched men in blue uniforms trimming the grass and hedges in front of the institution. There were no guards visible around them. I would learn later that these were trusties, and it would be many years before I would reach this status. Like many black men before me, I realized that it was ridiculous to worry about that which you couldn't change. I was confronted with the problem of making my mind accept the fact that I would be behind these forbidding gray walls until my sentence was served.

It is typical of man's nature that he can adjust to almost any environment. Prison life was no different. The only large problem was the absence of any females. Some men even adjust to this. I met men who had been sentenced to life imprisonment, and they had adapted to this abnormal condition. Many of these men went so far as to abstain from indulging in relationships with the various homosexuals who abounded in prison, while others quickly accepted this as the new way of life and fell in love with one of the boy-girls.

After we got out of the car they marched us inside. Here we undressed, leaving our civilian clothes behind and putting on the prison blues. Many of us would wear these clothes and similar ones for many years before we would have another chance to wear civilian clothes. From there, we were marched to Seven Block, a place in Jackson Prison that was used for quarantine. We were isolated from the rest of the prison population. We stayed in quarantine from one to three months, waiting to find out where we would be sent. I stared around the large brick building with trepidation. It was four floors high, and on each gallery there were single cells. As I followed my guard up to the third gallery, I noticed most of the cells had men in them. The men whistled at us as we passed. Some of them made smooching sounds with their lips. At first it was unbelievable to me. The thought of spending the next few years locked up in one of these cages was beyond my comprehension.

The guard stopped and opened one of the cages with his key. He waited impatiently until I walked in. Then he slammed the door behind me. As I sat down on the small cot in the cell, I realized for the first time what prison meant. This was the big house, and I had made it at the ripe old age of seventeen. As I lay there on my bunk staring up at the ceiling, I counted on my fingers how many years I would have to do. Since it was then 1957, I figured the soonest I could get out would be some time in the early sixties. Since there was no getting around it and I would have to serve the time, I made my mind up at that moment that I wouldn't take any shit from anyone. I knew there was only two kinds of people in prison. Either you were a man or a punk, or too old to have to worry about it. Since I was so young, I knew I would have to worry about it, so I made up my mind to be one of the pushers and not one of those that got pushed.

The first weeks in prison I spent receiving blood tests and shots. After that we were given lectures on prison life and constant warnings not to borrow anything from other inmates. We were let out of our cells to eat three times a day, then put back in and locked up. The only time we were allowed out was when we were on call or taking a shower at night. Once a week we were allowed to see a movie. Then they broke all the doors and we were let out to go downstairs and sit in the dining room. We had to remain silent at all times during this outing, but the men and young boys quickly learned how to talk without their lips moving.

At the movie, when the lights went out, it became a whorehouse. Punks went to work with their hands and lips. The men who stood on the side, because of lack of seating, would have sissies stand in front of them with slits in the seams of their pants. Before the morning chow line would begin, all the slit pants would have been repaired.

After I had been in quarantine a month, my first problem came up. While we were lined up to take a shower, the man behind me patted me on my ass. I knew it wasn't an accident because a light giggle went up and down the line. I ignored it. He did it again. I waited until after I had taken my shower and when we lined up to march back to our cells, I got behind the joker who had thought he was doing something clever. He was an older man who had done time before. At night I had heard him talking across the cells. I was next door to him. He had made a few remarks earlier about me, but I had ignored them. Now, he was pushing his luck.

As we walked down the gallery, I rolled my towel up so that I could use it to choke with. It was still bulky, but I knew it would damn well serve my purpose. I caught him from behind and put my knee in his back. With both hands I twisted the towel tighter

and tighter. When the guards came running up and
started to force me to turn him loose, in a last attempt
to finish what I had started, I tried to kick him off the
third gallery. For fighting, I was put in the hole. I spent
two weeks in there, and when I came out, I was
assigned to the main prison. They thought I was too
violent-natured to be allowed to serve my time around
boys my age.

Once inside the population, away from the restric-
tions of quarantine, I began to settle down. The every-
day routine of prison life became acceptable. The few
problems I had because of my age were quickly settled. The rumor that I would not only fight but kill if
necessary gave the dogs room for thought. There were
too many soft marks inside the wall for them to go out
of their way for me, and then I was considered a dog
myself. The days ran into months, then the months into
years. Boots and I corresponded with each other all
the way through her prison bit. After her release it was
another story. When she sent me ten dollars, I sent it
back. In the letter I wrote her, I told her if that was all
she could send, she needed it more than I did. When
I had come to prison I had brought one grand with me.
Since then, Tony and Big Mama had sent money off
and on. My prison account had over two thousand dollars in it after I had been in prison four years. After
Boots' release from prison, I received three hundred
dollars from her in one year. With the arrival of Ape
in prison, I found out that Boots had chose Tony.

18

WITH THE PASSING OF Christmas, my year was coming up. The parole board had given flop, but that didn't make any difference. I now had four months to go for discharge. Tony had come up to visit me twice in the past year, but each time he came, I had refused to go to the visiting room. In my mind I knew there was nothing he could tell me. He had my woman and that was that. I had left my jewelry and all my clothes for him when I'd gone into prison. That hadn't been enough; he had taken my woman. I didn't want the bitch back. If anything, I wanted to kill her. She could have chose anyone other than my only friend. I was not the only one who was mad at them. Big Mama, before she died, had barred Boots from her trick house. And some of my old friends who had just left the streets told me she wouldn't have anything to do with Tony since he'd copped Boots.

After Big Mama's death, I started running the yard until I would almost fall out, trying to forget and for-give, but it didn't do any good. There was a burning hate inside of me that no amount of running and train-ing would relieve. I practiced punching on the big bag until I could hit with either hand with devastating effect. An old con I had become close to asked me one day why I trained so hard. After listening to me explain, he laughed.

"Listen, Whoreson," he said, "you got too much on the ball, boy, to go out and resort to violence. If you goin' be a player, you got to act like one. If Tony stole your woman, fightin' him about it ain't the answer. Always remember this, what goes around comes around. You just wait and have patience, you'll get your chance to play on him, and when it comes, make sure you do it good and smooth."

I listened to what he said, and acceptance came slow but it came. Prison had taught me patience, and with calm endurance I knew that one day my chance would come to fix Boots and Tony. Some of my bit-terness vanished, so when they called my number to report to the front office for a visit, I hesitated for only a moment. Since I didn't have any kinfolks, it couldn't be anybody else but Tony. When Big Mama passed away, a lawyer came to inform me she had left five thousand dollars in his care for me, so there was no reason for him to come and see me again. Our business was finished until I was released.

Leaving the gymnasium I cut across the yard and reached the hall office. Thirty minutes later, I was standing in the visiting room waiting for my visit. When the door opened I recognized my visitor at once. It had been over six years since I'd seen her. Before she had been a cute young girl; now she was a very attractive young lady. I opened my arms and she stepped into them as though it were the most natural act between us. When she tried to speak I smothered her words with another kiss. I held her by the shoulders and looked down at her with genuine pleasure.

"Janet, how good the gods have been to you. Surely you know you have become a creation of art," I said graciously.

Her laughter was soft and gentle. "My, Whoreson, what have they been teaching you in this place?"

It was like the opening of a flood-gate. Given the opportunity to talk to a female after six years released a torrent of words. My vocabulary had become quite extraordinary for a boy from the slums, because of my eagerness to read. I had just about read everything in the prison library, plus completely finished all the courses in the prison school. For the past two years I had been taking college courses, and it had become noticeable in my writing and speech.

We stared at each other across the visiting table. "I'm really proud of you, Whoreson," she said. "You have got so big since you've been here." And then she smiled at me, and you've never seen such a smile.

"Why, your shoulders would make two of me."

She was just about right. She wasn't exactly tiny, but she was a thin, small-built woman, with delicate features, while her skin had a smooth texture that reminded one of a fine dark mahogany. After I finally ran down I looked at her in embarrassment.

"Damn, Janet, here I've been tellin' you about my schoolwork and all that junk and haven't even complimented you on all the records you keep putting out. Why, I lie awake at night sometimes just to hear them play some of your songs."

She smiled, pleased. "It ain't really nothing, we just been kind of lucky. We got a good songwriter, and the breaks have been coming our way." She remained silent for a moment, then continued. "Tony asked me to give you a message for him," she said. Her eyes scanned my face for any sign of anger before she continued. "He said to tell you that he thought you was too much of a player not to recognize game when it went down, and that it was part of the dues that all players had to pay "

However disagreeable what she said may have been to me, I had no intention of allowing her to see that I was irritated. She studied my expression closely.

To avoid an awkward situation I began to give her a snow job with plenty of bullshit on top. "You know, Janet, have you ever stopped and tried to figure out why so many of us from our environment, boys that is, don't try to be anything else but parasites, pimps and just plain dopefiends?"

Her mouth was wide open now, and I knew I had

her. She stared at me in wonder. I could see her brain racing a mile a minute.

"Many people think we're sick," I continued, "but it's not really a sickness. As I now see it, it is not the eccentricity of a single individual but the sickness of the times themselves, the neurosis of our generation. Not because we are worthless individuals, either, rather because we are products of the slums. Faced with poverty on one side, ignorance on the other, we exploit those who are nearest to us."

Her eyes were big now. She was so enthused over my words that I wanted to reach over and feel her leg to see if she had had a climax. "Oh Whoreson, this prison term has really done you good. I wouldn't have thought that I'd ever hear you talk like this. What you're saying really makes sense."

This had been the first time I'd been able to try out my new vocabulary on anyone other than cons or guards, and I could see what some of the smarter prisoners had said was true. If you used good diction, you could con a bee out of honey.

She was so naive that I couldn't help but amuse myself a little more. "Yes, I do have a much broader outlook on life than I had when I entered this institution, but now, back to my original line of reasoning. Now don't misunderstand me, Janet, this is not an attempt to disguise or to palliate this widespread sickness that pervades the black ghettos, but rather an attempt to try and understand why, why is it that so many of the youth of our generation have no higher goal in life than to be pimps?"

"Oh, Whoreson, I'm so proud of you." She hesitated for a moment, then went on. "When I first came to this visiting room, I had decided not to tell you something, but now, after listening to you talk, I feel as if I could tell you without being frightened of what you'll say."

The smile that I forced was fictitious. The last thing I wanted to do was smile. I had a premonition that whatever she had to say would remove the amiable mood between us and leave a breach that would be hard to repair.

She hadn't seemed to notice, because she announced, "You've heard of the pop singer, Johnnie Ringo, haven't you?"

I stared at her coldly. "You talking about the blue-eyed soul, the white boy with the number one record out right now?"

Her eyes lit up. "Uh-huh, that's him. We haven't announced it yet, but we're supposed to be engaged and...."

She froze in mid-sentence. My stare was so chilling it paralyzed her. There was a burning rage inside of me that defied description. "I'd rather see you on your deathbed first, bitch."

"Whoreson, I didn't know you were prejudiced," she said in a shocked voice.

"Prejudice hell, bitch. Every time one of you black bitches get some kind of recognition with a little money to go with it, black men ain't good enough for you. Then you ask us why we want to pimp. That's all one of you funky bitches is good for, to be used."

My voice dropped low, and it was full of scorn. "And to think, bitch, that you had enough nerve to tell me once about finishing school so that I could be something."

She started to speak, but I interrupted. "Shut up. You once told me you wouldn't have a pimp. Well, dumb bitch, just what do you think you're getting engaged to? It's for goddamn sure he wouldn't look at your black ass if you didn't have all that money in the bank from your records." I continued, not giving her a chance to speak. "I just wish it was possible I could see you when he took you home to introduce you to his people. They'd look at you like you just crawled out from under some rock. If it wasn't for your money, bitch, they'd probably ask you to empty the goddamn ashtrays."

There were tears in her eyes as she stared at me. "I thought you had changed, Whoreson, but I see a better education didn't really help you. You're still rotten underneath it all."

I grabbed her arm and almost pulled her across the visiting table. "Don't no black man want to see no black woman get played on, tramp, so if that's rotten, I'm rotten clean through."

With the back of my hand I wiped my lips. "I have ten times more respect for a whore than what I have for you, tramp. At least they are getting paid when they associate with a peckerwood, but you, pig, you don't have any excuse. And to think that you had the audacity to offer your lips to me." Again I wiped my lips with the back of my hand. Then I leaned across the table and spit in her face. I pushed back my chair and got up. The guard had seen my action and was bearing down on me. "Get me out of here, peckerwood," I growled at him.

As I walked towards the door, I could hear her sobs behind me. Before I left the visiting room, the last sight I saw was Janet with her head down on the table crying.

For my behavior in the visiting room, I was given seven days in the hole. Upon my release from the hole, I ran into my buddy, the old con. He shook his head in disgust.

"Man oh man," he began. "Whoreson, I don't really know what to say, other than that you're a damn fool. The whole prison is talking about you. The brothers who were in the visiting room recognized Janet Wilson, boy, and they say you really spit in that girl's face."

"The bitch had it coming," I stated harshly. "What do you think I should have did after the bitch told me she was going to marry a honkie, kiss her?"

He continued to shake his head at my ignorance. "So what, fool? Do you think it helped your cause any by spitting in her face?" He began to lecture me as though I were a child. "First of all, the girl had to like you or she wouldn't have wasted her time coming up here. Second, ignorant ass nigger, the girl got big stuff. I mean big stuff. Her cash is so long that the whiteys are playing for it. So what do you do? Instead of smoothing her feelings out and talking her into changing her mind, you spit in her face like some damn kid. And to think that I thought you might one day be a player. No wonder your partner stole your main woman, you ain't got no style about you."

It occurred to me to knock him down, but in my heart I knew what he was telling me was true. I gritted my teeth and listened.

He studied me solemnly. "Here everybody in the prison is dreaming of the opportunity that presented itself to you. All they hoping for is the opportunity to just meet a woman in her position, and here you is with one in love with you and you don't know how to handle it."

His scorn was blistering. "The only reason I took an interest in you when you came to this prison was because me and your mama used to be good friends, but if I had known you was this much of a fool, I'd never have spoke to you." He removed a cigarette and lit it. "Any time a nigger and whitey are shooting at the same woman and she's black, the whitey has to have big money to win. In your case, sucker, the honkie ain't got big stuff, he just another poor ass singer with one record out."

For several moments he remained silent. I stared at him and suddenly it dawned on me that he was taking this personally. Looking at it from his viewpoint I could understand his anger. For him, such a woman would be a precious possession. An opportunity of a lifetime. Naturally he resented my blunder. To him it seemed as if I were tossing away something he had searched for all his life without ever attaining. With me it was different. I was twenty years younger than

him, and I didn't have a doubt in my mind that I
wouldn't get over big when I got out of prison. There
wasn't any one bitch in the world that I felt I had to
bend over backwards for. What the other niggers in
the penitentiary thought about me didn't mean nothing. I was going home in less than four months. What
they didn't realize was that the bitch got away lucky.
If we had been anywhere else, I would have done
much more than spit on her. I grinned. I began to picture myself peeing on top of her head.

The old con scowled at me. "I don't know what
you find to grin about. I guess you think you done
something cute? Well, you sure in the hell didn't,
young ass, bitch ass, mother…."

That's as far as he got. I caught him upside the
head with a hard right hook. Then put two sharp left
hooks in his stomach that folded him up. Before he
could get himself together I hit him on the chin with
a straight right hand shot that laid him out cold.

For fighting in the yard, they put me in isolation
until I was discharged. That was all right with me,
'cause I knew if they put me back in population, I
was going to have a lot of trouble out of that con. He
wouldn't forget the sneak punch I'd hit him with no
time soon. And then to get knocked out by a younger
con like me, even though I fought on the boxing
squad, wouldn't make matters any easier. He would
have to retaliate, or his name would become pussy.
That's the way it was in prison, either a man fought
and proved he was a man or he played the passive
role and got fucked. To lose a fight in prison didn't

mean anything. To lose without fighting back spelled trouble. They had a saying in prison that all cons heard sooner or later: fuck, fight, or wash clothes. If you washed clothes to get out of fighting, you would just about end up being fucked before the week was out. Sodomy rape was a way of life in the penitentiary, not something that occurred on occasion. If you were weak or showed fear, you became fair game for the dogs. What they couldn't do with fear, they would accomplish with force. That's how some of the prisons get a steady supply of punks, the dogs turn them out. By rape if necessary, by persuasion when possible. Is there any wonder then that, when I left prison, I was more an animal than a man? My nickname while I was in prison shows more than words could do what kind of man I was becoming: Boss Dog.

19

MY RETURN TO THE free world was uneventful. No one really cared whether I came home or not. Big Mama was dead, and I didn't have anything in common with Tony since he plucked off my woman. In fact, I made it a point to stay out of their way. I didn't know how I would react if I ran up on Boots, so I kept my distance. The streets hadn't changed that much. There was a new group of young pimps hanging around on the corners, but besides that, it seemed as if the clock had stood still.

My first stop had been at the bank where the lawyer had deposited my money. I withdrew it and made a beeline for the nearest Cadillac dealer. I put four thousand dollars down on a new Caddie, with the promise to bring the other twenty-eight hundred on the date of delivery. Since I didn't have any credit I had to pay cash, but it didn't make any difference. When I left prison, I'd had close to three thousand dollars in my account, and with the five grand Big Mama left me, I still had enough to get a few rags to wear. Tony had my jewelry, and I was on my way to get my diamonds from him, without any static.

I spoke to the car dealer. "How about letting me use one of those old junks till my car is delivered?"

He shook his head. "I don't think I could do that. If you had an accident or something we'd be in one hell of a fix here."

I pulled out my bankroll and peeled off a fifty dollar bill. "Do you think that will cover your problem until my car is delivered?"

He pocketed the bill and called one of the colored men working on the lot and had him put a dealer's plate on one of the older cars.

I drove off the lot and headed downtown. After getting my license straightened out, I stopped at a clothing store and bought a few outfits. Dusk was just falling when I turned onto Hastings. Tony had moved all of his girls down to the lower end of the street because of his misunderstanding with Big Mama, and after her death, he was too settled where he was to move back to the neighborhood we had been raised in.

Since I didn't know where he lived, I pulled up in front of six girls working in a doorway to inquire as to his whereabouts. Five of them rushed up to the car. They all wore short skirts and their faces were heavily painted.

"Hi, honey," the leader of the group yelled. "Which one of us do you want to see?"

The leader was a large woman with an abundance of everything. You could look at her and see that she must have been cute before she allowed herself to gain so much weight. Now that she was going to fat, it was hard to discover anything attractive about her. But when she smiled, showing the tip of her tongue at the corner of her mouth, there was the promise of sweet sensuality and exorbitant delight.

There hadn't been the slightest thought in my mind of playing stuff, but since she had hit on me, I decided to teach her a lesson.

"Ya, baby. Why don't you sit down for a minute. Maybe you and me can reach some kind of agreement."

She tossed a wicked look over her shoulder at her friends, as though to tell them she had just pulled off a grand coup. Her attitude was one of authority; you could tell she was under the impression that she was the leader of the hen house.

I drove around the corner and parked. "What's your name, honey?" I asked softly.

"Most of my dates just call me Ruby, sweetie."

Appearances could really be deceiving. This bitch actually thought I was a mark. "I want to talk to you for a few moments, Ruby," I said while pulling my huge bankroll out. I scanned through the money for a second, then found a ten dollar bill and put it in her lap.

Her eyes had got big as a dinner plate at the sight of my bankroll. "Sure, sweetie, as long as you got the price, I got the time," she capped, trying to control the greed in her voice.

Assuming an air of embarrassment I put the little game into action. "Ruby, I don't know how to ask you this, but, uh, I, uh, want you to teach me how to pimp."

That really caught the bitch unprepared. She stared at me with her eyes wide and her mouth flopping like a caught fish. I continued before she had time to speak. "What I mean is, I'll pay you to show me how to dress like a pimp, act like one, and really carry myself like one." I rushed on, "You ain't got to worry about gettin' paid, 'cause my daddy died and left me twenty-five thousand dollars. I'm goin' buy me a Cadillac as soon as I get the rest of the money." I pulled the bankroll back out. "As you can see, I got five thousand dollars of it now." I flashed six one hundred dollar bills at her. Beyond a doubt, the bitch was hooked. She just stared at me dumbfounded. "You don't think you'll have any difficulty teaching me what I want to know, do you, Ruby?"

She shook her head. "Ain't no trouble in teaching you, but, I mean, you ain't bullshittin' about this, are you? This ain't some kind of joke you call yourself having on me, is it?"

"Is that money in your lap a joke?" I asked.

Again she shook her head. "You mean you don't

want to go to no hotel or nothing like that?"

"Absolutely not, young lady, pimps don't go to bed with a woman the first time they meet her, do they?"

For a minute I began to think I was laying it on a little too thick. She stared at me as though I was losing my goddamn mind. "That's right, honey, you don't want to go to bed with me if you want to be a pimp. They don't hop in and out of bed with every woman they meet the way a square would do."

It hadn't taken her long to catch on to the way the trend was going. She rumbled around in her pocketbook and came out with a pencil and small notebook. She had come to the conclusion that I was some kind of nut and decided to play on me for the ten dollar bill I had given her. I didn't want her to give me the wrong number so I aroused her greed.

Peeling off a five dollar bill, I put it in her lap. "You make sure I can get in touch with you now, Ruby, 'cause I want you to help me pick out my Cadillac and clothes, plus I'm going to pay you real well when I get the rest of my money, sometime this month."

The thought of playing me out of that money had become so exciting to her she could hardly breathe. When she tried to speak her words came out in blurts. Her features lacked any compassion; to her I was the once in a lifetime trick. I stared at her in amusement. This big out-of-shape cow-like bitch really believed she would end up beating me out of some money.

After I took the address she had written out, she staggered away from the car as though she was drunk.

At no time during our conversation had she even asked for my name. I pulled away from the curb full of confidence. This was one bitch that was getting ready to get faked completely out of her whore boots.

Now my immediate problem was to find Tony so I could get my diamonds. I drove slowly back up Hastings examining various faces in the late model cars I passed. The neighborhood hadn't changed much, unless it was even more decrepit than before I left. For the first time in my life, I didn't feel as if I was coming home. I could look at the sores of poverty and truly understand the meaning of slum life: the filthy streets, the wineheads sitting in doorways, the horrible shacks some unfortunate souls called home. I realized that there had to be something better in life for me.

On the opposite corner I saw a blood-red Cadillac parked at the curb. I pulled over and found a parking place. I had got the wire in prison that Tony owned a red Caddie, and I didn't think there were that many red Cadillacs on this side of town. I stopped in two restaurants first, without any luck, then crossed the street and entered Ed's bar. Just about the first thing I saw was Tony sitting at a table with two white girls. He saw me and waved a hand in my direction. I walked slowly over to his table.

"Whoreson, I heard you was out, baby. How come you didn't look me up so I could give you a coming home party?"

The people in the bar had become silent as students in a deaf and dumb school. I stared around at some of the familiar faces. Whores sat on barstools staring at us curiously, while behind the bar the white owner watched us closely for trouble. The cracked bar mirror revealed alcohol-flushed faces waiting in anticipation.

I stared coldly at Tony. "The only thing I want you to give me, nigger, is what you got that belongs to me."

For a moment he didn't quite understand what I was talking about. He stared around undecided for a second, then his face brightened. "Oh ya, you mean your jewelry, don't you?" His voice had taken on a chilling note. His two girls stared at us with frightened eyes.

There was no doubt about it. If I pushed it, Tony wouldn't back up an inch. He would meet me on any terms I wanted. I knew in my heart that all I had to do was pull up a chair and we would resume our friendship as though nothing had happened. I wanted to, for a fact, but something inside me wouldn't allow me to bend and grasp the outstretched hand of friendship.

Again he tried to bridge the gap between us. Removing my watch from his arm, he spoke quietly. "Dig, Whoreson, ain't no whore in the world worth the friendship between two men." He slid the watch across the table towards me. "If you think I'm bullshittin', dig this. I've had these two whores with me for the last two days looking for you. These are two of the best whores in my stable, Whoreson, and you can have either one of them you want. She's yours, man. I'll send her clothes over to your joint if you'll just say the word, plus you can take her on with you."

Both women started to complain but he silenced them immediately. He removed my ring and shoved it across the table at me. I stared at the women. One was a blonde, while the other one had dyed her hair bright red; both were still in their early twenties. From his point of view, he probably thought he was offering me a damn good substitute for Boots, but when I looked at the two palefaced white girls, I knew that neither one of them could ever take the place of the black queen he had taken from me.

I shook my head, rejecting the offer. Even if he had offered Boots, I would have turned it down. "What goes around comes around, Tony," I said, slipping my ring on. "I just hope you can recognize game when it comes your way."

He sighed, deep and slowly. My open refusal of his offer had hurt him. One of his white girls, the blonde, had been watching me closely. She gave me the impression that if I had chosen her, she wouldn't have objected to the trade.

I turned on my heel and walked away. I hadn't had a woman since I'd been home, and it had been well over six years since I'd slept with one, so I didn't want my weakness to show. The women he had offered were very beautiful, not tramps. It wasn't hard to believe him when he said they were the best of his stable.

My conscience was starting to act up. Should I have accepted his offer of renewing our friendship? I couldn't see where it benefited me to ruin our relationship, but my pride had been hurt. I meant to repay Tony for what he had done, whether I was right or wrong. Some way, somehow, the day would come when he would experience payback.

As I crossed the street, I could hear the sound of high-heel shoes running behind me. When I got to the car door, she caught up with me. I looked over my shoulder at the fine blonde. She smiled up at me. She was small, with large legs. Her skin was smooth, milky white, with no blemishes.

"Hi, honey, I hope you don't mind me following you? It was my idea, not Tony's. I didn't appreciate the way you rejected me in the damn bar, so I asked Tony if it would be all right if I came out here with you."

"That's all you wanted to do," I asked coldly, "is come out here in the street and watch me drive away?"

Her laughter rang out merrily. She was the first woman I had heard laugh in quite a while. The sound was more pleasing than I could have anticipated. After a man has been locked up for a long time, he will appreciate the small things a woman does, things that he probably wouldn't have noticed before.

"No, Whoreson, I want to do a little more than just watch you drive away, but it's your decision."

It was too much temptation, she was too attractive for me just to walk away from. I held the car door open. She climbed in from the driver's side, and her skirt rose up above her thighs as she slid across the seat. Words would fail me if I tried to explain how I gaped at those big pretty thighs. How can I describe how a man feels, after being away from something so long, to have it laid out on a platter for him?

My first stop after pulling away from the curb was the drugstore. After purchasing a fifth of whiskey, my next stop was the motel I had been staying at. We undressed slowly, sipping on the whiskey and smoking up some reefer I had stashed around the room.

Whether or not it was the alcohol I don't know, but as we drank, I began to turn mean. She had told me her name was Ann, but the more I drank, the more I began to call her Jerry. At the beginning I hadn't meant to abuse her. Each drink I took convinced me that it was my right to dog her. After we had had relations a brutal idea began to grow in my mind.

She lay there beside me nude, on her stomach. I rolled over on top of her and she started to squirm. "Not so soon, Whoreson. Damn, you'll wear me out at this pace."

"Shut up, bitch," I said. "I'm gettin' ready to teach you something new."

"Uh-uhh," she said, "ain't nothing new about doing it like that, and it hurts besides."

She began to try and squirm from under me, but I had all my weight on top of her, and she was still on her stomach. Using my feet, I put them between her legs and began to spread them open. Hastily I fumbled around until I got the spot I wanted. With my finger as a guide, I pushed deeply into her rectum. Her scream shattered the stillness of the room, but it didn't interfere with the act of violence I was com-

mitting on her body. Taking a towel from off the back-
board of the bed, I wrapped it around her head, covering her mouth, then continued to force my desire on
her helpless body. She cried and moaned, but the
towel muffled her attempts to call for help. With each
succeeding lawless act I forced on her, I moved that
much closer to the edge of madness.

For the next three days I kept her with me, not
allowing her out of my sight. The only place she went
was to the toilet, then back to bed. When we got hungry, I called out and had food delivered. Whenever
someone knocked on the door, I made her go into the
shower and turn the water on.

At times when I was raping her, I could hardly recognize my own voice, cursing and muttering inco-
herently. On a rare occasion, I would commit a normal act of intercourse with her, but my preference was
for the abnormal.

When the morning came that I grew tired of her,
or rather, returned to sanity, she was a poor specimen
of the opposite sex. Her face was tear-stained from
constant crying, while her body was a mass of blue
bruises; discoloration had set in around her nipples
from my treatment.

When she realized that I was really going to let her
go, she jumped into her clothes. She waited until she
was standing in the open doorway before speaking.

"You dirty sonofabitch," she snarled, "you ain't no
man, you're an animal, and a dog at that, you bastard,
you."

There was nothing attractive about her face now.

Fatigue and hate had distorted her features into a mask of hatred. Without makeup, there was nothing left of the cute blonde I had entered the motel with. Her face was a blueprint of hell.

My booming laughter beat at her in the empty doorway. "When you see your man, bitch, tell him my only regret is that it was you I fucked in the ass instead of him. Tell him not to worry, though, 'cause he's got his coming." Before she could slam the door, I added, "Don't go away mad, bitch, just go away."

She slammed the door so hard I thought for a moment the glass would break. After that, the room became silent as a tomb. I found my wallet and pulled out Ruby's phone number. Here was another smart bitch that had one hell of a sunrise coming her way.

20

THE PHONE BY THE SIDE of the bed began to ring. I rolled over and sat up slowly. My head was throbbing from too much liquor and too many pills. Those red devils I had been taking gave me violent headaches the following morning. For a brief moment I held my head between my hands, then glanced around for my temporary bed partner. The bed was empty; she had departed sometime that morning without my knowledge. "Damn," I swore. It was no surprise she was gone. I began to remember flashes of my behavior. No wonder she had left the first opportunity she got. I was beginning to develop an obsession. Some people were hooked on drugs, others had alcohol to worry about. My problem was starting to be an obsession to commit sodomy. I knew I had developed the desire while spending those six celibate years in prison without a woman, but it was one problem I was going to have to overcome.

The shrill ringing of the telephone ended my brief attempt to analyze my strange preference. "Hi, Ruby," I said into the receiver. "No, woman, I wasn't lying when I told you today was the day to pick up my Cadillac. What? I was supposed to call you at two o'clock? What time is it now? Damn, Ruby, I just overslept, I'll pick you up on the corner of Hancock and Woodward. Give me about twenty minutes to get dressed." As an afterthought, I added, "Don't forget, I'm goin' take you downtown and get you a hell of a new coat today."

I hung up, then took a quick shower. After that, I proceeded to dress with leisure. I knew she would be waiting, because she thought she had a genuine trick in me. Well, today would be the day of enlightenment for her. My attire was immaculate. A cold black silk mohair suit, with white-on-white, long-collared dress shirt and pure silk midnight black tie. I slipped my jewelry on and stared in the mirror. A man's face stared back at me now, not the features of a boy. Golden complexion, not one gained by lying in the sun but one of nature's gifts, topped off with cold black eyes and jet black hair. A mischievous smile came to my lips but not to my eyes, when I thought about the game getting ready to go off. Ruby's pimp didn't know it, but he was getting ready to be played right out of a good whore.

When I slowed my car down at the corner of Hancock, she was standing right on the corner, waiting impatiently. "I didn't mean to inconvenience you, Ruby," I said when she got in the car, "but I had one hell of a party last night and just couldn't get up

She was studying me closely. "That's all right, Billy," she said.

It had been over three weeks since I'd met her, and she still hadn't found out what my real name was. Well, today would be the end of all that. Before tomorrow this time, she would have a new outlook on life, and also a new program to work out of. All that damn fat she was carrying around wouldn't be on her a month from now, either, I thought ruthlessly. I put her at wearing a size sixteen dress, and that was giving her the benefit of the doubt. Our short journey quickly came to an end as I drove up to the car dealer's lot. It didn't take long to complete our transaction. When I paid the dealer the rest of his money, Ruby's eyes almost popped out at the sight of my large roll. One of the porters drove my new Caddie up. Powder blue with a white convertible top and sky blue upholstery.

Whatever doubts she may have harbored in the back of her mind were gone as we settled back against the luxurious seats on our way downtown. "Billy, this really is a beautiful car," she said for the tenth time as we drove slowly on, accompanied by the murmur of soft music.

I parked in front of Detroit's finest furrier. As I

entered the store, Ruby was right on my heels, staring around in fascination. Up until this moment, I
don't think she ever really believed I was going to
buy her a coat, let alone a fur. I sat back in a large
soft chair while she tried on a dozen different furs. At
last she found a mink stole she liked and brought it
over for me to look at.

I nodded in agreement and stood up. "Will this be
enough to put it in your layaway?" I asked the salesla-
dy, removing three one hundred dollar bills from my
pocket.

The saleswoman took the money and made out a
slip for me. When we left the store, Ruby's eyes were
shining and she had a tight grip on my arm. She had
been played on just that quick.

My next stop was at my motel. She took her clothes
off quickly, while I stared at the abundance of fat
hanging from her sides. Her belly protruded
grotesquely. I made love to her slowly, indifferently.
Her obesity had killed any desire I had; now it was
just a matter of satisfying her. She moaned and
groaned under me until I felt her reach her climax,
then I pretended to reach mine.

Hastily I rolled over on my side of the bed. "You
know what I want you to do now, don't you, Ruby?"

"What you want me to do, Billy?" she asked innocently.

For one moment I was about to send her on her
way and forget about playing on her, but I needed a
whore, and since I'd started to play on her, I decided
to see it on out. "Take this money and go back to your

apartment and get your clothes. I need a whore now, not a girlfriend."

She stared at me in surprise. It seemed for a minute that she wouldn't go for it, but her greed got the better of her. She stared at my big roll lying on the dresser, and at the five dollar bill I had pulled off of it. "Sure Billy," she said and started to get dressed. "I won't be long. You'll be here when I get back, won't you?"

I didn't bother to answer, I just lit a cigarette and watched her squirm as she tried to wriggle all that fat down into her tight dress. It was a sight to behold, and I watched her curiously, wondering if she would make it or not.

After she left, I waited five minutes, then rushed back downtown and got a refund from the furrier. The saleswoman didn't like it; in fact, she called the manager, but after fat-mouthing for a while, he returned my money.

I drove back to the motel thoughtfully. It was going just like I planned, except I hadn't realized she was that fat. Well, there was one remedy for that. She would just have to lose the extra weight, and I was going to see she lost it damn fast.

When Ruby returned carrying her suitcases I was ready for her. "Oh, Billy," she said. "You should have heard my ex-pimp yell when I started to pack my bags. He swore he couldn't live without me."

I stared at her coldly. "He should have did more than just run his mouth," I said harshly.

My words only amused her. "Shit," she said fiercely, "if that nigger had tried to do something to me, you'd have had to call an ambulance for him."

Her attitude towards her last pimp was no news to me. It was common knowledge up on the track that her pimp had been scared of her. She had a reputation for being quick and good with a knife and had been known to cut a few people of both sexes.

"But you ain't got to worry about nothing, Billy, honey. I like you, and I know with all that money you got, we ain't goin' have no problem at all gettin' along."

I waited until she had finished speaking before coming off the bed in one smooth motion. The way a man started off pimping a whore was generally the way he ended up. If you didn't make a whore realize that you were the man, she'd end up in the driver's seat, while you'd be more of a bitch in her eyes than a man.

My fist landed upside her head in one solid thump. She fell up against the dresser, then slid to the floor cursing. "You sonofabitch, don't no bastard hit me like that."

She came up off the floor, eyes blazing. When she made her move it wasn't fast, it was unchained lightning. Her hand dipped down inside her bra in a blur of motion. Before I could move she had popped the button and a long blade shot out the end of her knife. For a woman her size, she moved with blinding speed. She came in towards me, not in a stabbing stance, but with the knife held low so she could gut me with one vicious swing.

Without hesitating she stepped in and swung the blade upward. It was the moment I had been waiting for. I turned sideways and chopped down with the side of my hand, catching her wrist with a solid blow. The knife fell to the floor and, before she could stoop to reach it, I slammed a brutal combination of blows to her head. I have to give credit where it's due; she didn't go down, she hit the wall and came right back at me with her nails. She was swinging her arms like a windmill. I went under her wild swings and stuck a left and a right to her stomach as hard as I could. She folded up like a big bag. Grabbing her hair, I pulled her to me. With slow deliberation I ripped her dress off. When she was down to her panties and bra, I grabbed the front of the bra and snatched it so hard that it popped loose in the back. Tossing her on the bed I began to pull her panties down around her legs. When she raised up, I backhanded her in the mouth.

When I got her pants off one leg, she opened her legs wide and stared up at me. Her eyes were full of scorn as she coldly revealed herself to me. But I had one hell of a surprise for her. Cunt was the last thing in my mind. I moved to the head of the bed and reached under the pillow. When my hand came out it was holding my pimp sticks, two coat hangers twisted together. She lay as though paralyzed, her eyes getting big with fear. "Bitch," I stated coldly, "there's a few things you got to know and you got to learn. The first one is that my name ain't Billy. It's Whoreson, if that means anything to you. The second thing you should know, bitch, is that you can't teach me nothing 'bout pimpin', whore. I was born to pimp. Now, we'll start with the things you got to learn, and first on the program is respect. A good whore always has respect for her man, and you definitely are going to be a good whore."

Before the words were out of my mouth, I had lit into her with the coat hangers. Her screams fell on deaf ears as I continued to beat her. She fell off the bed and tried to squirm under it. I grabbed her leg and pulled her out to the middle of the floor and continued to beat her. When I got tired I took her in the bathroom and made her take a bath, then snatched her out of the tub and beat her again. I beat her until her voice became hoarse, then tossed her on the bed and stuck my jones in her big wide butt.

Later that same evening, I took her down on the track. When I saw her standing in the doorway talking to two other girls, I walked over and knocked her down. She stared up at me from the ground. There was stark fear in her eyes, and when I saw that, I knew half my battle was won.

Now all I had to do was stop her from stabbing me while I slept. This problem I went to work on at once. I ran down the pill man and bought out his supply of beans. I made her stand on the corner and work for three days and three nights without a drop of sleep. I kept her full of beans and black coffee. The morning I pulled her up and took her home to sleep, she was out on her feet. She walked into the side of the motel, mistaking it for the door. I kept Ruby going at this pace for one month. In that time she came down from

a size sixteen dress to a size twelve. When I saw her
with her clothes off now there was nothing repulsive
about the sight. She had always been tall, now she
was graceful, too. Her skin was smooth, and her face
had always been cute. Now, with the loss of her dou-
ble chin, she had turned into an attractive young
woman. I still took her up on the schoolground some
mornings and made her run it till she became exhausted. Whether or not she disliked the treatment I put
her through, she was proud of the end results. I constantly caught her looking in the mirror smiling at herself.

We sat in the motel sipping wine. "You know,
Whoreson, if you didn't get mad so quick and beat
me so hard, I'd really like you." She rushed on before
I could speak. "I mean, I like you now, honey, but if
you just wouldn't fight me so much, I'd be so happy.
I ain't never had no man like you before, and it just
takes a little time for me to get used to your ways."

I stared at her coldly. "Bitch, if I treated you any
different you would end up trying to put shit on me.
This way, whore, you know if I catch you putting your
little funky game on me, you know beyond a shadow
of a doubt I'll break both your legs."

She tried to fight back the sleep that was tugging
at her. Her head dropped down on her chest, but she
jerked it up. "You know, Whoreson," she said in a
drowsy voice, "if you was a little more kinder, a whole
lot of the girls on the corner would choose you." She
added, "They see how hard you work me, and it scares
them, 'cause don't nobody's pimp work them the way

you work me."

"Ruby, stand up and take off all your clothes." She jumped at my command as though I had kicked her. Her eyes got large and she stood up hesitantly.

Her voice shook with fear. "Whoreson, I didn't mean any harm," she said, pulling off her clothes. Her hands trembled as she pushed her panties down and stepped out of them.

I beckoned to her. "Come on over here." I ran my hands over her smooth body. There were still a few flabby spots, but on the whole she was becoming one beautiful brown-skinned girl.

"Quit all that shaking, Ruby," I said softly as my hands traveled up and down her body. She was trembling like a frightened doe. Under my smooth caresses she slowly quieted down. I pulled her onto my lap. Gently I ran my fingers in and out between her legs. She emitted a low moan and lay back against me.

I picked her up in my arms and carried her over to the mirror and stood her up. "What you see in the mirror, bitch," I stated coldly, "is my creation. Not something you did for yourself, but what I had to force you to do for yourself." I continued, "So from now on, when some bitch comes up to you and begins crying on your shoulder about how hard I work you, you laugh in her face, bitch, 'cause I ain't did nothing that didn't need doing."

"I wasn't complaining, Whoreson."

My sarcastic laughter rang out in the small confines of the room. "I know you wasn't, Ruby, you was just building up to trying to think, trying to get around what I told you. You don't think, woman. I do your thinking for you. 'Cause whenever you try, something's bound to end up gettin' fucked up. Now ain't that right?"

She grinned at me shyly, then nodded her head in agreement. "Whatever you say, daddy. You know I'll do whatever you want me to."

With a smooth motion I stood up and picked her up in my arms. Her nude body went tense in my embrace as I carried her over to the bed and laid her down. With slow deliberation I ran my tongue up and down her golden brown body. I could feel her muscles tighten unconsciously as I began gently to make love to her. The more elaborate pains I took, the more excited she became. Soon Ruby was moaning as she began to feel thrills I had never before taken the time to arouse in her.

21

THE STREET WAS STILL wet from the early evening rain. I watched the people scurrying around downtown, some rushing to catch late buses, others just rushing home, hoping to get inside before it rained again. I parked in front of an ofay bar and wondered if it would be interracial.

Quite a few pimps from my side of town were coming downtown, cruising around the bars and copping white prostitutes that they couldn't have gotten next to before the bars integrated. Actually, I wasn't looking for a white girl to cop. What I wanted was for a white whore to hit on me to spend some money with her, that way I'd have a chance to "georgia" her out of some cock. I had two envelopes in my pocket, one a dummy, the other empty. If her man hadn't tightened her game up for her, she would be an easy mark to switch envelopes on.

The Devil's Den was the name of the bar I finally decided to enter. It was dark inside so I stood at the bottom of the stairs until my eyes became accustomed to the darkness. The bar curved like a half-moon, with a tiny stage set right off from it. I walked to the end of the bar so as to get away from the blaring noise the mixed group was playing. Apparently the musicians thought the louder they played, the better it sounded.

I took the very last stool at the end of the bar. I glanced around casually; the club was semi-crowded. Most of the customers were coupled off. The only single people at the bar were males. Before I could get up and leave, a woman stopped beside me and asked for my order. I ran my eyes up and down her body until she started blushing. She must have been all of forty years old. A little under five feet four, a little over a hundred-and-twenty, with a body that God had built for one purpose and one purpose only, encased in a form-fitting knit dress. Her heart-shaped face with carmine mouth and huge black eyes was topped by jet black hair parted at the side, hanging long over her shoulders. Even though she was gettin' old, she still looked like a movie queen to me. As I stared at her, I knew that this was one white lady I was going to stick the golden rod in. Soon.

"May I take your order, please?" she asked, still blushing.

"Do you always turn that pretty pink when you wait on a customer?" I asked politely.

"Well," she stated frankly, "I'm used to men looking at me, but for some reason, you have a very disconcerting stare, young man."

"I hadn't meant for it to be disconcerting, miss, but when I saw you, I wondered if in this lifetime I would ever be allowed to pluck the fruit from a woman in the autumn of her years as beautiful as you are."

Her eyes lit up; before she could lower her glance, I saw the hunger in them. She wanted a young man, and I meant to find out just how much loving her capacity could stand. When she brought me back my drink, I held her hand longer than necessary. She blushed again, then looked around to see if it was noticeable. When I turned her loose, she went to the end of the bar, right up under the band, to get away from me. Several times I caught her looking back down the bar at me. Two could play at that game as well as one. When I finished my drink, I got up and left. I knew there wouldn't be any chance of ripping her off tonight, but it would go down anyway, I was willing to bet cash money on it.

After the loud music in the bar, I really didn't want any more noise. I found a station playing soft music and left it on as I drove through the downtown district. I turned off of Woodward and drove over to Hastings; it was like entering another world: the crowded street, whores working on each corner, drunks staggering up and down the street, filth and poverty staring you in the face no matter where you looked.

Once I had loved this neighborhood, now I only tolerated it as a means to an end. One day I would drive away and never look back. At the moment, I didn't know how, but I knew that one day I would.

I pulled up and parked in front of the trick house Ruby worked out of. Two girls standing in the doorway stared at me coldly. I didn't give a fuck about what they thought about me; to me they were just something to be used. I walked past them without a glance and went up the stairs.

The house man opened the door and let me in. The dining room was full of people. A card game was going on, on the dining room table. Ruby, with her back to me, was pulling on a white trick's arm, trying to pull him away from the gambling and take him into a bedroom.

The card dealer snarled at her. "Bitch, I done told you to leave that man alone; don't you see he's playing blackjack."

There was something familiar about his voice. I stepped up to Ruby and put my hand on her shoulder and stared at the dealer.

It was New York! After all these years, here was New York in a trick house in Detroit. There seemed to be a change about him, and as I stared at him it hit me. His clothes. Before he had been immaculate in his dress; now there was a difference, not too noticeable but still there. As I stared, I noticed tiny dark spots on his gold hi-lo shirt. Blood!

"Well, well if it ain't Whoreson. Fatima, baby," he spoke slowly with a slur in his voice, "do you see who

I see, girl? Grown tall as a tree. Man, you done come right on up there, ain't you?"

Immediately after he spoke, I noticed Fatima standing behind him. If he hadn't called her name, I don't think I would have recognized her. Damn, I thought sourly, six years of whoring couldn't have done all that to her. She looked like a bag of bones stuck down inside a dress. Her hair was dry, while her skin had a dead color to it. As I examined her closer, I could see sores on her arm. When she looked at me she barely opened her eyes. There were the same revealing stains on her dress. Blood spots. It dawned on me all at once. Both of them were dopefiends, junkies.

I stepped in front of Ruby. "I see you still got the same habit, telling other pimps' whores what to do."

"Oh, so you're a pimp now, huh?" he said sarcastically.

"Well, I sure the fuck ain't no dopefiend," I replied coldly. His eyes narrowed and he shuffled the cards quickly. I removed my large bankroll and pulled off a ten dollar bill. His hungry eyes followed the roll.

I held the bill out to Ruby. "Go get us both a drink, baby." She took the money from me and walked back to the kitchen. I edged over to the card table. I watched New York as he dealt the cards around to the black and white tricks. When the player in front of him asked for a hit, he pulled seconds from the deck. I knew then that the cards were marked.

"Why don't you take a hand, Whoreson. Give me a chance to win some of that good whore money you're so proud of," he sneered. Some of the prostitutes in the room looked at him oddly. It was seldom that a pimp got in a game that was already rigged to rip off the tricks, unless he was a fool.

I stared at the pile of money in front of New York. He had over two hundred dollars in the bank. He hit his hand and turned up twenty-one. The other players cursed and tossed their hands on the table. I saw an ace in the discarded hands, so I reached over and began to shuffle the deck. The cards were a new Bicycle deck, with the fan on the back, and someone had taken a red pencil and darkened certain lines on the fan. You could see the mark all the way across the table, but you had to know what you were looking for.

When I set the deck down in front of New York, I swung out with the ace and three other cards. While he reshuffled the deck, I palmed the four cards. When he set the deck down for me to cut, I reached over and split the deck in half. I set the four cards on top. The top card was an ace, the second was a face card, the third was another face card, and the fourth was an eight.

I removed my bankroll and knocked on the table. "Deal me all that money in the bank. Just four cards, New York. You and me, big time."

He spotted the ace on top and grinned. "Okay, baby boy, just four cards between you and me," he said, dealing me the second card off the top of the deck.

All the girls who didn't have customers crowded around the table, watching the game silently. New York tried to get the most out of the moment. "Seems as if I'm always teaching you something new, boy. This time I'm goin' teach you never to buck a hustler's game." His lips turned down in a sneer.

Ruby set my drink down in front of me, then stepped back from the table. Soon as he finished dealing, I reached over and turned up his hand without bothering to look at my cards.

"You got nineteen, Bossgame," I said harshly. "Are you hittin' it or sticking?"

A look of surprise came into his eyes and his expression changed. "I'm paying twenty," he said slowly.

Before he could move, I reached over and picked up the money in front of him. "Well, that's what I got, slick daddy," I said and stepped back from the table. My cards were still face down on the table. He reached over and snatched them up. Then slowly it began to dawn on him that he had been played on.

"You never even looked at them," he stated. "I ain't going for no shit like that, Whoreson, from you or any other motherfucker."

Before I could reach him, he kicked over his chair and snatched up Fatima's pocketbook from the end of the table. His hand darted inside the half-opened purse.

As fast as he had moved, Ruby had moved faster. Her voice was chilling in the suddenly silent room. "Should I stick him, daddy, should I stick him?"

There was no doubt in anyone's mind about whether or not she would stab him. They were both frozen in position: New York, with his hand half in and half out of the purse, Ruby one step behind him with her long switchblade pressed to the side of his neck.

As I watched in fascination she pushed the knife

deeper into his throat. A small stream of blood began to trickle down his neck. He stared up at me with his eyes pleading. "Push that purse over here," I growled. He complied.

I removed a snub-nosed .38 police special from the pocketbook, then stepped up and cracked him in the head with the handle. He fell out of the chair on the floor.

His face was full of fear as I walked up to him. "Nigger," I said, "I ain't goin' do nothing to you, for the simple reason that ain't nothing I could do to you as bad as what you're doing to yourself. All I want you to do is make sure that whenever, wherever, you happen to see me or my woman, you put some distance between us." As I stood there, staring down on him, the years flashed back and the humiliation of what he had done to me filled my soul with shame. "You might get the impression that I don't mean what I'm saying, New York, so this is just to give you the message."

Before he could move I grabbed him by his collar and began to pistol-whip him about the head. When I released him he slipped back to the floor unconscious, his face and head covered with blood. Everybody in the room was staring at me in shock. It had been a brutal act, but I wasn't ashamed. He would have shot me if it hadn't been for my woman. "Come on, Ruby," I said and started for the door. I had the door open when Fatima caught up with us.

"Whoreson," she said, "take me with you, please. I'll do whatever you want me to do, please, and I'll work hard. Just let me go with you."

Her pleading didn't move me at all, 'cause I didn't give a fuck about her. But the thought of slick ass New York waking up and finding out I had taken his whore, too, was too good an opportunity to pass up. I nodded and she solemnly fell in behind us and followed me out to our waiting Cadillac.

It had taken more than seven years before the chance had presented itself for me to strike back at New York, but as they say, what goes around comes around and, goddamn, I felt good after gettin' the chance to play payback. And after glancing out of the side of my eye and seeing Fatima sitting so unconcerned against the car door, I had an idea I was going to feel a hell of a lot better after I fixed this dirty bitch's wagon.

I saw the bean man walking down the street so I blew at him and parked. When he got to the car window I bought all the pills he had on him, red devils and secos, and a few dexis. Next, I stopped on Canfield and sent Ruby in to buy me a can of reefer. While she was in the house I sent Fatima to the drugstore to purchase two fifths of Johnnie Walker Red. I watched her wave to somebody across the street, then Benny the dope pusher crossed over and followed her into the store. The bitch was gettin' a fix to take with her. Well, she would sure in the hell need it before I was finished with her this day.

Fatima beat Ruby back to the car. When she got in, I said, "Bitch, get your ass in the backseat next to a window, and keep that dope you bought in your hand.

If the police break down on us, I want you to eat that shit or throw it away before they stop us."

In the ghetto any black man or woman driving a Cadillac is fair game for every policeman with a badge in his pocket. Tickets were the least of your worries. What you had to do was make sure they didn't catch you dirty. Sometimes they would stop you on just G-P, or to give you a bullshit ticket just so they could try and tear up your car on the pretext of searching for drugs. I had a speeding ticket in my glove compartment that I had received while sitting in front of the trickhouse waiting for Ruby to finish with a trick.

Ruby came out of the building and ran down the stairs. She jumped in the front seat and put the window halfway down. I started the car and pulled out into traffic. I looked up and down the street closely for any police cars. If one hopped out behind me, he would have one hell of a race before he caught me, because I wouldn't stop until I gave the women time to clean up.

We made it to the motel without any difficulty, and everybody relaxed. An hour later, with one fifth of whiskey gone, we started getting down to the nitty gritty. Both women had removed all their clothes, while I was down to just my pants. My jewelry and bankroll were lying on the dresser beside what was left of the reefer. I staggered up from the bed and walked over to the dresser to roll another joint.

In the dresser mirror I saw Fatima run her hand up and down Ruby's body intimately. Ruby didn't seem embarrassed by the caress. I didn't allow my expression to change when I walked back towards the bed. Fatima snatched her hand back at my approach. "You didn't have to stop because of me, bitch, you done stole one whore from me, you might as well try for two."

She started to make some sort of excuse, but I reached for her and she squirmed away and fell on the floor. As I started towards her, she rolled up in a ball, with her arms around her head. I slowly opened my fly and pulled out my jones. Before she knew what I was doing, I got a steady stream of piss going and spattered her head and arms. She rolled away quickly and when I tried to hold her steady with my foot, I pissed all down my pants leg.

"Bitch," I screamed, "you done made me pee all down my pants leg." She jumped up and ran for the bathroom. I tried to piss on her as she went by but missed her and peed on my watch and bankroll on top of the dresser.

I stared angrily at Ruby. She was sitting up in bed laughing so hard that tears ran down her cheeks.

"Bitch," I said drunkenly, "I don't see a goddamn thing funny about me pissing on myself."

"I wasn't laughing at you, Whoreson," Ruby said, lying through her teeth, then started laughing again. "You don't think you messed your watch up, do you?"

"Hell no," I stated and walked over to the dresser and picked up my watch. I wiped it off on my pants, endeavoring to look stern. Suddenly the mood hit me and I started laughing. Maybe it was the weed. Whatever it was, I fell on the bed and Ruby and I laughed like two fools.

The sound of the shower came to us, and a little later Fatima peeped out of the door. "Come on out, girl, I ain't goin' do nothing to you," I said slowly.

She came out and stared at me angrily. "You ain't had no reason to do that to me, Whoreson."

"Shut up, bitch," I said. "Here, catch." I removed a ten dollar bill from my roll and tossed it towards her. "Take that, bitch, and let the door hit you in the ass. I don't need you, don't want you, and wouldn't have you, so get the fuck out of here."

That kind of took her by surprise. The angry look disappeared. "Whoreson, wait a minute, daddy, and let me talk to you. I know you was mad 'cause I left you, but we should be even now." She continued before I could interrupt. "And if you're worried about me using, I'll kick if you want me to."

I sat up in bed. "Listen, Fatima, 'cause you use stuff don't mean a thing to me, I wouldn't have you no kind of way. Don't no bitch ever leave me and then come back thinking I'm goin' take her back. The truth of the matter is, I don't need you. For what? You ain't nothing. All you'd do is bring me grief, and that I don't need. Take that money, baby, and buy yourself a trip to cloud nine." Then I added, "When you go out the door, woman, close it easy, please?"

"You dirty sonofabitch, you," she yelled and ran out the door, leaving it wide open.

22

I PULLED UP IN FRONT of the Devil's Den and stared at the bar moodily. I had been trying for over a month now to cop Stella, the owner of the bar. It hadn't taken me long to find out she wasn't just another barmaid. I knew that she wanted me, but for some reason she held back. I meant to break through the wall of reserve she kept putting up, and I had reason to believe I just might break luck tonight. Generally she didn't come to the bar except on weekends. She wouldn't commit herself to a real date, but she had decided to come downtown tonight just to see me.

Stella was sitting on the corner stool when I entered. "Hi," she yelled and waved in my direction.

I smiled to myself. It was apparent that she had been drinking. I felt sure that half the battle was won.

"Hi yourself," I said as I sat down beside her. "Did you save enough for me."

She smiled and stared at me mischievously. "Yeah, Johnny, but let's not waste our time sitting around here drinking." Then she added as an afterthought, "You did say your name was Johnny, didn't you?"

There was something about the way she said it that made me glance up immediately. She was staring at me in a peculiar manner. All at once it came to me. She was damn near out on her feet. I felt taken aback. It wouldn't help my plan if she was too intoxicated to realize what was happening.

She leaned over towards me. "Come on, honey, let's get the hell out of here."

That was just down my line. I stood up and took her arm so she wouldn't stagger. The bartender gave me a cold look as we walked out, but the hell with him; he was the least of my worries.

I steered her towards my car and helped her in, then got in the other side. She pushed the armrest up and slid across the seat so she could be under me.

The street was nearly deserted as I drove through the downtown area. I started to stop and put the top down, then decided against it; it would sober her up too quick. I could feel her hand rubbing my leg up and down, until she got up the nerve and began to massage me intimately.

As far as I was concerned, that clinched things. I wouldn't have to wonder about her reactions when I pulled up in front of a motel. I stopped and bought a pint of whiskey, then headed for a motel on the out-skirts of town. I wanted to make sure we weren't seen by anyone.

She sat in the car and sipped on a cup of whiskey while I checked us in. "Come on, baby," I said light-ly, jingling the motel key in my hand.

Her skirt rose about her thighs as she got out on the driver's side. Again I marveled at her ripened per-fection.

We entered the room holding each other tightly. I closed the door and kissed her passionately, then picked her up and carried her to the bed. When she returned my kiss, her tongue darted in and out of my mouth like a burning spear. Hot, stabbing jolts of sen-sation ran through me as I lowered her gently to the bed. I undressed her and kissed her feverishly on her neck, shoulders and beautiful white breasts. Her nip-ples became hard under my probing lips. When I went down lower and kissed her on her navel she shud-dered and her stomach grew tight. She began to mur-mur words of endearment as I worked down lower and lower. I proceeded to make love to her with slow deliberation, tantalizing her with the promise of joys she had never before known. Before she could become too accustomed to my lovemaking that way, I raised up and penetrated her at just the right time. She was tightly built, and a small scream escaped from her. I took her tiny waist in my hands and pulled her to me firmly yet gently.

Irresistibly she clung to me in frenzied, delirious

madness. "Please, Johnny, please don't stop. I've-never-before-had-an-orgasm." The words came out of her in a gasp. She tossed her head from side to side, then dug her nails into my back, screamed, and shook violently.

Much later, I lay back and examined her nude body as she slept beside me. I grinned to myself. I had even surpassed my own expectations while making love to her. I had evoked sensations I didn't know women had.

We got up the next day, late in the afternoon. When she first awoke, I played with her until she became aroused, then made love to her again, once more making her reach orgasm. Her eyes lit up from the fires I kindled in her. My skillful handling had given her astronomical pleasures and sexual sensations never before imagined. She was hooked. She couldn't keep her hands off of me.

I had planned on waiting before I started to press her for money, but her behavior gave me an immediate opening. "Stella, it might be three or four weeks before I see you again," I said, starting to get a good lie together on the spur of the moment.

She snatched at the bait. "Why, Johnny, here we are just really getting acquainted, and now you're telling me you've got to go."

Her hands kept rubbing intimately, until I stood up and walked to the dresser. I knew then that she would become a nuisance. Whether or not it was a flaw in my makeup, I didn't know, but after I'd made love with a woman, I didn't like to be bothered. In fact, I became downright annoyed if my bed partner didn't take the hint and give me some distance.

"It's not that I want to go, Stella, but I got a car note due, and my rent's been overdue for the past month. I need something like four hundred bucks to get myself together."

"Where are you going to get the money at when you leave here?" she asked point-blank.

"My father owns a store in Cincinnati. If I go back home and hang around for a few weeks or months," I added, "he'll loan me the money."

She hesitated for a moment, then said just what I knew she would say. "If you stay here, I'll loan you the money."

My first reaction should have won me an Academy Award. First I pretended shock, then became indignant. My technique was beauty in motion. I allowed her to persuade me to accept the money against my better judgment, I stated with a straight face.

Her face lit up with happiness. "Johnny, you stop by the bar tonight and I'll have it for you. Better yet, why don't you just let me rent this room. That way the people down at the club won't have any idea what's happening," she continued, not giving me time to answer. "Suppose we just meet here, say, around eight o'clock. I'll have the money ready for you."

Eight o'clock hell. I could read the bitch's mind. She meant to wear me out for that four hundred. "I'll tell you what, I got some business to take care of, so make it ten o'clock." Before she could answer, I leaned down and kissed her. That closed the deal better than words could have.

When she started to breathe heavy, I pulled her from the bed and slapped her on her rump. "Get dressed so I can drop you off downtown at your car. If I let you, we'll still be here at ten tonight."

She grinned and ran into the shower. I relaxed a little. I don't think I could have stood another bout with her so soon.

A while later I dropped her off and continued on home. For the past few weeks, I had been neglecting Ruby. I would have to give her a little attention before she got out of hand.

For the next month I played both ends against the middle. Stella had become wise to what was happening, and Ruby knew I had a square girl for her wife-in-law. Even though I tried to explain to her I was gettin' big stuff from my ofay, it didn't sit right with her. I think what really dragged her was that Stella was white. Black girls just don't like to stable up with white girls, no matter how much money their pimp is getting from the ofay. And the shoe fit the same way on the other foot.

I had started a bank account now, and I had over five grand put up for a rainy day. Three thousand of it had come from Stella in the last month. Two days ago I had just got two grand from her, and when we met tonight I was going to hit for some more.

I stared out of the motel window. The weather was beautiful, but I didn't feel in the mood to ride down on any bitches. I had just heard on the news that Janet was back from abroad, and she had called her engagement off. That should have made me happy, but for some reason I couldn't build up any sweat over it. Right now, Janet was in a different world from the one I lived in. I had enough problems with the two women I was living with to last three lifetimes without dragging Janet into the picture.

Stella had given me an outright, no-bullshit choice. Either I married her or no more money. I would have fired the bitch outright, but she had sweetened the pot with the promise of twenty thousand dollars cash on the day we were married. Perhaps to some men this wouldn't have been a problem. For me it wasn't that simple. I was a pimp, inside and out, and marrying a bitch wasn't in my program. Stella had presented the opportunity and I meant to take advantage of it. If the bitch didn't think I could play her out of that money, she was crazy. I didn't have it absolutely together, but I had a plan.

The phone rang. I picked up the receiver and spoke for a few moments, then hung up. I smiled. It was coming together. The pieces were falling into place. I put two joints in my pocket and stepped outside. It was just dusk dark. Not too hot or cold. I let the top down on my Caddie and headed for the west side.

I appreciated this big expensive car as I drove across town. When I stopped at a red light, four teenage girls waiting for the bus flagged me down. The women standing at the bus stop stuck their noses in the air as the young girls ran over and climbed in my car. Those old bitches were just mad because I didn't pick them up. All the teenagers had on shorts, and I mean short shorts. The young girl who sat down in the front seat beside me had big pretty brown thighs, and I stared at them in appreciation.

"Hey, baby, this sure is a hip ride, ain't it," one of the girls in the back yelled. I caught her reflection in the mirror and she didn't look to be over thirteen. "You need a woman, honey?" she asked.

I smiled at their frankness. "No, honey, you might be too old for me," I capped right back.

She grinned. "If you was to get some of this hot stuff I got, I bet you wouldn't think that."

I laughed out loud. "You probably got a point there."

One of the girls in the front seat began to turn the knob until she found a soul music station. They all began to dance in their seats and pop their fingers to the music.

When I got to Twelfth and Warren both of the girls in the backseat got out. Four blocks later, the one sitting by the door in front yelled out it was her stop.

After letting her out, I turned to the one beside me. "How far do you go, honey?" I asked.

"I go all the way over to Linwood if you're going that far," she replied.

"I got to make a stop first, baby, then I'll take you on home. That is, if you ain't in a big hurry."

She looked up at me out of some of the prettiest eyes. "What are you, a Mexican or something?"

I laughed. "No, baby, I ain't no Mexican, but you can bet I'm something."

When she laughed it wasn't the laugh of a child. It

was the sound of a young healthy woman coming into her own. She hadn't bothered to move over to the vacant spot by the door, either. She sat right up under me, as though she belonged to me.

Her behavior led me to believe we might make one hell of an evening out of it yet. One way or another, it would amount to pure delight to lay up with this young devil, cute and tender.

I pulled up in front of a poolroom on Warren and stopped. One of the loafers in the doorway walked over to the car. Before he reached it, I got out and met him on the sidewalk.

"Preacher, baby, I see them white folks finally let you out."

Preacher grinned. He was a short, fat, dark-skinned Negro with a deep, booming voice. "Ya, baby, them honkies damn near got the nitty from the gritty before they let me out. Man, five years in that place without nothing but some fags to help me pass the time ain't my cup of tea."

I took him by the arm and walked him away from the car and poolroom. "Dig, baby," I said, "I got a thing on the fire, and if you help me take it off, I'll give you one grand."

He stopped and looked at me closely. "You know I'm still on parole, Whoreson, so I can't stand no stickups, baby, but other than putting that candy stick in my hand, you got your man."

"It ain't no stickup," I said and grinned. "And you ain't got to crack no heads." I studied him for a moment. "You know, I got to thinking about you,

Preacher, about how you used to carry that Bible around up there in the joint, and went to wondering if you brought it home with you."

He smiled. "Man, when I got out, I gave it to the screw at dress-out. I told that honkie he should try reading it, he might find something in it to help him."

"What about all that bullshit you used to talk up there in the yard, Preacher? What happened to all your plans on starting you a church and trimming all them sisters out of their money? You done forgot about it already, huh?"

He scratched his nose "No, baby, I ain't forgot. I just ain't got no green to get started. I sent all the way to California to get me some bullshit license statin' I'm an ordained preacher-man. But it ain't doing me no good, Whoreson. I ain't got no money to get started with."

Two old women passed us. "Just look, man, all them sisters just waiting for me to trim them, and I can't get my goddamn church off the ground."

"Well, dig this, Preacher, I got good news for you." I put my arm around his shoulder. "How much will it take for us to rent a storefront, put a second-hand organ in it and a few chairs so we could get by for a few days."

"What's this few days shit, Whoreson? If we set up we might as well go for the long gallop."

"That part of it is impossible, baby, and I want you to realize it," I said sharply. "I'm gettin' ready to play stuff on an old white bitch, and as soon as I take off the cash, she goin' run to the man. But you'll have at least twenty-four hours to get what you want out of the joint and get in the wind."

We walked together until we came to a drugstore. "Wait a minute, Preacher, I might as well run in here and cop some things I'm going to need." He followed me into the store. I walked around the counter and found some white envelopes. No one was watching except Preacher, so I pulled two loose from the pack and put them in my inside pocket. We walked over to the stamp machine at the beer and wine counter, and I bought two stamps and put them on the envelopes.

Preacher looked at the wine counter wistfully. "You want to kill a fifth with me?" I asked.

"Do I want to get rich? Do I want to go to heaven? Ask me that, Whoreson, but don't ask me about a bottle of wine. You know goddamn well I want some sweet red."

I bought two bottles and we walked back towards the car. "Man, don't tell me you goin' play on that young kid in your car, Whoreson."

"Don't look at me like that, Preacher. All I'm doing is keeping my game tight."

He snorted. "Game tight hell, man! All you want to do is georgia that young kid. That ain't cunt, man, that's still peehole."

I looked at him in disgust. "Looks to me like you read too much of that goddamn holy book while you was doing your last bit."

He studied me closely. "You ain't changed none, Whoreson. I had forgot that you was a genuine snake." He continued as though he was reading the gospel.

"The white race won't have you, and the black race don't want you."

"Fuck you, nigger, in your black ass," I stated angrily.

He ignored me and opened the wine and took a long drink, then passed me the bottle. "I remember, Whoreson, while we was in the joint you was strange fruit. While some of the dogs ran around raping white boys, you went them one better. You raped white and colored, it didn't make you no difference. If you saw a weak man, he was goin' be had."

I turned up the bottle and drank deep and long before replying. "That was only because I was young and wild, Preacher. You can't hold that against me."

He shrugged his wide shoulders. "I don't hold nothing against you. It ain't my place to judge, nor would I judge you if I could. I done did some rank things in my life. But I ain't never tampered with no child."

I cursed. "Call me in the morning, man, if you ain't changed your righteous mind," I gave him the open bottle and walked on over to my car.

She greeted me as soon as I got in the car. "I thought for a minute you was goin' stay up here all night."

I set the second wine bottle down between her legs. She opened the bag and sniffed. "Shit, I don't drink no wine, man. I drink scotch, mister; I don't drink nobody's wine."

"Just pour me a cup of wine, girl. I didn't hear nobody say it was for you, did you?" She poured out two cupsful and drank hers down fast.

As soon as I caught a gap in the traffic I pulled away from the curb. I stared at her thighs again. Shit, Preacher had to be insane. This damn sure wasn't no child.

She spoke up suddenly. "We sure had some good pot yesterday. My cousin's boyfriend brought some home when he came home on leave and it sure was good."

On the left side of the street I saw a gas station, so I made a U-turn and pulled up in the driveway. "Fill it up," I yelled to the attendant. I removed my bankroll and fanned it out, making it look larger than it was.

Her eyes grew big. "Damn, I ain't never seen so much money. What you do for a living, stick up people?"

Slowly I removed a hundred dollar bill from the roll and dropped it in her lap. "How would you like to have that for your very own?" I asked lightly.

Surprise and greed leaped from her eyes. "You wouldn't give that to me, would you?" she asked in a husky voice.

"It's all yours if you want it," I replied softly.

"What would I have to do for it?" she asked.

I smiled coldly to myself. There was the bait, and she was nibbling at it greedily. I put my hand down between her legs and rubbed her intimately. She didn't pull away or resist.

"No," she said, more to herself than to me. "If you gave me that money you'd just take it back as soon as you got through doing whatever you wanted to do."

The gas station attendant came to the window and

I paid him. "I'll tell you what I'll do, honey. I'll let you put the money in an envelope and mail it to your mother, or if you want, mail it to yourself."

The fish was caught; she leaped clear out of the water. "I ain't goin' mail nothing to my mother, 'cause she wouldn't give it back to me."

I pulled an envelope out of my pocket and handed it to her. She stared at it for a moment. "Put the money in it," I said quietly.

She dropped the bill inside it as if in a trance. "Now close it up and seal it," I said, leading her right down the road to the butcher shop.

She wet it with her tongue and sealed it. "Here, let me see if you got that sealed right." I removed the envelope from her hand, made my switch and handed her the dummy back.

"Ya, it's sealed. Reach in the glove compartment and get a pencil out and put your name and address on it."

She started to hand it back to me, but I refused. "No baby, I don't want you to give me the envelope. I don't want you to get the notion I might switch on you, so you hold on to it. You know the money's in it now."

She clutched the envelope to her. "I ain't never did nothing like this before," she said while writing out her address.

I drove slowly and watched for a mailbox. When I saw one I parked beside it. "Well, baby, here we are."

She looked scared for a moment. "You sure you

want to go through with this?" she stalled.

"Give me back the money then, if you don't want to go through with it," I said bluffing.

She bit down on her lip. "How long have I got to be with you?"

"About five minutes. It shouldn't take longer than that, should it?" I asked, amused.

"I don't know, should it?" she replied. I could tell she was way out of her program.

When I reached for the envelope, she opened the door and got out hesitantly. I watched her closely until she mailed the letter. If she had tried to run, I'd have run her little ass down and probably jumped on her for trying to put shit on me.

She climbed back in the car and sat over by the door nervously. I put my foot in the gas tank, making a beeline for the nearest motel. Even though I had two motel rooms, I wasn't about to take this tender young thing to one of them and have one of my warhorses walk in on me.

I pulled up behind a motel on Linwood. When she saw me park, she shook her head. "I ain't going in that place."

"Well I don't know what you're planning on doing, girl. You done took my money, and I guess you know I can't get it back out of no mailbox."

She shook her head. "I know that, but I just ain't going in none of the motels."

"What you want to do, then?" I asked. "Do it in the car someplace?"

"I don't care," she answered in a frightened voice.

For a few moments I just sat and thought about that. Well, it would save me the motel money, I reasoned. It was good and dark now, so I wouldn't have any difficulty finding a good spot to rip this sweet meat off. I slammed the car in gear and backed out. After my third alley I found just what I was looking for. An old dilapidated garage with the house vacant.

I backed up into it and pointed to the backseat with my thumb. "Climb over the seat," I directed. I wasn't taking any chance of her getting away this close to the finish line.

She climbed over obediently, then sat in the corner like a frightened kid. "Take them shorts off, everything," I growled.

I removed my sportcoat, shoes, shirt, then climbed over the seat. She hadn't taken anything off, so I straightened her out on the seat and removed her shorts and pants. The sight of such a young tender thing excited me, so I just stripped her down. Her breasts were small and hard, and I kissed them affectionately.

My breathing became deep and broken as that beautiful sight aroused me. When I put my finger inside of her, she began to cry, but I was beyond any feelings of concern. I unzipped my zipper.

She became aware of what was about to happen and cried, "Wait, wait, I didn't tell you, but I ain't but sixteen."

At that moment it wouldn't have mattered if she wasn't but ten. I was beyond the point of caring. I removed my finger and used it to guide myself with.

She screamed piercingly as I entered her, causing me to come instantly.

"Damn," I swore and sat up. "Instant cock. I could make a fortune off of you on the market." I straightened up my clothes and climbed back in the front seat.

She sat in the corner, slowly dressing. "You hurt me," she said angrily.

"You hurt my pocket, you ever think about that," I said, amused.

She smiled. Now that her ordeal was over she was happy. "I'm going downtown and buy me ten dresses when my money arrives."

For a moment my conscience nagged me, but not enough to make me part with a hundred dollars. "Would you do that for another hundred dollar bill?" I asked curiously.

She hesitated for a moment. "If you promise to do it as fast as the first time," she replied coldly.

I started to laugh and continued to laugh until she climbed up in the front seat. "I don't see nothing funny. What's so damn funny?" she asked and punched me in the side.

"Nothing," I said, holding back my laughter. I pulled out my bankroll and gave her a five dollar bill. "I'm goin' put you out at the bus stop. You can either take a car or catch the bus. Suit yourself. I just don't have the time to drop you off."

She clutched the five-spot to her. "Do you always spend this kind of money on the girls you go out with?" she asked. When I didn't answer, she continued, "If you want my address, I'll write it down for you."

I looked at her and smiled. "No thank you, honey. When you get old enough, I might run into you somewhere."

When I pulled up in front of a bus stop, I looked at her and said, "Instant cock," and began to laugh until my sides hurt.

She looked at me and shook her head. When she got out of the car she was smiling to herself.

23

THE WAITRESS BROUGHT my dinner and walked away, her hips moving provokingly. Her walk had the same effect on the men sitting around the restaurant as a snake, swaying back and forth, would have on a bird.

I glanced at my watch again. Three more hours. Stella had met Preacher twice now. This evening was the night for the big play. She had been to the false church we had tossed up and accepted it without too much fuss. After she saw his license she had been almost convinced, and when I took her by his church one evening and she walked in on a fake marriage, all doubt left her mind. She was more than ready to have him marry us, and when he put her off, causing us to postpone it another day, she started sleeping the sleep of the contented.

Getting a young man almost half her age was a middle-aged woman's dream. Impatiently, I glanced at my watch again. The door opened and Boots walked in. I stared at her coldly as she spotted me and started to walk over to my table.

She hesitated for a minute. "Do you mind if I sit down with you?"

Her carriage was as proud as ever. She walked as though she possessed something other women didn't have. She was the floating dream of many a man.

"If you're not afraid of someone telling your old man about us being together, knock yourself out and sit down." I watched her closely as she pulled out a chair. There was something on her mind. She wouldn't dare arouse Tony's displeasure unless she had something important worrying her.

I remained silent, waiting for her to speak. "Well, Whoreson, I heard about your bad luck. I'm sorry to hear that Ruby ran off."

"Ya, I can just look at you and see it," I said sarcastically. The sleepless morning a week before when I awoke to find that Ruby hadn't come home; my frantic telephone calls, first to women's division at the police station, then the hospital; the fear that something had happened to her; all this and more rushed back to me because of her comment. But to hell with Ruby, I thought. It was good riddance. I had bigger plans.

"Perhaps I didn't say that quite right," Boots began again. "What I really wanted to know, Whoreson, is what you plan on doing now that you ain't got nobody."

"For some reason, bitch, I can't seem to figure out where you're coming from. You know without my telling you that that ain't none of your business, but you still wouldn't put yourself on front street for that reason. What's the real deal? You done got fed up with the large stable you're living in, or is it that Tony wouldn't dare make a black bitch his main woman over all them white girls he got?"

She stared around the restaurant with unseeing eyes. I knew I had hit the tender spot. "Since you're so curious," I went on, "I'll tell you my plans. Sometime in the morning I'm going to pack my bags and hit the highway. I haven't made up my mind yet to where I'm going, but Detroit will be three hundred miles behind me this time tomorrow."

It would have been impossible for a blind man not to see that my words hit home. She let out her breath slowly. "Take me with you, Whoreson. If you do, I'll be yours for life."

"Why?" I asked her point-blank.

The question caught her by surprise. She looked up at me sincerely. "Why? I'll tell you why. Tony don't need me. All he needs is a banker. That's all I am to him."

Somewhere in the back of my mind her words rang a bell. "Banker! What you talkin' 'bout, Boots?"

With a sigh, she began to talk, and I listened real

close. "You know, you and Tony got a lot of ways alike. Maybe that's why I picked him while you was gone. Anyway, he's always gambling, so he don't put all of his money in the bank. He gives it to me to put up for him in case he runs into a crap game or something out in the street. That seems to be all I can do for him nowadays, just hold his money."

"How much?" I asked softly. She hesitated for just a second. "Six thousand dollars. He said he was going to buy his new Cadillac with it."

"Where is it?"

Her eyes met mine for a moment, then she looked away. "I got it put up at my apartment." She caught her breath and asked, "Are you really leaving in the morning, Whoreson?"

The jukebox began to play the number by John Coltrane, "These Foolish Things." I sat back and smiled. What goes around comes around. I could see it in the bitch's eyes. That money belonged to me.

"All you got to do is walk out to my car and open the trunk. All my clothes are already packed, sitting out there waiting for me to ride out."

Her voice was hoarse. "Let's get up and walk out and make one stop. I'll run in and get the money, and then we can hit the highway. Right now, Whoreson. I'll give you every penny of it." She stopped long enough to get her breath. "It don't make no difference when we leave. If you was going, we can just as well leave now."

Now that was just like a bitch, I thought to myself coldly. She didn't stop to think that I might have some business of my own to take care of. I knew she was on the borderline and could jump either way, so I pushed her. I wasn't going to allow her time to think, 'cause if she did, she might change her mind about that money. She knew as well as I did that once she took that money Tony would break her back, wherever he found her. Her only chance would be to put many miles between her and Tony.

I manipulated her like a puppy on a leash. "Let's go," I said sharply, not giving her time to reason.

She stood up bewildered. "Where?" she asked in a shocked voice.

The people at the tables and the counter watched us closely as we left. There would be much talk, and it wouldn't be long before Tony was informed about us leaving together. If I knew Tony, he'd make a bee-line for his money stash. No pimp with anything on the ball would trust his woman in the company of her ex-pimp.

There was no time for any bullshit, so I drove straight to her apartment. "Get the money and whatever clothes you can toss together at once," I ordered.

She jumped out of the car and ran up the stairs. I glanced at my watch. I wasn't afraid of Tony, but I didn't want any static from him until I got that money in my pocket. After that, I didn't give a damn what he did. I wasn't planning on kicking back no six grand.

It didn't take her long. She came out with two suit-cases under her arms, walking fast. Before she got to the car, another girl came out of the building behind her and ran down the steps.

Their voices came drifting to me. "Boots, you know what you doing, girl. Tony goin' kill you. At least leave his money. You know how he is about that."

Boots hesitated. I yelled out the window, "Bitch, if you don't get your ass in this car, I'm goin' kill you myself." I stared at the girl holding Boots' arm. "And if you don't turn her arm loose and get the hell out of my game, bitch, I'll get out of here and break one of your funky legs."

She released Boots. "I know you, Whoreson. I'm going to tell Tony just what you said."

"It don't make me no difference if you tell your black ass mammy, bitch," I yelled and jumped out of the car.

Boots ran over and pushed her suitcases into the backseat. I climbed back in and started the car up. "Set it out, woman," I said and held my hand out for the money.

If you have never had a woman give you six thousand dollars it will be hard to understand what I felt at that moment. When she set that money in my hand it was like I had just taken a heavy drug. The blood raced to my head, and I believed I owned the world. How sweet it is!

"Where we going, Whoreson?" she asked.

She had tried to sound cheerful, but I could feel the fear gnawing at her. I couldn't blame her. I knew that I was the only thing between her and a broken back. If she had had a hint of what I was thinking, she would have jumped out and run for dear life. I hadn't made up my mind yet on what to do with her, but one thing was sure: whenever I told a whore they couldn't leave me and come back, I meant every word of it. I wasn't a bus driver; a bitch couldn't catch a ride with me whenever she made up her mind to do it.

Since I didn't want any trouble from Tony until after I took off my big sting, I found a motel on the outskirts. Boots' eyes got big as I pulled up and parked. "We ain't goin' check in here, are we?"

"Well, I don't know what the hell you're going to do, but I'm sure in the hell goin' check in," I said.

She stared at me angrily. "Whoreson, you lied to me just to get your hands on Tony's money."

I leaned over and slapped the shit out of her. "First, bitch, don't call me no liar. Second it ain't Tony's money, it's mine." Whatever inconvenience the bitch was going to cause me, I had to put up with it for at least the next few hours.

She followed me docilely into the motel. I checked us in, and we settled down. I made her go out and get her bags. When she returned, I was counting my money. She glared at me.

"Listen, whore, I ain't about to have you walking around me rolling your eyes, so just keep all them goddamn funny looks to yourself."

Being cruel to her was really unnecessary. This was the first time in my life I had ever seen her broken. There was no doubt in my mind about that, she was completely lost.

Her head hung down and she looked at me sadly.

"Why, Whoreson, why? What did I ever do to you to make you want to do this to me? When I was with you, I gave you every penny I ever made. Don't that mean something to you?" Her voice broke. She started crying silently. "What is it, Whoreson, what is it? Do you hate women or something like that? A man just don't be cruel like you're being for no reason at all."

"Bitch, let me tell you something. Your tears, your name-calling, it ain't nothing but humorous to me. You can talk from now on, it ain't goin' mean a thing, 'cause as far as one of you funky bitches is concerned, my understanding is completely zero."

For several minutes she just stared at me. "I guess you can be tough when a woman's concerned, but I wonder how you'll act if Tony rides down on you."

"If you're trying to make me mad, Boots, forget it. I got Tony's money in my pocket, and if he rides down on me, it's goin' still stay in my pocket."

She swore bitterly. "Goddamnit, you Detroit niggers ain't no earthly good." With a jerk she pulled her blouse off, then loosened her bra. I watched her coldly as she wiggled out of her skirt and panties. Without a backward look, she marched off towards the shower. The sound of running water filled the room.

I stretched out on the bed. I still had two hours to go before picking up Stella. We would have to arrive at the church at the exact minute. I went over my plan again. Everything depended on the timing. Preacher had a bunch of wineheads lined up. He promised them ten dollars each just to sit in the church, so I could figure on it being full when we arrived.

Boots came out of the bathroom and lay down on the bed beside me. I had taken my shirt off to get comfortable. She twisted around so that her head was on my chest. Her hands began to wander up and down, promising temporary pleasure.

Her body was too tempting, even after so many years. I got up and went in and took a shower. When I returned, she stared at me strangely. I didn't mind. I dressed slowly, putting on a midnight blue silk suit with powder blue shirt.

She remained silent as I dressed. When I finished, I said, "I'll be back sometime in the morning. If you ain't here, I'll figure you done rode out. Do whatever you want to do. It's your decision." She watched me silently as I went out the door. To me, it didn't really make any difference. She could stay or leave.

24

IT WAS A CLEAR, STARLIT night. Most of the traffic was gone; it was that in-between hour of the evening. When I got downtown, Stella was standing in front of Hudson's department store. When I blew my horn she came running over, her black silk dress hugging her hips provocatively.

Her eyes sparkled at the sight of me. "Oh, Johnny, I was so worried you'd change your mind." She stepped into the car, displaying more class than I was accustomed to.

I let my eyes run up and down her body slowly. It made her happy when I looked at her like that. She knew she was gettin' old, so I guess she figured she was losing her looks. The dress brought out her complexion, though, and when she smiled, it made her look ten years younger. We stopped and had dinner at Harry's supper club before continuing on our way. When I pulled up in front of the church I saw by my watch that I was two minutes early. I pulled her to me and kissed her.

She complained happily. "Stop, Johnny, you're going to mess up my makeup."

When a woman is really in love, she looks desirable or maybe it was just the twenty thousand dollars I was about to get. Whatever it was, something made her look very good that night. I got out of the car and opened the door for her. She smiled her appreciation as she got out. It's so easy to make a woman in love happy.

We walked into the church hugged up tightly together. She was lying in my arm as though she had been made there. Preacher had to wave frantically at the organ player to stop him from belting out one of Jimmy Smith's latest numbers. Stella was too far gone to notice.

The people sitting around the church played their parts well. Most of them were too drunk to know what was going on, while others thought it was the real deal going down. I glanced around and noticed one winehead holding his woman in her chair; she was too drunk to sit up by herself. I held my breath, prayed that it would end in a hurry, and rushed Stella towards the front of the church. If Stella had been black, she would have been hip immediately, but she had never

been in a black church before, so whatever she saw
was bound to look strange.

The organ player began to play "Here Comes the
Bride." I stared at Preacher, hoping like hell he would
hurry. My stomach flipped over on me as though I
was standing in front of a judge getting ready to be
sentenced on first degree.

Preacher mumbled out the words and I managed to
get my yesses in at the right place. As soon as it was
over, I kissed the bride. I let out a sigh of relief. One
drunk came up and tried to kiss the bride, but I pushed
him away. I didn't give a damn about him kissing her,
I just didn't want her to smell that goddamn booze on
his breath.

I handed Preacher a fat envelope. "Here you go,
Reb," I said. "Maybe this will help you get a larger
church."

He grinned and accepted the sealed envelope.
"Good luck to both of you happy people; may you
get what you both hope for."

Stella was beaming with happiness. "Thank you,
sir!" she replied sweetly. Her face was full of joy, and
for a moment I hated myself for the lowdown trick I
was getting ready to put on her.

I glanced over my shoulder and saw one of the
drunk ass bitches trying to do a striptease. I damn near
shit on myself until I saw someone pull her back down
to her seat. After that I didn't waste any time gettin'
the hell out of there with Stella. She seemed to enjoy
my dilemma.

When we got outside she acted like she wanted to

go back in. "All I want to do is thank all the nice people for showing up," she said happily.

"The hell with the nice people," I replied quickly. "They would have been here anyway. It's a church night."

Again I held the door for her while she got in. A little more kindness wouldn't hurt a thing this late in the game. She gave me directions as I drove. When we got to the suburbs it was like another world to me. No broken-down houses staring you in the face. Everything neat and clean, the streets unlittered with tricks accosting every woman that walked past. Yes, Stella, I thought coldly, you're going to pave the way so that I'll never have to live in another slum again. From here on out, it would be penthouses with the best of everything tossed in. I had experienced enough filth and poverty to last me four lifetimes.

When I pulled up in her driveway, I could see that her house was in the fifty thousand dollar bracket. It was far more than just a modern ranch-type home with a beautiful lawn. There was enough room on her property to hold ten inner-city homes, with room to spare.

The inside of the house turned out to be just as beautiful. Wall-to-wall carpet, rooms big enough for a man to really live in. I felt good at the thought of all this being mine now, if I wanted it. But I had my cap set for bigger prey. This was just a beginning. Stella was just one more woman for me to use on my way to the top. Right then I came face to face with myself. I didn't care for no one woman, black or white; they were all just stepping-stones. Life had become a giant jungle for me in which the coldest, most brutal animal won. To fight your way out of the quicksand of the slums, you had to be ruthless. Maybe Preacher was right when he said I was a man caught between two races with neither one wanting me. If so, I didn't give a damn. I didn't need to be anyone or anything but me.

Stella had everything prepared. "Here, honey," she said and held out a champagne bottle for me to open. I took a towel and wrapped it around the cap and opened it without a pop.

We drank up the bottle, then moved to something a little stronger. I rolled up some weed and gave her a joint. The weed on top of the whiskey lit her up. Before she got too high, she grinned at me and got up.

"Here, honey. I want you to see I'm holding up my end of the deal."

She got up and staggered towards the bedroom. I followed her and watched closely as she opened up her wall safe. She flashed the money at me, then started to close it back up.

"Wait a minute, baby," I said quickly. "That's mine, ain't it?" She nodded drunkenly. I removed the money and set it on the bed. It was the first time in my life I had ever seen so much money. I slowly counted it while she staggered out to refill our drinks. When she returned I was drunk on power. Green power.

I stacked the money on the dresser. Stella now wore only her slip. I caught her around the waist. If I hadn't known myself so well, I would have sworn I was in love. I pushed her down on the bed and pulled one of her straps loose, revealing one of her beautiful pink tits. I put my mouth over it and slowly ran my tongue up and down on the nipple until it became hard. I could feel my penis rearing like it was about to bust out of my pants. The money had excited me more than anything else in my life. I mounted her with my pants still on and rammed myself down into her. She caught her breath quickly but loved it all at the same time. I took her roughly, pounding up and down in her until she moaned. When she reached up for me I clutched her tightly in my arms and gave her the best twenty thousand dollar fuck I had ever given. We lay beside each other, breathing heavily. Soon her light snore came to me. I rolled over and stared down at her face. Gently, I kissed her cheek. I really liked Stella, but I couldn't allow my emotions to come between me and the bright lights. Playing heavy game was part of nature.

I washed up, then came back and picked my money up and took it into the front room. I counted it again; when I finished, I wrote Stella a brief note, trying to say good-bye as gently as possible. This one small act of kindness was ruined for me as I thought of her waking up in the morning alone. When she found out she had lost her one opportunity to satisfy her sex drive, and that that one fuck had cost her twenty grand, she would be one mad bitch. As I walked out the front door, uncontrollable laughter escaped from me. Mocking laughter, filled with bitterness and hate.

After locking the money in my car trunk I went

back to the motel. I was filled with an intoxicating
drug, stronger than drink, more pleasing than drugs:
the ripening fruit of greed. If Boots was still at the
motel she would really find out what payback was all
about.

Boots met me at the door. "Get your bag, whore,
I'm ready to ride out." Joy leaped in her eyes. She
ran back in the room and came out with her bags and
mine. I peeled rubber as I left the motel parking lot.
Life was beginning to look sweeter and sweeter.

I drove out to the city limits and pulled up in an
all night gas station to get the tank filled. While waiting, I made a phone call to Tony.

One of his girls answered the phone. "Honey, I said
he was taking a bath and I don't think he wants to be
disturbed." Her voice was low and polite.

"Bitch!" I snarled into the receiver. "You tell him
that this is Whoreson on the phone."

I could hear her relaying the message to someone
else in the room. Almost instantly Tony's angry voice
came over the line. "Whoreson, dig, baby. Don't play
games with me." Before I could answer he rushed on.
"Listen, man! I don't give a fuck about that whore,
but I do want you to return my money. You understand what I'm talking about? I can dig where you're
coming from, baby, but having that funky bitch steal
my bread is going too far."

I laughed loudly. "I just called, Tony, to find out if
you knew payback when you saw it. As you know,
baby, the game ain't cop and blow. It's cop, block and
lock." I waited until he quit cursing. "I just want you

to know, Tony, that I done blocked your game, copped your whore, and locked up your gold. Can you dig it, player?"

His voice was deadly as he replied, but I ignored him and continued to laugh. "All that shit about killin' the bitch when you catch her is bullshit, though I couldn't care less what you did to her. I just wanted you to really know, Tony, that I repaid you for what you did to me, and you can rest easy on the bitch's account, 'cause I'm going to fix her little red wagon, too."

"I ain't goin' never forget this!" he yelled wildly. Then his voice changed and he begged, "Just bring me my money back, Whoreson, that's all I want."

"I don't want you to never forget it, Tony, and I don't want you to ever forget that I'm the one who did it to you, baby," I said harshly and slammed the phone down on him.

When I reached the car Boots smiled hesitantly. "That was Tony, wasn't it?" she asked, a tremor in her voice revealing her fright.

"He just got a taste of payback, baby," I replied as I started the car up. I gave the gas station attendant his money and pulled away from the pump.

The stars were still bright as I hit the highway for New York. We drove most of the way in silence. Boots attempted to make small conversation, but I ignored her, so she cuddled up in the seat and tried to sleep. When morning came I was almost there. I kept my foot in the gas tank, eating up the miles.

It was noon when I finally reached New York. As

soon as I got past the city limits and off the freeway, I pulled over to the curb. Boots stared at me in surprise when I stopped.

"This is the end of the road for you, bitch," I stated brutally.

For a brief second she just stared at me, too dumbfounded to understand what I meant. "What you mean, what you talkin' about, daddy?" She stared around at the unfamiliar city. "Honey, you don't expect me to get out here?" Her features were frozen with disbelief. She stared more closely to see if I were joking. "Whoreson, you wouldn't do this to me, would you?"

For an answer I reached across her and opened the door. "It ain't about nothing, bitch," I replied. "Just a little payback."

She shook her head mutely. She fumbled with her tiny purse and held it under my nose. "I ain't got a penny, Whoreson. I gave you every penny I had in this world, man." Her eyes filled with tears. "I'm asking you to please don't do this to me, Whoreson." Her voice was broken as she continued. "I don't know a soul in this goddamn city, man, and ain't got a dime to make a phone call with."

I laughed mockingly in her face. "You don't know how sweet that is to my ears, Boots. The only regret I got now is that you ain't covered with gasoline so that I could have the pleasure of tossing a match on your funky ass."

She stared at me, fighting for control. "Then you really mean to keep all that money that I gave you? You ain't goin' give me none of it, not even enough to rent me a room so I could work out of it and get myself together?" Her voice was beginning to get firmer, to take on a frosty chill I should have paid heed to.

"A room!" I laughed. "Bitch, if you could buy a house for one nickel and had to get it from me, you wouldn't have enough to buy the doorknob on the back door."

She didn't bother to answer. She reached over the seat and got her bags. She tossed them out on the ground, then leaned over and spit. Before I could react she jumped out of the car. I removed my pocket handkerchief and wiped my face. As far as I was concerned, I had come out on top. I watched her in my mirror as I pulled away, standing on the curb, staring after me, her hands on her hips, until I lost her from sight.

25

THE WIND RATTLED my windows and I cursed this New York weather. I rolled over in the bed and sat up. I shook my head to shake off the fuzziness. I had been in New York for over a week now, and ever since I had gotten in touch with Janet, it had been one merry-go-round. I lit up a cigarette and thought about her. She was playing one of the most expensive nightclubs in the city now, and some of the people I had met through her had really been big stuff. I grinned to myself as I remembered the way she always introduced me: Mr. W.S. Jones. She was afraid to tell them my first name, but that was understandable. In the circle of white people she moved in, my name would really start some gossip. Even so, I could see some of the more experienced men staring at me closely at times. I knew that they were trying to figure just what the hell the deal was with me. I smiled. Just the thought of the twenty-five grand I had put in the bank made me feel legitimate as hell.

The phone rang suddenly. "Hi, honey. Are you awake yet?" Her sweet laughter came tingling along the line.

"Hell no! I'm dreaming that Janet just called me and wanted to know if she could come up to my apartment and wake me up properly."

"Whoreson, dear, I really do wish I could come up, but I know that once you get me in that apartment, you never will behave yourself, so I think I'll take a few precautions, like having you meet me uptown for lunch. Can you make it?"

"It depends on what time you're having lunch," I replied, glancing at my watch. "Since it's after two o'clock now, wouldn't it have been better to just say supper?"

Her rich laughter came through the phone again. I was beginning to really enjoy myself with her. Janet was the first woman I had ever dated without having it in the back of my mind to beat her out of something. Since I had reached her after arriving in New York, I had experienced some truly shocking changes in my life. I didn't have to worry about any phone calls in the middle of the night telling me my woman was in jail or the hospital, so I had begun to relax. For the past few days, I had been wondering more and more what I could invest my money in. Something legitimate for a change....

"Say in about a half an hour, honey. Wouldn't that give you enough time to get up and get ready?" she asked sweetly.

"More than enough, Janet." I hesitated briefly. "Listen, sugar, can't we go somewhere besides those expensive places you like to go to? No, it isn't the money I'm worried about," I said quickly, cutting off her question. "I just don't feel comfortable when I'm sitting in Sardi's." That was really an understatement. When I went to places like that with her, I felt like a lackey; I felt everyone could look through me and see I didn't belong.

"I'll tell you what, Whoreson. I'll meet you in the lobby of your hotel in half an hour, then you can choose wherever you like."

"Honey," I said, trying one more time, "if you're coming this far, you might as well come upstairs and help me dress."

"Don't forget, half an hour," she said and hung up, not even bothering to answer my question.

Again I wondered if it could be possible for Janet to be a virgin. I would have known if she was fuckin' when we grew up. There had never been any wire out on her making it with anyone, but you never could tell about those things. Since she was in show business, I couldn't imagine all the men she came in contact with not being able to get her pants off. No, someone somewhere had to have copped. I'd find out in the near future, I promised myself.

I took a quick shower and dressed carefully, putting on a sky blue silk suit with dark blue matching suede shoes. It was chilly out, so I draped my fall coat over the arm of a chair while I lit up a joint. I had just about finished smoking it when she called from the lobby. I didn't even bother to try to get her to come upstairs. Everything would come to the man with patience. I grabbed my coat and hurried down to the lobby.

She was standing against the desk when I got there. She was still thin, with large lovely eyes. I looked at her with affection. Two young ladies sitting in the lobby stared at her openly. I believe they recognized her but hadn't made up their minds if it was Janet or not. I rushed her out of the hotel and into my car. I removed the ticket from off of the windshield.

"If I don't start paying these goddamn things soon," I said as we got in the car, "I'll have enough of them to start a collection."

She turned to me and smiled. "I know you don't like to eat at some of the places I go, Whoreson, but I've got an appointment with some people at Harry's Supper Lounge."

I couldn't keep the irritation out of my voice. "I guess it doesn't make too much difference, Janet."

"Honey, I didn't mean for this to happen, but before I left my place they called, and since it was important I decided to have them meet us." She continued to explain. "One of the men we're meeting happens to own a booking agency, so I thought you might want to meet him." She added quickly, "You know these are the kind of people you're going to have to know,

Whoreson, if you want to make it in any part of show business."

For a while I remained silent, thinking over what she had said. "You know, all I'm really thinking about opening is a small record company, Janet. To these people you talk to, that's small peanuts. I hate to give them the impression you're wasting your time with someone who's still on the ground floor." Once again I was filled with that feeling of insecurity. I wondered if I was that far out of my depth.

She reached over and clutched my arm reassuringly. "Don't worry about it, honey. They're nothing but flesh and bones. You came out of the slums, Whoreson. Here you are, not even twenty-five yet, with money in the bank. Why, all you have to do is pick out a field you like, and you're young enough to learn by your mistakes. By the time you reach thirty, you'll have a full knowledge of what you're doing." She smiled at me and continued. "Most of the people you'll meet will be men and women just like yourself. People who wouldn't believe that all life had to offer them was a small paying job in someone else's office or plant. They had ambition and confidence in themselves. That's why they're where they're at today."

A doorman opened the car door for us when I pulled up in front of the place. My knees trembled slightly. It was another world to me, but I knew I was buying chips in the game and I planned on playing my hand to a tee. I got out and we walked inside the club. The headwaiter knew Janet on sight. He led us to a table where three men and one woman were already sitting.

The men stood up as we approached. Janet introduced me to the men and I shook hands with all of them, then nodded slightly towards the woman.

One of the men pulled Janet's chair out and held it for her as we sat down. I gritted my teeth, wishing I had thought of doing it first.

Once or twice I caught the woman's eyes on me, appraising me openly. She was in her early thirties and had sharp, keen features. Her eyes were a pale green that matched the flaming red hair she wore in a huge beehive. I wondered idly if it was really her hair or a dye job.

"Janet, dear, you're just going to have to tell me where you found this beautiful specimen of a man. Just look at him," she exclaimed as I blushed. "He even blushes beautifully."

The men around the table laughed. I put on my most charming smile, hoping it would cover up my embarrassment.

"You won't have to worry about Martha now, Mr. Jones," the young man who had been introduced as Ringo said. "If she likes you, she won't write anything nasty about you in her column."

I stared closely at the blond young man they called Ringo. Something about his name had rung a bell in the back of my mind, but because of my nervousness, I couldn't put my finger on it.

"Don't worry about anything Ringo has to say, darling," she replied, patting my arm affectionately. "He's probably still carrying a grudge over the loss of Janet. You already know, don't you, darling, that Janet and

Ringo were engaged to take the big jump?" She smiled brightly at everyone at the table, but I hadn't missed the bright glitter in her eyes as she told the old news. She watched for my reaction, but I was beginning to get on firm ground now. I was used to the sharp claws of malicious women.

"Yes," I replied cheerfully. "Janet told me earlier that Mr. Ringo would be here. I have been aware of him, but I haven't had the opportunity to meet him until today." I glanced up at Janet and saw the relief in her eyes.

After that, the conversation became more formal. They discussed the idea of having Janet and Ringo go on a three-month tour of the West Coast after she completed her bookings in the East. I could tell from the look in Ringo's eye that he was all for the tour. He and Janet had the same agent and the agent was all for the trip. It wasn't hard for my inexperienced mind to grasp what was behind the scheme. Ringo hadn't had a record in the top one hundred in the past two years. With Janet drawing the crowd, they would be able to cash in on the rumors about their past romance, plus rebuild his image.

Ringo was hungry. I watched his cold blue eyes search Janet's face. She kept her eyes away from him; she was up on what was going down. She glanced at me shyly. I shook my head, wanting her to know I didn't want her going for the deal at all.

Martha caught my motion and smiled. "Mr. Jones, I believe you might have a surprise for a lot of people in this town."

I grinned at her in return, staring into her eyes until she looked away. I wanted her to know that I was a man and not some woman's playtoy.

I decided to put all my marbles in the pot at once. When a man has dealt with women all his life, he has a feeling about them that is seldom wrong. I knew that many women were slow to make a decision, but if you backed them in a corner they would accept it. I decided to put Janet in a corner. I really didn't have that much to lose. Either she went for it or I started to pimp everything that wore a skirt in New York.

"I don't think Janet will be able to accept that offer," I began and waited until I was sure I had everyone's attention. "Because we are getting married next month." Just like that, I laid it on the table. Everything was hanging out. Janet's mouth dropped open and she looked like she was having trouble breathing.

Martha was the first one to regain her composure. "Is that correct, Janet? Can I quote you on that?" Her questions were sharp and to the point.

Janet nodded her head in agreement and continued to stare at me in utter shock. Martha jumped up and ran to the phone. The gray-headed agent ordered a round of drinks for everyone, while Ringo shot daggers across the table at me. I returned his stare. Up your ass, peckerwood, I said to myself coldly. This was one little black girl you gray boys wouldn't get a chance to play out of a million.

When Martha returned we had a few more drinks, then got ready to go. When Janet got up and came around the table, I took her arm.

I began to steer her towards the door. Before I could react, a flashbulb went off in my face. I jerked my head back, but I was too late. The damage had been done. I stared angrily after the girl with the camera.

"What's wrong, Mr. Jones? A man as handsome as you are shouldn't mind someone taking your picture," Martha said lightly. "Besides, I want Janet's fans to see the wonderful specimen she has managed to latch onto."

Outside the club we shook hands again, then I managed to get Janet away and into my car. We rode in silence for a few blocks.

"Why did you do that, Whoreson?" she asked slowly.

"Why! I don't know why you even bother to ask me something like that, woman. Unless you were interested in making that tour with that high-paid pimp," I replied, fighting for time to get my answers together.

"You don't have to call Ringo any names, Whoreson, and it sure wasn't necessary for you to go and put your foot in your mouth like that," she replied. The anger was coming now.

"If you didn't like the idea, why didn't you just tell your lily-white friends that I was lying?" If I could get her on the defensive, I reasoned, I had a good chance of winning more than I had bargained for. Even though I had mentioned marriage on the spur of the moment, I was by no means a fool. I knew marriage to Janet would put me on easy street for a long time.

"First of all, Whoreson, I didn't want to make a fool out of you by denying it. If you had asked me about it, I would have probably agreed to marry you anyway, but this way you make me feel as though you're playing on me." She glanced up at me and her eyes were filled with tears.

"Playing on you, hell," I replied sharply. "Was pretty Ringo playing on you when they tried to get you to go on that goddamn tour?"

"I could have handled that myself," she explained softly. "Anyway, it's understandable. Ringo wanted to marry me and still does for that matter. Why shouldn't he want to go on a tour with me? He probably thinks it will help his chances out."

"Marry you, my black ass. You black bitches kill me. Every time one of you gets a little bit of money and a white man looks at you, you really think he wants to marry you. Bullshit. All he wants to do is play you out of that cash." I reached over and pulled the car shade down so she could see herself in the little mirror on the back. "Look in that and tell me what you see. No, that's all right. I'll tell you what you'll see. A black woman, not the most beautiful black woman in the world either, just a young cute black girl. Now, not counting all the fine ass white girls out there, let's talk about the fine ass black ones." I stopped and caught my breath. "Wherever Mr. Ringo sings at, you can bet money there's some pretty, not cute, but pretty, beautiful, black girls in the audience listening, and some of them girls would jump out of a ten-story window just to be able to carry Mr. Ringo's shorts, yet you don't find him taking any of them home to mama, do you? You bet your goddamn ass you don't," I stat-

ed, not giving her time to answer. I pulled up in front
of my hotel and parked. "I want you to come upstairs
for a minute. I got something I want to show you."
Without waiting for her answer I got out and walked
towards the entrance. She followed meekly behind me.
We remained silent until we got out of the elevator on
the fourth floor and entered my apartment.

"I don't see any difference, Whoreson, in you or
Ringo. You say he wants to marry me because of my
money, but I'm supposed to believe the only reason
you want me is because of my just-fair looks, as you
put it." Sarcasm dripped from her words. "You may
not know it," she continued, "but Ringo happens to be
Jewish, so he knows all about being discriminated
against. I happen to know he came from a poor background the same as I did."

"You better damn well bet he did," I said harshly.
"Let me tell you something, little mixed-up fool. When
I was in prison I learned something about white folks,
and Jews in particular. Dig this first, baby," I said, waving her quiet. "Out of all the ofays in prison, the only
ones I wouldn't mess with were the Jews, baby. And
you know why? Well, I'll tell you. A poor Jew catches damn near as much hell as a black man in this country, honey, you hear me. If he goes South they might
beat his goddamn ass if them hillbillies feel like it, you
know what I mean?" I stared at her closely, then continued. "That's why I say this. When a poor Jew starts
climbing, baby, he knows he has one strike against him
already, you dig. Just because he's a Jew. Now I want
you to look me in the eye and tell me, do you really

believe a young Jew boy who was raised in a cold-water flat, rats running all over the motherfucking place, will intentionally go all out of his way to marry a woman with two strikes against her? Not one like he got, but *two*. Do you really believe he would?" I stared at her as though she was losing her mind. She held her head and staggered over to the couch and sat down.

"I just don't know, Whoreson. I really don't. What you say may be true, and then again it may not." She dropped her head.

"Okay then, baby, just think about this and try to answer it for me," I went on, realizing I had her going. "If you think I'm lying, why don't you go with me this evening and I'll show you damn near every white boy we see who's really pimping, and I mean pimping, with white girls and black ones, is Jewish." I stared at her intently. I had just told her one of the damnedest lies. If she asked me to prove it, I didn't have the faintest idea where to find any white pimps at, let alone any Jewish ones.

She jumped up and ran over and hit me in the chest with her small fists. "I don't care!" she screamed. "You're no better. All you want me for is my money, too." She was crying and screaming.

I grabbed her arm and pulled her into the bedroom. I held her as I opened up the dresser drawer and removed my bankbook. I pushed her on the bed and tossed it in her lap. She stared at it dumbly.

"Open it, goddamn you," I screamed. I should have got an Oscar for my acting ability. I grabbed her and opened the book, making her see where I had close to twenty-five thousand dollars in the bank.

She stared at the figures, not really believing her own eyes. The tears stopped flowing as she tried to understand what she was seeing. She had known I had money in the bank, but by no stretch of the imagination would she have believed such a large figure.

"Now do you still believe I want you just for your money?" I asked slowly. I sat down and pulled her in my arms. She was still shook up.

"But, but, Whoreson," she managed to say before I interrupted.

"But, hell," I said and kissed her. "It's your choice, now, baby. Either you want a black man or it's really true that you done got color-struck and you won't be satisfied unless you get your own white owl." I was dealing them at her now from the bottom of the deck, and I didn't believe she was fast enough to catch on.

She tried to deny it. "Whoreson, you know that ain't true."

"Prove it, baby," I said flatly and pushed her back on the bed. Before she realized it, I had her out of her blouse and was working on her skirt. I kissed her around the neck as she tried to stop my searching hands.

"Please, Whoreson, please. Not like this," she managed to say.

I found the zipper on her skirt and opened the button over it. With one smooth motion I removed skirt and half slip. She glanced down at herself surprised. I had her undressed down to her panties and bra.

"Stop, Whoreson, stop!" She started to squirm but I pinned one of her arms behind her head, while lying on the other one.

Without allowing her time to think, I pushed one side of her bra up and stared down at her one small breast. Quickly I covered it with my mouth, slowly releasing her arm as I felt her struggles cease.

"Please, Whoreson, please. Don't do this to me. Not like this." Her pleading was in vain. I could feel her hand on the back of my head as I slowly ran my tongue around her tiny nipple, making it harden.

Her breathing became louder and louder. I removed her pants slowly, kissing her navel as I went down. She tried to close her legs, but it was only her last resort against the inevitable. When I mounted her, I had to force an entry because of her tightness. She cried out in pain. I kissed the salty teardrops from her eyelids as the wonderful discovery of her virginity dawned on me. Later, I made love to her slowly and tenderly, helping her over her awkwardness, until she finally realized the beauty of lovemaking. She lay in my arms, cuddled up tightly, happy and satisfied. As I lay back and stared at the ceiling, a feeling of tenderness came over me. For once in my life I knew the meaning of the word love.

26

ACROSS TOWN IN A small, dingy hotel room, Boots stared at the ceiling, too, but her thoughts were not of love and tenderness. She was remembering the harshness of the treatment she had received when she arrived in the big city. It had become like a growing cancer in her mind. No matter how much she drank, her mind came back to that morning. Never in her life had she felt so rejected. No man had ever managed to make her feel so low. Only one thing kept her in this cold city, and that was the thought of revenge. At no time did she ever doubt her ability to revenge the wrong done to her. The only problem was how.

She blushed as she remembered how she had broken down and cried inside the car of the man who had stopped to pick her up. He had been an elderly white man with glasses, and he had watched her silently for a few minutes. After she had blurted out like a young schoolgirl how she was stranded in New York without any money, he had offered her train fare home. She had refused the fare but had accepted ten dollars so she could get a room. He had refused to come up when he let her out. It was one of the few kind things she had ever had done for her. She would have liked to have been able to return his ten dollars, but he didn't leave an address. He told her to accept it as a gift and not to worry about it. He had blushed when she leaned over and kissed him on the cheek. How beautiful life would have been, she thought at that moment, if her father had been any way like that. Kind and gentle and, most of all, understanding.

Boots dressed slowly. She tried to remember the good times she had had with Whoreson, but it didn't do any good. Her mind was firmly made up. She stared at the open newspaper again. There he was, big as life, holding Janet. "Well, Mr. Whoreson," she said loudly to the empty room, "you have a few surprises coming to you, my friend. Quite a few surprises."

The bar was dimly lit when she entered it. She stared at the few male customers sitting around on the bar stools. Only one of the men had taken any interest in her as she walked across the floor. The rest continued to stare in their drinks. She walked past the bar and joined two women sitting in the rear at a table.

They glanced up at her as she approached. She smiled at the two young black prostitutes as she joined their table. One of them was a lesbian, and the other belonged to the lesbian.

The lesbian stared at Boots coldly. Ever since Boots had started working out of their bar, she had been trying to figure her out. The first night she had come in, the lesbian had spent ten dollars with her, hoping to cop another girl. But to her surprise, she quickly found out that Boots was just as experienced in the art of making love to another woman as she was. Boots could take either the top or bottom, without the least show of emotion. She could sense something hard about this young hustler out of Detroit, and she didn't want to bring it to the surface. Most of the other women who worked out of the bar gave her plenty room. They didn't care to become involved in any arguments with her, but Boots, on the other hand, would quickly come out and tell her she was full of shit, then laugh at her harshly.

Boots sat down without waiting for anyone to invite her. "Hi, Billy, dear," she said, smiling at the lesbian.

Billy managed to smile back and glanced out of the corner of her eye at her girl, Ann, who was staring at Boots in fascination. She was quick to notice the byplay that always started between Billy and Boots. She remembered the night when Billy was busy. She had approached Boots and let her know that she might be interested in changing pimps. Boots had laughed at her and told her she wasn't a lesbian.

Ann stared openly at the tall dark-skinned woman who aroused her so much. Her avid interest was not missed by Billy. "Ann," she said sharply, "you run down to Lee's bar and see if any tricks are there!"

Ann started to object, but Billy reached across the table and slapped her. The sound was like a shot going off in a small place. People turned and stared as Ann jumped up and ran out of the bar.

Billy stared coldly at Boots. There was a look in her eyes that said, if you have any objection, spit it out.

"She's young yet," Billy said quietly. "She has a lot to learn."

"Don't blow your whore over me, Billy," Boots said coldly. "I wouldn't have her if you gave her to me, so don't push it."

"I just don't understand you," Billy said, laughing to cover up her confusion. "Boots, I ain't never seen no bitch in my life that acted like you do. What do you want?"

"I want a yellow nigger's ass locked up so long he'll have cobwebs on his dick when he gets out," Boots answered. Her voice trembled.

Billy glanced at her nervously, then said jokingly, "If that's all you want, you ain't got too much of a problem. There's a detective sitting at the end of the bar now, trying to catch some poor whore for soliciting."

Boots glanced up at the young detective at the end of the bar. Something clicked in her mind. She smiled coldly and got up.

The chilling look in her eye made Billy even more nervous. She watched Boots make her way across the bar floor towards the policeman.

"Hi there," Boots said and stopped beside the officer. He glanced up at her and smiled. His eyes were a mild brown, and he wore his short brown hair in a crew-cut.

"What can I do for you, young lady?" he asked easily.

"How much money you want to spend?"

He stared at her curiously. There was a brightness in her eyes that made him wonder whether she was on dope or something. "What about ten dollars?" he asked slowly, watching her face.

She glanced over his shoulder and saw the bartender shaking his head at her. "That will be just fine," she answered and started walking towards the door.

The policeman caught up with her, and when they reached the street, he flashed his badge.

"You're under arrest for accosting and soliciting," he informed her.

She smiled over her shoulder at him and never broke step. "That's just fine with me," she replied, then asked, "Do you think I might be able to get the charges dropped if I give up my pimp?"

The officer's heart skipped a beat. He wondered if he had heard correctly. It was rare for a prostitute to even admit she had a pimp, let alone propose dropping her charges if she busted her man.

"If we can get a case on him, I'm quite sure we can work out something in your favor," he answered.

Boots smiled coldly. It didn't really make any difference whether they dropped the charges on her or not. The main thing was racking up Whoreson's goddamn ass.

27

I WALKED OUT OF MY apartment, stopped and inhaled deeply. You could smell the coming of winter. I smiled to myself. 1965 had the outlook of being a beautiful year, I thought. If we got married before Christmas, we could spend the rest of the winter on the West Coast. The first part of next year, I'd go into the business end of show business. There was no doubt in my mind any longer as to whether I could make out. It was just a matter of playing for bigger stakes.

My car was kind of slow starting and I decided I'd have it checked the first chance I got. I drove slowly uptown. Janet would be waiting for me at her apartment. It was one of those days when I believed that I had the world in my back pocket. I parked in front of her hotel and smiled condescendingly at the doorman. He smiled politely and held the door open. This was something I was getting used to, and it was really sweet.

The bell captain smiled and nodded politely at me. I was getting to be known by sight from all the times I had come in with Janet. The thick carpet sank under my feet as I crossed the lobby and entered the elevator. I rode up to her expensive suite, my head in the clouds.

My brief knock was answered immediately. When I stepped into the large apartment, I froze instantly. There were two white men standing there, and police was written all across their faces.

Janet closed the door slowly behind me. "Here is Mr. Jones now," she said in a low voice. I looked at her and there was shock written all across her face. The first thing that flashed across my mind was that she had found out where I had gotten the twenty thousand big ones at.

How the hell had Stella found out so quick where I had gone? I cursed silently. I'd have to play it by ear until I found out how much they knew.

"Whoreson," she blurted out, "they want you on another pandering case." Tears welled up in her eyes.

At the mention of "another," both policemen glanced quickly at each other. "It's not pandering we want you for, Mr. Jones," one of the well-dressed young men said. He flashed his badge at me. "We are federal officers and we want you for transporting prostitutes across the state line."

I was stunned. For a minute I couldn't believe what they were saying. I grinned. I knew they had me wrong. I hadn't brought any whores here—but Boots. Boots! The name exploded in my mind. What had that bitch done to me? The smile slowly disappeared as I was beginning to get a glimmer of what had happened.

"We have the statement of a young lady who says you bought her here with you from Detroit. Is that correct?" the younger of the two asked.

I could only nod my head. "I just gave her a ride, that's all," I said, more for Janet's benefit than for any other reason. She was staring at me in horror. She put her hand over her mouth to hold back a sob.

"Oh Whoreson. Whoreson. Why? You didn't need the money," she screamed and ran towards her bedroom.

"Goddamn," I cursed, the bitch believed me guilty already. She hadn't even bothered to ask me if it was true or not.

"You better come downtown with us, Mr. Jones," one of the officers said. "I must advise you that anything you say now may be used against you."

I turned silently and followed them to the door. "Janet," I yelled back across my shoulder. "Call me up a lawyer, baby. At least wait until you know what's really happening before falling apart on me."

It was a sickening ride downtown. I sat in the backseat and remained silent. When we got to the Federal Building, the two officers put me between them and

led me inside. They took me somewhere on the third
floor and put me in an office. I sat there for about ten
minutes, until a fat, round-faced white man came in.

He smiled at me. "My name is Mr. Lopdall, Mr.
Jones, and I'm the man assigned to your case. Before
you say anything, I want you to know that whatever
you say might be held against you." He sat down.
"Now that we've got that bullshit done with, we can
get down to business." He lit a cigarette and offered
me one. "I guess you know we have got you by your
balls."

"I don't know a goddamn thing," I snarled angrily. "You got some kind of fuckin' statement by some
silly ass bitch, and you think I'm supposed to con-
fess." I glared at him. "You can take that statement
and shove it up that bitch's ass, for all I care."

The smile came off his face. His eyes glittered dan-
gerously. "Well, now that we understand each other a
little better, Whoreson," he dragged the name out, "we
can lay all the cards on the table. I not only have you
by the balls, boy, but if you give me any bullshit, I
will personally see that we rack your ass up."

"Screw you and that bitch," I replied hotly. I didn't
give a damn what he said, I wasn't planning on copping out.

He took another approach. "You seem like a pretty bright kid, son, so let's look at what you're up
against. First of all, we do have the lady's statement.
Now I'll admit you could fight it, but here's what kills
your shit. We got your record, boy, and we know for
a fact that this woman was your whore. You went to

prison in 1957. After doing six years and three months you were released." He smiled at me coldly. "How do you think a jury will react when they find out that this same woman who went to prison with you as your rap partner is now pressing charges on you for the Mann Act. Do you really believe they'll find you innocent?"

I stared at him too shocked to speak Up until now, I had still believed I would be able to walk out of here and return to my bright future. His last words had brought my small world tumbling down around my head.

He stared at me for a few seconds, then dropped the crusher on me. "Don't think this is your only problem. It seems as if this young lady really wants your ass."

I stared at him in surprise. I couldn't think of anything else she could do. She didn't know anything about the twenty grand I had ripped off, thank God.

"She happens to be pressing pandering charges against you with the State of New York. You could get ten to fifteen for that alone, not counting the time we're going to give you."

I slumped down in the chair. I felt as though someone had beaten me with an iron pipe. If you have ever been in a fight and it continued until you couldn't hold up your arms, you have an idea of what I'm talking about. I just wanted to lie down somewhere. I couldn't even think any longer. I stared at the officer, defeated. I knew I was finished. If I got time from the state, then got sentenced by the government, they could run the time wild. What I mean by that is, after you finished doing ten years for the state, the feds would be waiting for you; they would pick you up at one prison and transport you right back to another one to start the second sentence.

"I guess you realize that, if we want to, we can run your two sentences wild," he said. I could hear his voice coming to me as though we were miles apart.

"We don't want to give you the short end of the stick, though, Mr. Jones. I have already talked to the detectives on your case, and they have agreed to drop the charges against you if you will plead guilty to the federal charge."

I came awake then as if someone had poured cold water on me. In the past ten minutes I had accepted the fact that I was going to prison. Now we were bargaining on how many years of my life I would have to spend there.

"How much time would I get if I pleaded guilty?" I asked hoarsely.

He tapped his fingers on the edge of his desk, watching me closely. "I can almost promise you, off the record of course, that you won't get over five years in prison."

I smiled for the first time since entering his office. Five years wasn't too bad. I'd still be in my twenties when I got out, even if I had to do all five. It would be damn near 1970 by the time I got out, but that was better than a lot of people I knew. There were some men who would never get out.

"You just made yourself a deal, Mr. Lopdall," I said

as I leaned across the desk and shook his hand. Then I sat back in the chair and started to plan my future. It wouldn't pay to make bond, because if my picture got in a paper again and Stella came across it, I'd have another case to fight. No, the best course would be to lie in the jail and wait for sentence. After that, I'd have no problem, except doing the time.

They carried me across the street and locked me up in a bull pen. I ignored the five men who were there when I arrived. From parts of their conversation I gathered that the three young Negroes had been caught trying to hold up a bank. The two older men, both Italians, sat huddled together, speaking in low tones. I sat down on the end of the bench, away from the others. It was a bitter pill I had to swallow. Another meatball. Here I was going back to prison again for something I hadn't done. Technically, I had been innocent the first time. I hadn't received a dime from that particular prostitute, but I had been sent to prison nevertheless.

The very thought of it was so ironic that I tossed my head back and laughed. The men inside the bull pen stopped gossiping and stared at me curiously. My laughter carried the sound of all the bitterness and loneliness I had experienced in my short existence. Mockery was the answer to my stupidity, for what else could I call it? Not cleverness. What could be clever about a man who wasted over ten years of his life behind prison walls. By the time I got out, I'd have over ten years in, and for what? Twenty thousand dollars. A man working at a carwash would make more than that over a ten-year span.

"Mr. Jones. Whoreson Jones. Are you back there?" The voice came from the cell door. I got up and made my way over to the door.

"You're Mr. Jones?" the elderly man asked me as soon as I reached the bars.

Before I could answer, he held out a small white card. "I'm Mr. Winestine," he said. "Miss Wilson has given me a retainer to handle your case for you."

The mention of Janet's name filled me with warmth. "I couldn't think of anything I need right now more than a lawyer," I replied and smiled at him.

He grinned in return. "Good, as soon as they take you over for arraignment we'll have you out on bond."

I shook my head. "I don't want any bond, Mr. Winestine. As far as I'm concerned, I don't think I've got a chance of beating this case."

He scratched his small, graying mustache. "You haven't made a statement yet, have you?" he asked quickly.

"No," I answered, then continued to explain why I believed my best chance would be to plead guilty.

He remained silent for a few seconds. "If that's the case, you had better work it like that. I can see how they got you. We would never be able to break down her testimony once they revealed both of your records. No doubt about it, they're going to find you guilty." He hesitated briefly. "You can still make bond, though. You might as well have a few months on the street."

I shook my head. "For every day I do in jail waiting to go to trial, when I get sentenced, it will come off my prison sentence. Isn't that correct?" I asked, not bothering to give him the real reason why I didn't want to get out.

"Oh yes. You'll get every day you spend in jail. I can guarantee you that you'll get that, even if you don't want me as your lawyer."

"Oh, yes, I want you," I replied. "In fact, if you'll make the proper arrangements, I'll see to it that you get your money today."

"That's not necessary," he answered quickly. "Miss Wilson gave me one thousand dollars as a retainer and informed me that money was not the problem. She said to tell you that she would handle the financial end of it. In fact," he continued, "she's waiting down the hall. I'll try and see if she can get back here for a few minutes when I leave."

"I'll see you in court then," I said abruptly. I knew as well as he did that I didn't really need a lawyer. It was all a matter of show. You were supposed to have one; if you didn't, the courts would just appoint you one.

He turned and walked away. I clutched the bars tightly as I waited for Janet's appearance. I could hear her heels clicking as she came down the hallway. I waited with my heart thumping loudly until she came into view.

She covered my hands on the bars with hers. I could see the circles under her eyes from where she had been crying. "Hi!" she managed to say with a forced grin.

"Hi, baby." I couldn't think of anything to say. Just

to stand there and look at her was enough for me.

"I talked to the lawyer, Whoreson. He says you're going to have to plead guilty. I don't understand."

"Listen, baby," I said and stared at her earnestly. "I ain't goin' try and give you no bullshit. You know that me and Boots ain't been together ever since Tony copped her while I was in prison, don't you?"

She shook her head in reply.

"I ain't got no reason to lie to you now, Janet, so this is the truth, baby." I gathered up my wits and began to lie fluently. "Before I left Detroit, baby, I saw Boots and told her I was leaving. Now, she wanted to get away from Tony, so I told her I would take her with me. I didn't say anything about us going back together, honey, but I will admit that we stopped on the highway and checked into a motel and had sex. I don't know if she got the idea in her head that I wanted her, but when we reached New York I paid for her hotel room and gave her fifty dollars to make it with. Then I stepped out of her life." I watched her closely to see if she was going for it.

Her eyes were large and she stared at me with complete sincerity. "I believe you, honey. I really do. Maybe she was just mad about us getting together." She dropped her head and muttered quietly, "I can't help myself anyway, Whoreson. I missed my period."

For a minute her words didn't ring a bell with me. Then it came to me like a flash. "What, baby? Are you sure?" I wanted to pull the bars down and take her in my arms.

Two of the young brothers came up to the bars and

stared over my shoulder at Janet. I could hear them talking amongst themselves as they walked back to give me some privacy. The third one walked over to make sure, and I could hear them exclaiming that it was Janet Wilson, the singer.

She shook her head and smiled up at me. "If I am pregnant, the baby has to have a name, Whoreson. I mean, I'm not going to bring any children into this world without a father."

"See the lawyer, baby," I said happily. "He can arrange it so we can have a quiet marriage in the jail. We won't be able to have a honeymoon for at least three or four years, but when we do, it will be beautiful."

"That's all for now, miss," the guard said quietly as he walked up. "We'll be taking them over to the courtroom shortly, so if you want to see him again, I advise you to wait over there."

I watched her walk away. She glanced back over her shoulder and I managed to get my hand through the bars far enough to wave.

As I watched her leave, it didn't disturb me any longer that I was on my way back to prison. That was the way the cookie crumbled. I had played the game and now I had to pay the dues. There were no more tears of frustration in the back of my eyes, because I knew I would not do this time alone. I had a woman who would be there right with me, writing and visiting until I came home. And now I knew there would be a real home somewhere in my future, a house full of love.

The many lonely nights that were before me
wouldn't be lonely any more. There would be no need
to reach down inside myself in the darkness, seeking
strength, fighting back the tears of loneliness and
despair, as I told myself that a man didn't cry.

The stark reality of the bars and gray walls that
would be part of my life for the next few years held
no fear. If Janet had me a boy child, how beautiful
the world would be! He would never have to experience the poverty and vice of the slums. I bit my lip
as I tried to remember the old toast an old con had
once told me. It fitted me to a tee:

"The jungle creed, said the strong must feed, on
any prey at hand. I was branded a beast, and sat at
the feast, before I was a man."

Yes, that was it, and that had been my problem. I
had been introduced to too much game at too young
an age. As I stared through the bars, I began to see
myself more clearly. In the past four hours I had finally grown up. I knew now that I'd never again put
myself in the position where a woman could send me
to prison on a whim. Not again in this lifetime. I knew
where I was going now. Maybe I didn't know when
I'd get out, but whenever I did, there would be another way of life waiting on me. One I didn't know anything about, except that there would be truthfulness
between me and my woman, and deceit would be a
thing of the past. I smiled at the thought. I had a lot
to learn, but I had a lot of time to learn it in. I glanced
at the three young boys huddled together on the bench.
They were young and wild, and life had been unkind

to them. Maybe one of them would find his way while in prison to a life away from vice and corruption, and most of all, away from the streets of broken dreams.

Donald Goines
SPECIAL PREVIEW

WHITE MAN'S JUSTICE, BLACK MAN'S GRIEF

This excerpt from White Man's Justice, Black Man's Grief *will give you an inside look at prison life in America. Considered "one of the most revealing books ever written about prison life and the bigotry built into our system," this is the story of Chester Hines, who thought he was the baddest man to come down the street. Behind prison walls he was nothing more than fresh meat.*

THE LIGHTS ON WOODWARD Avenue glistened brightly as the evening breeze blew away the last of the day's stifling heat. People walked the streets alone and in pairs, savoring relief from the blazing heat that had been their lot earlier in the day when the temperature had reached one hundred and ten in the shade.

The driver of the inconspicuous black Ford drove slowly and carefully. He didn't want any trouble before reaching his destination. That was his first mistake: driving too carefully. As he pulled towards a green light, he hesitated, then decided to speed up so that he could make the light. But as he did so, the yellow caution light came on, and again he hesitated, touching the brake, then the gas pedal, letting up to touch the brake again, then changing his mind and stomping on the gas pedal in an attempt to beat the light. Too late. The light turned red before he had reached the center of the intersection. He cursed, then stiffened when, out of the corner of his eye, he saw the patrol car parked thirty feet or so down the cross street.

Before he was completely through the intersection, he saw the squad car's headlights come on and the flashing red light. He glanced into the rearview mirror and it confirmed what he already knew. The squad car had turned the corner and was dead on his case. The thought flashed through his mind that he owed two overdue parking tickets. If they ran a make on him, he realized that his next stop would be city jail.

He removed the pistol from the shoulder holster he always wore when going out on a job, and for a second he debated the merits of trying to outrun the law. All he needed was enough time to rid himself of the gun, but the old Ford he drove didn't have the speed to outrun them. He had an extra large motor put in the car for just that purpose, but they were just too close. He glanced in the mirror and saw that they were right on his bumper.

"You better come up with something quick," he mumbled aloud, angrily. He resorted to the only thing that came to mind. He dropped the pistol to the floor and kicked it as far back under the seat as he could.

The squad car pulled up beside him, and the officer on the passenger's side waved him towards the curb. As he pulled the old Ford over he shrugged philosophically. Better that it happened now than later, he thought coldly. If it had happened on the way back, there would have been a shoot-out with no holds barred.

The policemen got out of their car and walked towards him, and he thought how easy it would be to knock them off as he pulled his wallet out and removed his driver's license. He put on his best honest-John smile, and held out the license, being helpful.

One of the officers took the license and walked slowly back towards the squad car. When that happened, the driver of the Ford knew that it was all over. They were calling in on him, doing exactly what he had hoped they wouldn't do. If he had been white, he reasoned, the chance of them doing that was small. All they would have done was write out a ticket and send him on his way, apologizing for detaining him.

In a matter of minutes the officer was back, but this time he had his hand on the butt of his gun. He nodded to his partner.

"It seems like a couple of warrants are out for you, mister," the policeman informed him quietly.

His partner had moved into position on the other side of the car. The officers worked as a unit, without bothering to speak. Each knew what the other expected from him.

"If you don't mind, sir, please step out of the car." It was an order but politely given. The white policeman remained polite, but there was a firmness in his voice that showed that he wouldn't take any shit.

If there was one thing Chester Hines had learned when he was a young man in his early twenties, it was not to get smart with police. It was something he had learned from experience. If you acted civil with them, sometimes they would treat you fairly decently.

People walking past slowed down so they could allow their curiosity to run unchecked as they watched the policemen search the well-dressed black man in the middle of the street. One of the officers opened the car door and began probing around inside the car. Seconds later he straightened up, and in his hand was the pistol Chester had tried to conceal.

The officer pulled out his handcuffs. "Okay, buddy," he drawled, watching Chester's every movement. "Turn around!" There was no disguising the disdain in his voice, and Chester turned slowly, daring not to make a quick movement, and extended his arms behind him.

"Don't make them so tight, buddy," he said as the policeman twisted the handcuffs tightly on his wrists.

"I'm not your fuckin' buddy, mack!" the policeman said harshly.

After that, Chester remained quiet, not wanting to provoke the officers of the law, and he spoke only when spoken to. When they arrived at the precinct station, he went through the mechanics of booking with a cool detachment; he'd been through the procedure so often that it had become second nature to him.

Irene! The name exploded in his mind like a burning flash—there one moment, gone the next. If it hadn't been for her goddamn nagging, he thought, he wouldn't be in the fix he was in, and he silently cursed the day he had met the tall, buxom show girl.

He had been on his honeymoon with his first wife, a large, plump beautician who owned her own beauty shop. They were honeymooning at a black resort in upper Michigan, where he had rented a small cabin for two weeks of bedding, boating and fishing—until the night he ran into Irene at the resort nightclub.

She had been one of the girls in the chorus line. Their eyes had met across the dimly lit room, and something intangible passed between them. That something grew until there was nothing for him to do but to kill his bride of two weeks. The idea wasn't new, it had been his master plan before he even married Marie, but Irene caused him to do it quicker than he had planned.

* * *

"Coffee, my man? Get it while it's hot." The trusty stood in front of his cell peering in. Chester nodded his head, not bothering to speak. He watched coldly as the man poured him a cup and pushed it beneath his steel door, through the little opening that was just large enough for a small bowl of food or cup of coffee.

"Today's your day in court, ain't it, my man?" the trusty inquired, trying to be friendly. He put his hands on his hips, which in a woman would have been sexy, but in this thin, aging homosexual, was hideously grotesque.

Chester bent down and picked up his cup, then turned his back on the trusty, not bothering to answer. In the three days he had spent in the precinct cell, he had heard the word through the grapevine that the man was a paid informer, serving his time at the county jail instead of being sent to the farm or prison. He had busted too many people, so the prison authorities feared for his life. He was too valuable to them.

Slowly Chester sipped the bitter tasting coffee. The tin cup was scorching hot. As he let the coffee cool off, he made a mental note of the informer's name: Paul Robbins. That would be a name he wouldn't forget. It always paid to know the informers, especially the professional ones. Even though Chester wasn't a dopeman, he liked to stay aware of such things. One never knew when it might just pay off.

A tall white guard stopped in front of his cell. Chester glanced up at the turnkey.

"Hines, you're going over to court in about a half an hour, so be ready," the turnkey said, then walked on down the long corridor, informing other men who were due in court.

Chester finished his coffee, rinsed out his cup, then sat down on the edge of the iron cot and let his mind continue its idle rambling. One thing was sure, he thought, he wouldn't be coming back this way. After he went to court, he'd be taken to the county jail, and if he was lucky, he'd get a chance to sleep on a mattress that night. It might not be much, but after three days on the iron cot he'd been using, it would feel like a waterbed.

There was no sense in fooling himself about bail either, he thought. That bitch of his, Irene, wouldn't be able to raise the money. Again it crossed his mind that if it hadn't been for her, he wouldn't be sitting there. Her constant nagging about money had been the main reason he had taken his pistol and left the house. True, he had been planning to knock off a whiskey store that week, but it wouldn't have been that night. Now, because he'd allowed the bitch's nagging to get on his nerves, he was on his way to court to fight a concealed weapon charge, and his funky bitch wouldn't be able to raise his bond.

With his record, he knew he didn't stand a chance in court. The judge would jam him; there was no doubt about it. But it could have been worse, he reasoned. It could have happened after he stuck up the store, then his ass would have really been fucked up. Instead of just a c-c-w to fight, he'd have had an armed robbery on his back, and that would have meant *big* trouble.

Taking his time, Chester dressed in the clothes his wife had left downstairs for him. He didn't have a mirror, but he knew that the tight black pants fit him nicely. He still had a small waist even though he was in his late thirties. The only things that showed his age were the circles under his eyes and the bags that had formed there from keeping late hours. He put on his white shirt; then, as he heard the guard opening the doors, he slipped on his sports coat. In minutes the turnkey was in front of his cell.

The men lined up against the wall. Two more guards came along and handcuffed the men two abreast. For something to do, Chester counted the men in the line. There were ten other doomed asses, he told himself, as he wondered how many of them had spent half the celibate years in prison that he had served during his life of crime.

The guard came back and ran a thin chain down between them, making them all chained to the same piece.

"Goddamn it," the man handcuffed to Chester began, "this is the one thing I hate about this shit! They chain you up like you're a fuckin' dog or something!"

"What do you expect?" Chester replied. "If they didn't take precautions and chain you, when they walked us through the tunnel they'd have to have fifty guards out there to keep the guys from running."

"Well I sure as hell wouldn't run," the man answered. "I ain't did nothing, not a goddamn thing no way. They got me down here for nothin'! These white folks just fuck over a man, if you ask me."

"I didn't ask you," Chester said under his breath, then decided to ignore the man. He had seen too many like him. Always talking about their innocence. And besides, he didn't feel in the mood for loose conversation. His mind was too occupied with his appointment with the judge. Maybe, just maybe, he hoped, the judge might give him probation. Since he hadn't been arrested in the past two years, it just might go in his favor. He just as quickly laughed the idea away.

That was something he could forget. He'd never been that lucky before, so there was no reason to start hoping for a miracle now.

"What's so goddamn funny?" His handcuffed partner inquired, his voice full of self-righteous anger, as the line of men started shuffling along.

Chester glanced around at the heavyset, dark-complexioned man handcuffed to him. "Nothing that you'd understand, brother, nothing at all," he said quietly.

"You guys keep the fuckin' noise down! You're not on your way to a private dance or something," the tall red-faced guard leading the way yelled over his shoulder.

"We're not on our way to a goddamn funeral, either," a short well dressed black man yelled back at him.

The group reached an elevator marked for prisoners only. The line of men stopped. Two more white guards joined the first group, then they began the job of loading the men into the small elevator. The men on the front of the chain went in first and walked around inside the tiny elevator, making a complete circle and stopping in front of the elevator door. The men were loaded into the tight space like cattle. The guards were no better off; they had to squeeze inside themselves.

"Get off my goddamn foot, motherfucker!" someone in the rear yelled angrily. No sooner had the elevator doors closed, when the tightly packed bodies sucked up all the available oxygen. Chester fought to breathe. He thought he would suffocate inside the tiny space. He raised his head high, sucking at the stale air that seemed thick enough to cut with a knife. The odors from the unwashed bodies filled his nostrils, and he decided to hold his breath. Better to suffocate, he reasoned, than to die from an overload of funk. The elevator finally stopped. The guards stepped out quickly; they, too, wanted to escape from the strong odor and lack of air.

The walk through the tunnel was quick. Every now and then they would pass another guard, strategically placed so that the chain of men would be under constant observation. There were desperate men in the small group of prisoners. Some of them were fighting murder charges, and any opportunity to escape would set them in violent motion.

The precautions that the guards took showed that they anticipated all forms of trouble and meant to handle it if it should jump off. When they came out of the tunnel, the men were separated from the chain that held them all together. They were still handcuffed two abreast, though. As they were released from the chain, they were led off to small bull pens—depending upon what judge they were going before. The petty cases, misdemeanors and traffic violations were separated from what they termed the hardened crooks, the violent men.

Chester studied the faces around him. Some of them couldn't hide the fear in their eyes. They were terrified, and one could see the fear jumping out of their eyes. Their legs shook uncontrollably. One young boy had pissed on himself. Whenever anyone happened to catch his eye, he looked away or glanced down at the floor.

The guard pushed Chester and his chained partner over towards one of the bull-pen doors. He took out his keys and unlocked the handcuffs, then opened the large steel door. He beckoned for them to go inside. "You boys know the routine, so hop to it." He slammed the door behind them. Before Chester could find a place to sit down, the strong, heavy, steel door opened again, and another two men came stumbling in.

"Keep your fucking hands off me, screw!" one of the men cursed over his shoulder at the guard who had pushed him.

The two small benches inside the bull pen were already occupied, so Chester, after wiping off a spot on the floor, sat down. He knew that he probably had a two-hour wait before court opened. They always brought the prisoners over early in the morning, at least two hours before court convened. Chester wrinkled his nose and moved. He had sat down too close to the piss hole, a small hole in the floor that the men had to use for a toilet. The smell coming from it was enough to turn a person's stomach. Around the small hole was dried vomit that someone had had the decency to try to deposit in the hole, instead of just anywhere in the bull pen. There were spots in the corners where some men hadn't been so considerate, and at that moment, another started to piss up against the wall. The men sitting near him cursed loudly, but the man continued to piss. The urine ran down the wall, and a small stream of it began to flow across the floor.

"You better hope, nigger, that that piss of yours has eyes, 'cause if it gets on me, I'm kickin' you in your ass!" A short, young, black man growled at the older man who had pissed against the wall. The young man continued: "You can damn well bet they got you in the right place, you sorry motherfucker." He moved away from the spot where he had been sitting. The small stream of urine hadn't reached him, but it was getting within a couple of feet from where he had been sitting.

He paced up and down the bull pen, glaring at the man who had pissed. "I should make you get down on your knees and lick that shit up. You don't give a fuck noway. It don't make you no difference that other men have to come behind you and use this same fuckin' place. No." The more he talked, the angrier he became. The large muscles in his arm jumped, and from the looks of him, he was quite capable of doing just what he threatened.

"Now wait a minute, blood. I didn't mean no harm," the drunk said, trying to justify his action.

"No harm my ass!" the young blood replied. "It don't even cross your mind that the men that come in here after us might have to sit in that funky piss of yours. You ornery motherfucker. You could have walked over and pissed in the hole, just like the rest of the men. But no, hell no, you had to piss on the floor." Blood stopped in front of the drunk. "You know what you are, man? You're a self-centered, cruel, no-good bastard whose own mammy don't want him."

"Wait a minute, blood, don't talk about my poor old maw," the drunk said. Before he could add another word, the young man slapped him twice across the face, viciously. The sound reverberated through the bull pen and empty halls. "Now, you motherfucker, take your shirt off and wipe up that shit." The young man didn't crack a smile. His eyes were cold and his lips were pulled down in a violent sneer.

The other men fell silent. When they finally spoke, they spoke in whispers, as though they were afraid they might bring violence down on their own heads. Chester grinned as he watched the man wipe up the piss with his shirt but soon grew tired of watching and looked inward, filled with his own worries.

2

THE SOUND OF THE KEY in the lock caused all of the men in the bull pen to glance up at the door. The door swung open, revealing a guard, clipboard in hand. He stayed in the hallway, a few feet from the threshold, to avoid the bull pen's smell as he called out names: "Rufus Johnson, Billy Jones, John Caster, Donald Warren, James Sailor, Jim Jackson, Tony Towasand…."

He continued calling names in a bored, slightly nasal monotone and, as he did so, the men formed a line at the door. Chester was the last to be called, and he formed the end of the line and followed the men out into the hallway. Guards stood at each end of the corridor, holding shotguns, as the prisoners were led down the short hall. The guard that opened their door was the only one who didn't have a weapon of any kind. He led the men up to a huge oak door, where he stopped and removed his keys. When he opened the door for the men, he made sure they went in single file.

Chester blinked at the harsh light in the courtroom and peered around curiously. He had been in and out of courtrooms all his life, but he never got over his fear of them. The black-robed men who sat up high on the benches dispensing their so-called "justice" filled him with awe. It was not a feeling of reverence or of wonder caused by something sublime. It was a feeling of terror, inspired by the raw power that these hypocrites held over the helpless black men who came before them. He didn't fear the men themselves. He knew well that they were insignificant, even while recognizing how insidious they could sometimes be. He feared the power, the power of life and death these men held in their hands. Half of them were too old to keep up with the times; they tried to beat down the complexities of the seventies with their gavels, with their twenties- and thirties-spawned attitudes, with raw power.

The courtroom was full of people. The seats were filled with men in custody and with people who came to watch the wretched human beings squirm before the all powerful judges.

The line that Chester was in seemed endless as he stared over the heads of most of the black men in front of him. He started counting. There were thirty men in front of him, and out of that thirty, only three were white. Two of the white men had the look of the derelict about them.

The line moved faster than Chester thought it would. It seemed like only minutes before he was almost in front of the judge. The black man he had been chained to as they came through the tunnel stepped before the judge. As his charge was read off, Chester had to fight back a grin.

A large hardened black woman got up and came forward, pushing a young girl eleven years old down the aisle in front of her. Chester examined the young girl closely. Take the braids out of her hair and let it down and she'd definitely look older. Her young breasts were large and firm. She was overripe, even if she was under age.

"Is this the child that the accused is supposed to have molested?" the judge asked as he leaned down to get a better view of the young girl's breasts.

Chester watched the gleam in the old, gray-haired judge's eyes and knew without a doubt what the man was thinking. How was it? He'd probably give up his front seat in hell for a shot of that young black pussy, Chester reflected coldly as he watched the proceedings.

"Ain't no *supposed* to it!" the older woman screamed hotly. "I come home from work and when I entered the front door I could hear this child screaming her head off. Right then and there I dropped them bags I'd been carrying and run to help her. At first

I'm thinkin' the child done burned herself or something, but when I reached the back of the house, I see this bastard with his pants down and his goddamn thing in his hand!" As she related the incident, her voice rose several octaves until she was almost screeching at the judge.

The judge didn't bother to reprimand her for speaking out or swearing. He just nodded his head, then set a five thousand dollar bond on the man. As the accused tried to explain, one of the court-appointed policemen rushed him away from the judge.

The courtroom had fallen silent as the woman spoke. Now, with that case out of the way, the judge paused to drink a glass of water, which was poured by an attractive young white girl who kept going back and forth bringing him the different files on the men and women who had to appear before him. While they waited for the next case to come up, the people in the courtroom gossiped.

Chester wiped the sweat from his brow as he stepped in front of the judge. Since the baby raper only got a five thousand dollar bond, he reasoned, he stood a good chance of getting a low bond. His case was nowhere near as bad as the man who had preceded him.

He waited silently while the judge read off his record.

It took awhile because he had a long record.

"What were you doing with a gun in your car, Mister Hines?" Before Chester could reply, the judge continued, "From your record, sir, you're not sup-

posed to even have a weapon at your home, let alone
in your car." He stared down silently for a brief
moment." I see by your record you once killed a man,"
he said, holding up his hand to cut off Chester's reply.
"Yes, I can see here where you were released on jus-
tified homicide, but if you hadn't had a gun on that
occasion, you wouldn't have taken a man's life."

"If I wouldn't have had a gun at that time, your
honor, I wouldn't be standing here now. I'd be dead."
In the short silence that followed, Chester decided
that, if he were ever going to get anything said, he
had better start saying it now. "Your honor, if the court
will allow, I've been just recently married and I've
just gotten a good job. If you would give me a personal bond, sir, I'm sure I'd be able to afford the
money to hire me a lawyer for this case."

"I'm sure you would hire yourself a good lawyer,
Mister Hines. Your kind of man always seems to hire
the best lawyer around," the judge stated sharply, then
added, "but from your record, sir, it would be a trav-
esty of justice if I were to allow you out on a personal bond. Ten thousand dollars, with two securities,"
the judge stated, then hit the block with his small
gavel, his way of informing the court guards that he
was finished with the case and was ready for the next.
While Chester had stood before the judge, the court
officers had been busy. There was a new line of men
behind Chester, all waiting for their chance in court.

Chester stared up at the judge, dumbfounded. He
hadn't expected the stiff decision. It was too much.
He'd never get out on bond now. Even if his wife

came up with the money, she'd never be able to raise the two securities. He turned around and searched the sea of faces in the courtroom. His wife and kids were sitting three rows back. Tears were rolling down her cheeks as she stared at him. She had been in enough courtrooms to know just what the judge had done. There were few black men who could come up with the thousand dollars cash it would take, plus he'd need someone to put up a house for one of the securities. It was impossible, and his wife believed in her heart the judge knew that when he had set the bond.

An officer grabbed Chester's arm firmly and guided him from the courtroom. He walked along in a slight daze. It had happened. Even though he had thought that it would be hard, he hadn't really given up hope of making a small bond, something that he might have been able to raise, even if his wife had to sell the car.

When they reached the corridor, he jerked his arm from the policeman's grip. "Goddamn it! I can walk. You don't have to shove me," he yelled belligerently into the officer's face.

"Just take it easy," the officer said lightly. "I didn't set your bond, and I'm just doing my job."